NOVANGELIS
NEW ANGELS

Cover photos by Thomas Hodges, International Photographic Artist,
(www.photoconception.com) of International Fashion and Art model Chu Chiao
Wang (http://www.chuchiaowang.com).
Back cover inset: the author at Montsegur, France by A.Heitmann

ISBN   978-0-6151-9311-3
Comments, questions, reviews – contact:
a-heightspress@comcast.net

For Jeanne Quinlan Bastoni,
family nurturer, navigator, and courageous activist.

NOVANGELIS

NEW ANGELS

by Mark L. Bastoni

*The places in this story are real,
the history accurate. The groups and societies
– with a few dramatic exceptions – exist.*

PART ONE

1. SUNDOWN ON PLUM ISLAND
2. A NOT-SO-PRIESTLY PRIEST
3. MESSAGE OR MISTAKE?
4. JULES DISPATCHES HIS AGENTS
5. PARIS BAR
6. HEADQUARTERS: BERLIN
7. ACCUSED!

PART TWO

8. THE FLEEING PROFESSOR
9. THE SECRETS OF LINDOW ABBEY
10. ACCESSING ANFORTAS
11. THE VILLAGE OF MYSTERY
12. THE DOMAINE OF THE BEE
13. A GRASSY KNOLL

PART THREE

14. REFUGE IN THE VINEYARD
15. DINNER FOR TWO
16. THE RAID ON *LAND HAUS*
17. CASING *SAINT BRICE*
18. THE LODGE IN SATANICUM
19. IN THE SHADOW OF SACRÈ COÈUR
20. THE BAIT
21. THE DEAL

PART ONE

Not all true things are to be said to all men.
– attributed to a secret gospel of Saint Mark

Chapter 1. SUNDOWN on PLUM ISLAND

Friday, August 16th.
Plum Island, Massachusetts. 10:00 pm. Day 26.

Someone was lurking outside his door.

Linus was expecting two people tonight. The man he knew as Wolfgang Kohlhertz was the invited guest. The woman he knew as Melisandre was the crasher. Melisandre would do anything to keep his deal with Kohlhertz from closing. Maybe even shoot him, he thought.

But tonight was *his* turn to be the set-up guy.

In the weeks since they met, Melisandre lurched between trust and treachery. He wondered which Melisandre would show up tonight. When she ditched him last week at Orly Airport in Paris it was a good trick but extremely ill-timed. Melisandre had no idea how poor her timing really was. Doubtless she knew it now. He wiped his clammy forehead and lifted the pistol. There was another footstep on the deck. Then another, walking toward the door. This was it.

The steps paused. The door began to open. A tall, square mass filled the frame. It was Kohlhertz, right on schedule. He was holding a gun, surveying the room. Linus, invisible in his shadowy corner, moved onto the edge of the chair and planted his feet. "Right on time," he said out of the darkness. Kohlhertz startled and crouched.

"Who's there?" he demanded. Linus reached up and snapped on a lamp, revealing Kohlhertz's square, grainy face. It smiled wickedly. "I *knew* it was you," he said with great satisfaction. "I figured you had more sense than these other dip-shits." Linus wasn't flattered.

"My fee," he said, pointing to his computer on the desk, poised for some long distance electronic banking. Kohlhertz stepped forward and released the agreed sum from the escrow account then stepped back. Linus used a wireless mouse to click the money into his own account. Then Kohlhertz nodded at the shoebox at Linus's feet.

"That it?" he asked. Linus shoved the box across the floor and Kohlhertz opened it.

"Look familiar?" Linus asked.

"I should've known this was important," Kohlhertz said, shaking his head. "Right in front of me all the time. It's gotta be worth millions. So why sell to me? And why so cheap?"

"Because I think it'll turn out to be worthless," Linus said. Kohlhertz raised his brow.

"Worthless," he said, smiling. Linus smiled back.

"May even get you killed. Maybe even tonight," he chuckled. Kohlhertz wasn't amused.

"I'll take my chances," he groused. "You knew what it was all along. Why did you wait to make a deal?"

"I *didn't* know what it was," Linus said. Kohlhertz put the box on the desk.

"I knew that old bastard Gervan couldn't be trust..." he began but stopped short. His face filled with surprise and he moved a step forward. A woman's voice behind him said,

"Hands." Someone was jamming a gun in his back. It would be an interesting evening yet, Linus thought, with secrets revealed and surprises to come. A major historical event was unfolding right before his eyes, one which could speed-shift the world into a new era. Many of history's strangest chapters had been written in the name of God and religion, he knew.

And in a small cottage on the Massachusetts coast, another of those chapters was taking shape.

April 04, 2003.
The Iraqi desert, between Karbala and Babylon.
The Scrounger.

Crill leapt over a burning pit then dove into a crater beside a trench. The sickening, sweet stench of nitrates, charred flesh and burning rubber clung to the cold desert sand. He slid his lanky frame up the crater rim and looked out at the carnage and destruction – after two nights of pounding by F-18s and Tomahawks there wasn't much left of the Baghdad Division of the Republican Guard. A broad grin broke across his face. It was just as he had imagined – mangled vehicles and armor, body parts strewn everywhere, made all the more eerie in night-vision green. His unit had seen little action in their dash across Iraq and Crill was noticeably pissed that he hadn't shot at some ragheads. But finally corporal Crill was getting his taste.

He crawled to the edge of the trench and rolled in, dragging down a silent cascade of sand, then scurried to a corner and paused to listen. His heart raced. He could see a bunker entrance just ahead. He hustled onto its roof. A direct hit had torn a huge gash in the two-foot thick concrete and someone inside was moaning. He tossed in two grenades and dove for cover. The explosions hit a split second apart. *Ba-boom!* And the moaning was gone.

He jumped back into the trench and went down the shattered steps into the dark bunker. The inside was a huge blast crater. Everything was splayed out against the walls. Chunks of concrete dangled from twisted steel bars overhead. He had to hurry. The clock was ticking on his little looting expedition. He was miles away from his unit and didn't want to get caught in an ambush.

He searched the corpses for rings and watches but found little more than pictures, diaries, and religious medals. As he scanned for an officer's corpse, hoping it would yield better loot, something caught his eye. He crossed through the debris, his M-16 leveled, to a deep well-like shaft on the bunker floor. Fine smoky dust sparkled in the beam of his flashlight. The shaft was about twenty feet deep, straight down with what looked like an old rope ladder at the bottom.

He scrambled out of the bunker and retrieved a piece of a tow chain from a burning tank, wrapped it around some twisted steel overhead then rappelled into the stone shaft and gingerly set his feet on the sandy bottom. A narrow passage sloped away into the darkness on his left and led him into a chamber with bleached white walls. There were no maps, no bodies, and the ceiling was only five feet high. This was no military installation.

At the far end of the chamber a gilded box sat atop a squat stone altar. Crill's eyes widened as he got closer. This was something very unusual, he knew, and maybe very valuable. Something the Iraqis had been sitting right on top of, hidden from them until the bombs began to fall. He stowed his rifle and crawled into the chamber on his knees. A plain wooden chest about the size of a picnic cooler sat in the sand at the foot of the altar. Visions of Ali Baba treasure spooled through Crill's brain as he lifted the lid.

"Fucking paper!" he groused as he sifted the dried parchment flakes with his fingers. He dropped the lid then took the adorned box off the altar and cradled it between his legs. It was slightly bigger than a shoe box, heavy and decorated with carved tarnished metal. He unlatched the top. Something round with a wax-sealed end was inside. He tilted the box and a red clay jar ringed with ruby-like orbs slid out. Crill could feel it... he had stumbled onto something important.

He slid it back into the box and put it his rucksack. Suddenly he heard jet engines, then explosions. The Air Force had arrived to administer their nightly pasting. It was a stroke of luck. He shinnied up the chain and crawled out of the bunker, tightened the rucksack, then ran to the Hummer he'd stolen and floored the gas pedal. But he wasn't headed back to his unit. He had seen enough of Iraq. And he felt that the military – once his chosen career – had let him down. Now he had something better to do than take orders from women, West Point-ers and queers, he thought. The guys in his unit knew he was out breaking orders and bunker-hunting. If he didn't return, they'd figure he was a victim of his own lunacy.

As he sped away the bomb concussions got closer and seemed to push him faster. Rocks pinged off the Humvee's tail. He hoped the bombing would cover his tracks and destroy the secret chamber he had discovered. If he could get back to Kuwait, he knew he could get out of the middle east. Some unlucky mugging victim – like some journalist roughly his size – would provide him with a passport. ID photos or signatures wouldn't matter if he wrapped his head and hands in gauze – a perfect disguise for someone coming from a war zone, one that would get him a priority flight to a Frankfurt hospital from where he'd slip away.

And Corporal Mason Crill would quietly cease to exist.

July 22nd.
Berlin, Germany. Day 01.
A Celebrity's Nightmare, a Paparazzo's Dream

Linus crouched behind a few cleaved boards on an old gray fence. The empty acre behind Tacheles, the abandoned factory complex-cum-art colony on Berlin's Oranienburgerstrasse, was a weedy junkyard of leftover machinery and sculpture debris. A million glass shards sparkled like gems in the hot afternoon sun.

Across the lot Massimo Riccio, archrival of the paparazzi and Linus's archenemy since the night Diana died, was staked-out at the back entrance, disguised as a beggar. Linus had heard a rumor in Paris that Jamie Richards, America's screen sweetheart, was posing for new boy pal Klaus Krenz, the extreme German painter. Klaus was best known for his blood-soaked nudes in jackboots with swastika tats with hypodermic needles dangling from their pale limbs. Massimo was famous for his relentless pursuit of the starlet, so Linus now knew that the rumors were true. And Jamie Richards as a naked-Nazi-junkie dominatrix was an image straight out of a paparazzo's gold-lined dreams. Massimo had found Krenz's studio. Linus had found Massimo.

He checked his watch – it was just after three – morning for the avant-garde, drifting in to host their studios and do their work. He also knew that Richards liked to travel in disguise so he quickly marked a woman in a chador who had just entered the lot. She stopped and took some bills from under her garb and stuffed them into the beggar's cup before going inside, her face hidden behind the thick veil. But Massimo must've seen something. He jumped up, pulled his camera from his rucksack and followed. Linus gave chase.

He jogged across the lot and carefully entered the dark stairwell – if Massimo saw him, the shoot might be blown. Slowly he made his way up into the dull gray light coming through the clouded windows and dirty skylights. The white concrete walls were covered with graffiti and cartoons. He could hear sharp but slow footsteps on the stairs above – probably from the woman in the chador since Massimo's was too sneaky to make that much noise. Linus stopped on the sixth floor when the steps disappeared through a door, waited then craned for a look up ahead. Massimo was camped outside a door across the corridor, lighting a smoke and waiting for whatever was going to happen on the other side of that door to get set up. Linus checked his camera. When Massimo made his move, he'd be right on top of him.

After a few minutes, Massimo pushed himself off the wall, snuffed his cigarette on the floor then readied his camera. This was it. Massimo turned the knob then shoved the door open and burst in, camera flashing. There on a pedestal was Jamie Richards, naked except for an SS officer's cap, holding a death's head dagger. Linus came in over the top and bulled Massimo out of the way. Richards was frozen wide-eyed with shock. Her painter boyfriend, however, wasn't so stymied. He bowled over his easel and charged the cameras. Massimo tried to bolt but ran into Linus who shoved him back into Krenz's arms and kept shooting. Krenz had Massimo by the throat, grappling for his camera, while Linus pushed Massimo forward, using him as a shield.

They scuffled into the hallway. Linus retreated to the stairwell then stopped and shot. The wiry Italian was no match for the enraged Krenz, who ripped the camera from Massimo's grip and pulled out the flash card. Massimo tried to swipe it back but Krenz landed a punch. Massimo's nose exploded. Blood covered his face as he went down on one knee. Linus slipped back further out of sight.

"Tell your friend there is some of that for him if he tries to use the pictures, *ja?*" Krenz warned, standing over Massimo. He shoved Massimo hard with his foot then tossed the camera down the hall. It skittered across the floor and stopped at the edge of the stairwell as Krenz went back inside the studio and slammed the door. Massimo was lying on his side.

"Madonna mia! Son of a bitch!" he cursed, kneeling and pressing a handkerchief to his banged nose. Linus came out of hiding. Massimo looked up. "Linus, you son of bitch rat!" he railed as he staggered to his feet. Then he noticed that his camera was right beside Linus's foot at the edge of the stairwell. Massimo's eyes popped wide. Krenz had taken the flash card but the camera also had memory. Something would be saved. Linus looked down at the camera then up at Massimo.

Massimo charged across the hall and dove for his camera.

Linus flicked his toe and shoved it into the stairwell.

"Ahhhhgggg!" Massimo screamed, hanging over the railing as the camera splattered on the concrete six floors below. Linus looked stoically at Massimo and said,

"Oops." Massimo started shaking.

"I *kill* you!" he screamed. Linus shoved him hard and bolted down the stairs. A small crowd hanging near the exit slowed him down. Massimo caught him on the sidewalk and tried to tackle him but he just didn't have the size to take down Linus's solid six-feet-plus. Linus pinned him against the wall.

"You are a son of a bitch Linus! A rat son of a bitch!"

"Ya Massimo? It's pay-back time. How's it feel? How's it feel!?" Linus snarled, bouncing Massimo against the brick wall. Linus let him go and Massimo backed off.

"I *never* do that to you," he whined, straightening his torn shirt.

"Oh? Who told the *Gendarmes* that I drove a white Fiat Uno?" Linus accused, referring to the infamous "other car" that supposedly caused the Princess Di crash. "They took all my gear and kept it for four months! I had a French detective on my ass for a year!"

"I had to make a big lie Linus. They wanted my films too. I say *ask* you. That's all. So they don't get my shots. And you had no pictures to lose."

"I had no pictures because I was trying to help while you and the other assholes kept shooting! And who saved you from that angry mob that night?"

"I know, I know. I already tell you *grazie*, Linus."

"Sure. *Grazi*. Big deal," Linus retorted. "You *owed* me, Massimo."

"I thought the police leave you alone when they see I told them a big lie. Really, Linus. *Credo*. It's the truth."

"A *year* Massimo. You know how much I lost? And I couldn't even leave France!"

"I no meant it to happen that way Linus. Really. C'mon. We're *cugini*. Wha'd a ya say we split the pictures from this. Your shots are worth plenty. Plenty for you, plenty for me."

"Not a chance Massimo," Linus replied. He didn't hate the guy... rather liked him, actually. He just thought that Massimo had it coming. They stood staring each other down on the sidewalk. Massimo lunged for Linus's camera but missed and ended up sprawled on the sidewalk. The see-saw drone of a police siren ended the fray.

"You *wait*! I get you back!" Massimo sneered as he got up and started to run. Linus tossed off a little "ciao" salute and bolted. About a half block away, he turned off the Oranienburgerstrasse onto a small side street, ran a block, turned again then slowed to a brisk walk, shaking his shirt to vent some of the heat off his sweaty chest. He stopped on a shady stoop beside a small antiquarian shop to gather his composure and have a look at his shots. They were spectacular. He pulled out his Blackberry and called Dark Star, his agency in New York.

Chapter 2. The NOT-SO-PRIESTLY PRIEST

From high up in an attic across the street, Jules the priest had a commanding view of both the back alley and front door of the Gervan antiquarian shop. And right now his attention was on Linus, the stranger, sitting on the steps next to the shop, talking on a cell phone. He raised his camera and zoomed in and could see some blood on Linus's collar, which was curious but not suspicious. Jules shot a few images anyway.

A blue sedan with dark tinted windows turned into the alley and stopped at the shop's rear entrance. Jules re-trained his camera and began shooting as the driver got out and opened the back. A tall man in black pants and boots stepped out. His blonde hair was buzzed short except for a long ponytail down the back of his white tunic. This was the guy Jules was waiting to see – the guy who said his name was Kohlhertz, and who three weeks ago brought old man Gervan an ancient scroll of unknown origin.

Gervan, of course, immediately called Jules.

Over the years and through the many 'sacred theft' or *'Sacré Furta'* investigations Jules had conducted, the scholarly Gervan had become a valuable resource. His expertise and especially his ability to spot fakes was crucial.

But Gervan was also perfectly positioned to glean intelligence about the many artifacts which trafficked through the underworld of antiquity collecting, and the old professor became the center of a loyal network of consultants and informants.

He zoomed for a close-up of Kohlhertz's box-jawed face as it peered through Gervan's back door, then got a close-up of the skinhead henchman hovering at the car. A drop of sweat rolled into the corner of Jules's eye. He dabbed it with his finger and loosened his shirt. The attic was hot – too hot for the tight priest's collar he was wearing.

He zoomed out for a wider view and made images as Kohlhertz motioned for his henchman to wait then reached to the doorknob and turned it slowly, then slipped unnoticed into the back of Gervan's shop. Jules checked the stranger on the steps – still talking on his cell phone – then broke down his telephoto rig and hurried out of the attic. A car and driver was waiting for him on the street near the end of the alley. When Kohlhertz's car pulled out, Jules would be right on his tail.

An Agitated Antiquarian

Inside the shop, Gervan focused on the sallow parchment atop his study bench. It wasn't his, but it was his most prized possession. He had tossed all night then tried all day to punch holes in his theory. Finally he was certain he couldn't interpret it any other way. And only then did he call in an urgent message to Melisandre. It was enough, he knew, to make her call back the moment she got it. And though it had only been ten minutes it seemed like ten hours.

He sat up and stretched his short, hunched frame then wiped his glasses. It didn't clear the fuzzy vision in his tired seventy-three-year-old eyes, so he wiped his glasses again and scratched his stringy gray hair with both hands as he looked upon the scroll one more time. It was unlike any other ancient documents he had studied. But through tenacity and luck he believed he had it solved and was equally sure that he had it right. And that was a chilling thought.

He looked at the faint marks on the curled corners and knew that someone had weighed it down, probably to photograph it. It was the first thing he had noticed. But the scroll was otherwise in such good condition that his initial impulse was that it was a fake.

Yet as the document's language unraveled his interest grew. Soon he realized that it was a coded message. Several alphabets derived from a version of cuneiform were used along with a set of symbols, like primitive hieroglyphics, which didn't appear to match anything in any language he had ever seen – and he thought he had seen them all.

He thought that he had stumbled upon an unknown volume of the Apocrypha, the group of books omitted from the Bible – the last of which was discovered in 1945 near the village of Nag Hammadi in Egypt. Certainly there were others still undiscovered.

But then he made a chance discovery. He found one of the scroll symbols in another ancient text, which led him to a new hypothesis – that the scroll was sort of a crude technological manual with the cuneiform-like characters as text and the primitive hieroglyphics as scientific symbols. And gradually the code began to break down.

As the clues mounted Gervan became obsessed. Then the results of a carbon-dating test came back. To his astonishment the paper was approximately two thousand years old! And even though the message he extracted seemed too implausible to be true, he just couldn't find anything to change his mind.

When the character who called himself Wolfgang Kohlhertz came to him with the scroll it was enclosed in a red clay vessel circled with bright, ruby-like bobs. The original beeswax seal had been broken and it had been re-sealed with newer paraffin – Kohlhertz made no secret of the fact that the jar had been tampered with.

He claimed to represent an anonymous collector though, of course, wouldn't say who, nor how he had acquired the artifact, nor when, nor from whom. He was seeking a translation and appraisal. Naturally he insisted on confidentiality.

But more striking even than Kohlhertz's sinister mien was the enormous fee he offered – so big in fact that Gervan questioned whether Kohlhertz really intended to pay. He also issued a very believable threat if his confidence was betrayed.

Despite his misgivings Gervan took the job – not for money or adventure, but because it might be important. And he immediately told Jules, the priest-cum-investigator, who quietly began making inquiries to see if anyone was offering a reward for a missing scroll – stolen artifacts, like stolen artworks, were often ransomed on the black market. But there was no word of missing documents from any of the known or, for that matter, secret collections.

And though the evidence that a new discovery had been made was mounting, Jules still knew that something was amiss. So he told Gervan to keep working and to stall Kohlhertz as long as he could. But that was about to change. And the agent of that change had just slipped through Gervan's back door and was watching as the old man anxiously awaited a phone call from his colleague and confidant, Melisandre.

Gervan checked his watch again and again. It was five past four in the afternoon. The small shop, crammed to overflowing with books and antiques, was always empty at this hour. Closing time was at five. He sopped the sweat from his brow, again trying to cast doubt on what he believed the scroll said and its explosive possibilities. But he could come to no other conclusion. He got up from his bench and stood by the phone, stuffing his handkerchief back into his vest pocket and checking the time again. Four-thirty and still no call. Melisandre was never this slow. The broad-shouldered man lurking in the shadows of the storeroom just watched, listened.

Suddenly the phone rang. Gervan jumped and answered before the end of the first ring. "*Melisandre!*" he said excitedly. Kohlhertz leaned closer. "I've found something. Come *immediately*," the old man implored with quaking voice and uneven breath. His hand trembled uncontrollably as he hung up.

"I assume ... " Kohlhertz began. Gervan startled, spilled the phone and turned toward the grainy-faced menace emerging from the shadows of the shop's back room.

An Impatient Poseur

"I assume," Kohlhertz repeated. He was over six feet tall. His neck, arms and trunk looked too long for his thick thighs and gave him a mantis-like appearance. "... you weren't talking about *my* property?" Gervan, trembling, pulled the handset up by its cord and fumbled it back onto the hook.

"*Herr* Kohlhertz. You startled me," he replied. Kohlhertz stared. Gervan averted his eyes, leaned on his bench and sopped the sweat from his face and neck. "I've been making modest progress on your document," he said, pretending to examine the scroll.

"*Modest*? You haven't *solved* it?"

"I have managed to identify many markings," he stammered. "I'm confident I'll have a solid theory within the next month or so if I can ..." Kohlhertz stepped up. The old man braced.

"A month or so," he dismayed. Gervan knew his charade wasn't selling well. And he was sure Kohlhertz had overheard his call to Melisandre.

"*Herr* Kohlhertz, it's only two months. Even working night and day ... this is very unique ... sometimes it takes *years* ... " Kohlhertz grabbed a handful of Gervan's vest and slammed him against the brick wall. A large abrasion blossomed red on the old man's forehead.

"Who was on the phone?" he demanded, holding Gervan pinned.

"Nothing to do with your item," Gervan insisted. Kohlhertz rammed his face again. "I swear!" Gervan begged. Kohlhertz spun him around and throttled him.

"What does it say? Who did you tell?" he hissed as he squeezed then let go. Old Gervan plunged to his knees, gasping. Kohlhertz kicked him in the ribs and he tumbled onto his side, holding up his hand.

"I think it's a map, a hiding place," Gervan coughed. Kohlhertz pulled him up by his hair and started slapping him. "Wait! *Wait!*" Gervan pleaded as his glasses went flying.

"Hiding place for *what*?"

"I don't know ... maybe the Solomon treasure," Gervan claimed. His ruse worked. The word treasure captured Kohlhertz's attention. He backed-off to let Gervan breathe. "The treasure. Disappeared from the Temple before the Romans pillaged Jerusalem in the first century," Gervan tumbled onto a chair. "I don't have it all. It may be a map. The treasure was taken someplace and never found."

With Kohlhertz lost in fantasies of great mammon, Gervan was –

for the moment at least – safe. Kohlhertz had seemingly forgotten that Melisandre was coming. Gervan was wondering if she would get there in time.

Suddenly they both noticed someone looking into the shop through the front window. But it wasn't Melisandre. It was a stranger and he was talking on a phone.

Linus Interruptus

"Riccio was there but he didn't get anything. Just me," Linus said. He was on the phone to Dark Star, his photo agency in New York, telling them about his bombshell pictures of the actress Jamie Richards. They were beside themselves with glee.

"Yes. *Exclusive*. Never mind how. Yeah. Tonight," he said. It was hot and he was sweating but something seemed unusually wet on his neck. He stood up off the steps and looked at the sign over the sleepy shop next door. It said GERVAN and it looked like an antiques shop. Using the front window as a mirror he saw the blood and found the wound. "I'm *busy* now. I'll send them *tonight*," he repeated then cut off. "Aw for *cripes* sake!" he groused, tugging the bloody collar. He had been gashed behind the ear in his scuffle with Riccio, his rival paparazzo. He dabbed the wound with his handkerchief and mumbled, "I *hate* this damned job!".

Though hate was probably too strong a word, lately Linus had been having doubts. He had drifted a long way from his earlier journalistic ideals and each bump, bruise and cut was another reminder of just how far. For a long time, working for a newspaper as an investigative reporter buoyed his idealism. But by the time he hit thirty-five he had concluded that no one could really make a difference. Crooks prospered. Corruption flourished. Then, to make matters worse, the newspapers all got an agenda and even journalism seemed gone to hell.

With his ambition – like his pay check – steadily shrinking, he opted out. He stopped looking out for the welfare of mankind and started looking out for the welfare of Linus P. Mercator for a change. He put down his pen, picked up his camera and went hunting lucrative tabloid trash, resigned to the fact that thousands of stories and millions of carefully crafted words exposing society's deepest ills wouldn't earn one tenth as much as a snapshot of a celebrity or politician, pants down around their ankles and an intern under their desk. Those were the stories the public wanted and those were the stories that Linus P. Mercator was now all about. At least that's what he thought he believed.

Now, he wasn't so sure.

He squinted through the glass, couldn't see anyone in the dark shop but he could hear some noise – loud talking then something falling over. And two words – "Solomon treasure". He decided to go in, maybe pick up a bandage for his wound. He pushed open the door and a small bell jingled. The shop was oddly silent. He listened and waited.

In the back, old man Gervan and Kohlhertz heard the bell, too. "Get rid of him and close the shop," Kohlhertz whispered as he rolled up his scroll and slid it into a plastic tube. Gervan straightened his torn vest, retrieved his smudged glasses and hung them on his reddened face then went to greet Linus.

"Kann ich Ihnen behilflich sein?" he asked. Linus noticed the torn vest and fresh scrape on the old man's forehead. Gervan noticed him noticing, pulled out his hankie and dabbed the wound but offered no explanation. *"Kann ich Ihnen behilflich sein?"* he repeated quietly.

"Mein Deutsch ist nicht sehr gut. Sprechen Sie Englisch?" Linus replied. Gervan, who spoke many languages, nodded. "I was interested in this," Linus said, pointing to a vintage magazine with a picture of JFK on the cover.

"Those are two Euros each," Gervan replied, handing him the magazine. Linus had a quick look but his interest was turning more to Gervan's roughed-up condition. He sensed a story. He held onto the magazine and said,

"Danke. I'd like to browse around," then grazed along the

bookshelves. Gervan sensed that Linus was suspicious and that gave him an idea. With Melisandre missing and his time running out, Linus was probably his only hope. But he had to get rid of him quickly. Kohlhertz wouldn't wait long and Melisandre was maybe miles away.

"Something in particular?" Gervan persisted, glancing nervously toward the back room every few seconds. Everything Linus was seeing – the nervous twitching, the red face, the bloody bump on the forehead – added up to an interrupted robbery. It wouldn't be a first for him. He once walked into an armed robbery at a nightclub which turned into a gun battle. This had a similar queasy feel.

He crossed the shop and set the magazine on the counter, casually flipped the pages as he glanced toward the back room. It was just a quick flash in his eyes but he was sure he saw the silhouette of a man outlined against a window. He turned away and picked up an old book. "How much for this?" he asked. Gervan said,

"Three Euros." They were both out of Kohlhertz's view.

"Do you need help?" Linus whispered, motioning toward the back room. Gervan shook "no" then moved away. Linus was puzzled. He set the book aside and looked questioningly at Gervan. Time was running out. Gervan knew he had to get rid of Linus now.

"You admire my glass collection," he said though Linus had hardly noticed the old bottles and jars on the shelf. "This is an interesting one," Gervan said, offering a piece of *faïence* – German version of the Italian Renaissance ceramics known as *majolica*.

"I'm not really interest ..." Linus began.

"Or perhaps *this*," Gervan interrupted, offering a simple clay vase decorated with red orbs. "Rather common. A worthless vase I'm afraid. But very decorative."

"Looks like a wine chiller."

"A very good suggestion. And I can let you have it cheap." Linus turned it in his hands then began to set it aside. Gervan's puffy eyes narrowed. "I'm late for an important meeting and I have no time to haggle. Please make up your mind and go," he said, loud enough for Kohlhertz to hear, pushing the vase into Linus's hands.

"Okay. And the magazine, too," Linus said, not wanting to upset the old guy further but puzzled by his desperation.

"Five euros, and that's more than fair," Gervan said softly, looking directly into Linus's face. He began wrapping the vase in newspaper and, when Linus wasn't looking, slipped a note inside then bagged it with the magazine. Linus paid the five euros. Gervan just tossed it on the counter then grabbed his arm and led him toward the door.

"I am very late and I must close," he apologized as he shoved Linus out. "Enjoy your purchase," Gervan said then he closed the door, latched it, and pulled the shades. Linus stepped out of the entrance and looked up at the gathering clouds. A thunder shower was looming in the humid July sky. He checked up and down the street as though he half-expected Massimo, his outmaneuvered rival, to ambush him. Of course it didn't happen. So Linus he set out casually across town toward his hotel.

As he passed the shop's back alley he noticed a skinhead leaning on a blue Mercedes sedan. And he also noticed two other guys who looked like a police tail detail. It was Jules the priest and his driver, sitting in a parked car. Like they were waiting for something to happen... something that, for now at least, Linus wanted to avoid.

He quickened his pace down the street, staying ahead of the game. And ahead of the rain.

Chapter 3. MESSAGE or MISTAKE?

Linus reached the Friedrichstrasse and wove his way through the heavy sidewalk traffic. It was a broad thoroughfare clogged with cars bouncing over the badly patched pavement – scars from the operation to re-connect East and West Berlin.

He waited for a "walk" light at the corner of Unter den Linden. His hotel, the *Grand*, was two blocks away. He always went for the high-priced digs – better chance of ambushing an unsuspecting glitterati and, what the hell, it was a business deduction, anyway.

He went to his room on the sixth floor, fire-wired his camera to his laptop and uploaded the images from the afternoon's escapade. Pictures of Jamie Richards, naked in an SS officer's cap, and the fight between Massimo Ricci, master paparazzo, and Klaus Krenz, enraged artist-cum-boyfriend, would create a huge frenzy – not to mention a huge pay check.

But instead of writing captions and sending the pictures, something else was on his mind – the beaten-up old man at the Gervan Antiquarian shop. He took the newspaper-wrapped bundle from the shop, sat on the bed and began unwrapping. The old man's story about closing early for an appointment was fishy ... not by itself, but combined with the bruises, the torn vest, the skin-headed wiseguy in the alley and the box-jawed man in the back room, the whole episode had a sinister flavor.

He cleared away the paper then laid the vase on the bed. It was crude, reddish clay, ringed with some type of glass or glazed red baubles – big enough to fit a wine bottle, nice enough for the dinner table. But nothing else about it was striking. As he started re-wrapping, a small hand-written note slipped out. It said "*Blauer Apfel* restaurant tonight" with an address. But no date. At first he thought it was just a stray scrap.

Then he thought again.

Maybe the old man *was* in trouble. But why would he refuse help when Linus asked him in the shop that afternoon, then direct him to a restaurant that night? Certainly it wasn't a promotions gimmick. But what else could it be? Since he needed to have supper anyway he decided it would be at the *Blauer Apfel* restaurant, which the map showed to be just around the corner from the Gervan Antiquarian shop.

He put the vase back in the bag. He was leaving Berlin in a day or so after being in Europe for nearly six months. Most of his belongings – too much for a commercial flight – were packed in a big trunk at the foot of the bed, ready to be sent on ahead. He padded the vase with some of the clothes and added it to the trunk, then called the shipper. If he could get it to the office on the other side of town before six o'clock – an hour from now – his trunk would be on its way to Boston tonight. Linus called the concierge and asked for a bellboy, a luggage dolly, and a cab.

A Hot Plate, and Getting Hotter

Linus re-read the note he found in the antique vase he bought a few hours ago. It said *"Blauer Apfel* restaurant tonight". He was on his way there for dinner and to maybe find out if the old man had sent him a message, or just a stray scrap of paper. He stood on the bridge over the Schiffbauerdamm, one of Berlin's many canals, watching the lights of the Berliner Ensemble theater marquee shimmer on the black water. Afternoon thundershowers had brought a cool summer night and left a glaze of reflections on the sidewalks and streets. The restaurant was four blocks away in the area behind the theater. The Gervan shop was just around the corner from the restaurant so he could pass by on his way. The images of the disheveled old man, the square-jawed guy in the back room, and the sleazy chauffeur in the rear alley were driving his curiosity.

The city noise faded as he followed a canal-side esplanade into a quiet neighborhood of shops, apartments, and cafes. When he got to the antique shop there was a yellow fire truck parked outside, its red lights strobing. A man and a woman were talking to one of the crew. Behind them, a fireman wearing an oxygen tank was coming out of the shop. The beam of a flashlight was moving around the smoky, dripping interior.

Linus slowed his pace and looked into the open door but stayed across the street. The two civilians made him apprehensive and he didn't want to volunteer anything until he knew what happened. Suddenly the man looked his way. The red strobe flashed on a white speck at his collar, enough to see that he was clergy. Linus knew he was being stared at but didn't know why.

He didn't know that he'd just been recognized by Jules, the priest in the attic stake-out who had photographed him that afternoon. All he knew was that a fit, 50-ish, six-foot tall clergyman with graying pushed-back hair and a beautiful woman beside him was taking a long, hard look. So Linus took a hard look back.

He was struck by the priest's clothes. Not the black pants but the unique jacket, finely tailored in brushed silk and cut to resemble a cassock. And the woman he was with surely wasn't mother superior. She, too, was dressed in finery.

But most striking was her long mane of chestnut brown hair. It hung outside of her silk raincoat and was gathered with flowers at three places along the length of her back. She was focused on her conversation with the fireman and didn't notice Jules and Linus gawking at each other. Just as Linus was about to say, 'what'a you lookin' at Holmes', Jules turned away.

He wanted to know what happened but Linus decided against getting too nosy. The mysterious *Blauer Apfel* restaurant was just around the corner. So he picked up his pace. Details about the fire would have to wait until tomorrow's newspapers came out. Yet he couldn't shake the sense that he was being watched, and for good reason. Jules hadn't lost interest in the passing stranger after all and he urgently shared that interest with his companion – the woman named Melisandre.

Melisandre Marks Her Quarry

Melisandre was in mid sentence when Jules said, "Excuse us," and pulled her away. He pointed her in the right direction then nodded at Linus, who was walking away and went around the corner. They moved to the corner and continued watching. "Who is he?" she asked.

"Don't know. Maybe no one," Jules replied. "But I photographed him. He bought something here this afternoon."

"What time?"

"The right time."

The two watched then Melisandre said, "Gervan's missing. Kohlhertz has him. I'm sure of it." Her eyes were glued on Linus.

"We didn't see them get in the car," Jules explained. "We followed them to a garage. I got out to look for a way in and my driver went looking for another exit. Unfortunately by the time he found it they had slipped away." Melisandre nodded at Linus.

"Let's track him for now." Jules pulled his cell phone.

"I have someone nearby," he said as he began to dial. But Melisandre stopped him. Linus had arrived at the end of the street and entered the *Blauer Apfel* restaurant. Melisandre looked at Jules.

"That's convenient," she said. Jules smirked and pocketed his cell phone.

"I will be in the kitchen," he said. Melisandre nodded and said, "He'll be with me."

Dumped in a Berlin Canal

The black van rolled through the darkness at a slow, steady pace. At the edge of Bocker Park, near Landwehr Kanal, it pulled to the side of the road and stopped. It was one of Berlin's more infamous sites – the place where the opposition dumped the body of *Red Rosa*,

Rosa Luxembourg, organizer of the Communist *Spartacus* Party, in 1919. And tonight another notable Berliner would suffer the same irreverent fate.

They were well outside the center of Berlin and traffic was light. The driver waited until no cars were passing then turned onto a dirt path and headed into the cover of the thick trees. The van bounced to a halt at the edge of the canal. He got out and looked at the black, barely moving water, then opened the rear doors. Two accomplices jumped out and scouted around, checking for homeless people or lovers – anyone who might see them. But the park was empty and there were no witnesses.

They dragged a large, flopping object out of the van, hefted it over the railing and dumped it into the canal. It fell ten feet then made a heavy splash in the deep water. Without wasting another second the three climbed back into the van and beat a hasty exit.

Parry, Then Party

Linus pushed on the bright blue apple – the *Blauer Apfel* – painted on the door and stepped up into the restaurant. He surveyed the long bar and some small round tables on his left, then a larger room full of square tables on his right. He then sat at the bar, ordered a beer, and looked for anything that the old man might've wanted him to see. Three huge ceiling fans paddled the still air of the large dining hall. A lively dinner party was taking place in the far corner. There were more women than men and most had cropped haircuts. It looked like a club of some sort because they all wore a yellow accent – like scarves, breast-pocket hankies – and gold jewelry.

On the pale green wall above them, a huge Ingres-like nude reclining and reading a book by candlelight hung in an ornate frame. Sumptuous golden hair covered her from ankle to breast. The way it was centered and alone on the wall – and the biggest decoration in the place – lent it special eminence. He turned back to his beer and recognized the woman who was with the clergyman at the Gervan shop fire coming through the door. Her priest companion was missing and she was alone. She gave him a long look as she took the seat next to his. The bartender brought her a glass of port. *"Danke*, Karl," she said and slipped her arms out of her silk raincoat. Linus guessed that she was about his age – early forties. The quality of her clothing stood out – in this case her fine linen suit. Not a stitch out of place. Never had he paid so much attention to clothes. Now he was noticing them all the time. A distinctive gold bee dangled from a gold chain around her neck.

"Die Speisekart, bitte?" Linus asked and the bartender handed him a menu. When he saw the English translations scribbled in the margins he knew that his accent had betrayed him.

"You're American," the woman said, also picking up on the accent. And Linus thought, 'Not another lecture on why the United States suck.' The one thing he wouldn't miss about Europe was the anti-Americanism. He just nodded. But then she said, "Me too. From where?" Relieved, he replied, "Massachusetts."

"Oh. I'm from Boston," she said.

"I live on the north shore," he said. If she was a real Bostonian she'd know where he meant. As striking as her long hair were her shining green eyes, which seemed unnaturally bright. Once her coat was off a strong fragrance filled the air between them. Linus felt a familiar allergic twitch in his eyes. It was chamomile, his only allergy. Luckily is was a rare scent and his allergy fairly mild.

"What brings you here?," she asked.

"Work," he said and quaffed his beer.

"In Germany?"

"Paris, mostly. And you?"

"Work," she said. Linus set down his glass, stuck out his hand and said,

"Linus."

"Linus," she repeated. "I'm Melisandre," She shook his hand.

"Your German is good. I saw you talking to that fireman," he said. His fishing expedition, like her secret interrogation, had begun. He wanted to know what happened at the shop, but only casually.

"What was that, anyway?"

"A book either fell or was left on a hot plate. Made a lot of smoke and set off the alarms," she said dismissively. After what he'd seen at the shop that afternoon Linus was sure there was more to it than that.

"Anyone hurt?" he asked.

"No. They're trying to locate the owner now," she said. Then, watching him closely to gauge his response, she added, "No one has heard from him since noon." They both knew Linus was there later. Linus didn't bite.

"You know the owner?" he asked.

"I get books and things there," she said, nonchalantly as she studied the menu. Then she asked, "Having dinner?" He looked over his shoulder at the crowded dining room.

"Thinkin'bout it," he said.

"Join me. I have a table. The best in the house." He stalled a moment. Had it not been for the strange events which led him here her chumminess perhaps wouldn't have seemed so overly anxious. On the other hand, Melisandre didn't strike him as someone who would be picking up strangers at bars. He knew something else was up and wondered if this was a contact that the old man from the antiquarian shop wanted him to make. So he put down the menu and said, "Melisandre, as my dear mother would say, that would be *grand*."

She led him through a beaded curtain and into a large private dining salon. Three vases overflowing with fresh flowers were set upon a table big enough for eight, but only set for two.

"All this just for us?" he said. Melisandre smiled.

"There'll be others," she assured, taking her place at the table's head. The hostess, a well-dressed middle-aged woman with the bearing of ownership, brought in their drinks, smiled politely at Linus and left the room without speaking.

"So Linus ... does everyone call you Linus?"

"Unless they're pissed."

"It's unusual. Family name?"

"No," he said with a half smirk. "I'm actually named after my father's hero. My middle name is Pauling."

"Linus Pauling. Two Nobel prizes, wasn't it? Chemistry and... "

"Peace, for promoting disarmament."

"Was your father a scientist?" she asked. He nodded.

"M.I.T. guy. Worked mostly on the space program."

"So what's the rest of it? Linus Pauling ... what?" He was sipping his beer.

"Mercator. Linus Pauling Mercator," he said.

"Mercator. Another assumed name?"

"Sort of. I'm a distant relative of Gerhardus Mercator, the cartographer, whose name was really Gerhardt Kremer. He changed it for some unknown reason after he mapped the globe with latitudes and longitudes. My family tree can be traced all the way back to 1512."

"Are you interested in genealogy?" she asked.

"Only if someone else does it. In this case, my mother, rest her soul."

"Your father?"

"Gone. Presumed resting peacefully as well."

"So you are Linus Mercator, the great navigator."

"That's right. Charting a course of righteousness through the world's moral minefields," he quipped. Melisandre discreetly pressed a call button under the table and summoned a young waitress who filled their plates from a large soup tureen. She handed Melisandre a check-folder and a pen. Linus didn't give it a thought and assumed the obvious ... she was signing for something, perhaps the meal.

Melisandre wrote "Linus Pauling Mercator. Massachusetts north shore" on the pad and gave it back. The waitress hurried out.

"L.P. Mercator. Wasn't there a journalist from Boston ... ?" Melisandre continued.

"Not any more."

"You. But you quit?" He nodded but spared her the details of his professional disillusionment – at least for now.

"There was a series, on women's shelters," she said. "I'm

involved in women's issues and I remember it led to some funding reform, didn't it?"

"A few speeches were made but I doubt if anything significant was ever really done," he dismayed.

"No," she said. "Someone went to jail on corruption charges. I remember it well." Her memory was good. She had him nailed.

"For embezzlement," he said. "But that was a rare result. Most of the stuff I did was long forgotten by the time the newspaper hit the curb on trash day," he said sourly.

"So what are you doing now?"

"Nothing. Celebrity photographer," he mumbled. It surprised her.

"A *paparazzo*?"

" 'Fraid so," he admitted. She couldn't hide her frown. "C'mon. It's not so bad. Look, these celebrities make obscene millions off ordinary people. I think they owe the public."

"Sure. But *how much?*"

"The market dictates. If there's a buyer there'll always be someone there to sell. It may as well be me," he opined. Melisandre wasn't convinced and, from his cynical tone, didn't think he was either. "It's truly Fellini-esque," he continued. "You know the original *paparazzo* was a celebrity photographer in Fellini's *La Dolce Vita*? His name was *signor Paparazzi*. The word means to "buzz about like an insect." That's what we are ... blood-sucking insects. All very *a propos*, don't you think?"

"I guess. But not very noble."

"Well, you know, all that time I was fighting crime, crime was fighting me back. And guess what? I lost. And this is far more profitable anyway." Melisandre just stared. Were it not for the good work that she knew he had done, he would've been easy to dislike. "Hey, at least I *tried* to make a contribution. Gotta be worth *some* points," he said.

"I'll give you that," she conceded. "But maybe you just need a break. Think of this as just a break..."

"Ya," he chortled. "It's been seven years."

"A *long* break. It's a good idea, lest we become *cynical*," she said. Linus chuckled again. He knew his cynicism was always on display. "Where are you staying? Do you need the name of a good hotel?" she asked.

"No thanks. Got one."

"Where?"

"The Grand. I'm leaving Berlin soon anyway," he said. Again, Melisandre's finger found the call button. The waitress came and cleared the soup plates and again Melisandre signed. This time she wrote "Grand Hotel". A woman in a cape and dark black veil appeared in the doorway and the waitress said, *"Dort ist eine Frau für Sie."* Melisandre looked up and saw the waiting women.

"Vera," Melisandre said and Vera glided into the room, raising her veil, her black satin cape flowing open behind her, its gold lining the same color and fabric as her svelte gown. They seemed like fashion opposites. Both were beautiful but Melisandre was more natural and simple whereas this woman Vera defined elegance and *haute couture*. She looked and walked as though she was born on the runways of Paris and Milan. "I'm so glad you could come," Melisandre said as they embraced. Linus stood up. "Veronica Franco, meet Linus Mercator," she said. Veronica nodded and said "hello" as she draped her cape and scarf over a chair. The waitress brought another glass of port and Veronica sat next to Linus.

As they chatted Linus noted her Italian accent though her English sounded more American than British. She said she was from Milan and now living in Venice. She was a tad younger than Melisandre, maybe mid-thirties, and her unpretentious charm rendered her elegance infinitely approachable. He complimented her on her dress and she said she had just come from the inaugural reception at the new Italian embassy in Berlin.

Linus wondered what was so important that it had drawn her away from an affair of State.

Chapter 4. JULES DESPATCHES HIS AGENTS

Jules hung back out of sight in the kitchen while the women kept Linus busy in the salon. He sipped his coffee as the waitress handed him the message from Melisandre that said only, 'Grand Hotel'. Two young women in black slacks, white blouses and yellow scarves stood beside him. He showed them the note. They nodded and exited through the kitchen door. Jules finished his coffee, stood up and straightened his jacket. He tore off the note page, pocketed it and gave the folder back to the waitress. Then he went to join the others in the salon.

The Spectacle of Adulation

A long procession of visitors followed Jules into the dining salon that evening – though to call them mere *visitors* was a stretch. Fawning acolytes was a more apt description. Melisandre introduced Jules as Father Doinel but he insisted on being called Jules. And though he and Linus had seen each other only briefly just an hour earlier at the shop fire, his handshake somehow had a greater familiarity. Linus didn't guess why. Veronica, who said *"bon jour"*, apparently knew him already. Jules's introduction was the last thing Melisandre said to Linus all evening. A few minutes later she and Jules withdrew to a corner for a private conversation while Veronica kept Linus occupied and entertained.

"So, *signor* Linus Mercator. You are a writer. Why don't you write a book about me?" she urged half-seriously. "I have had many enchanting experiences," she said with a glint in her eye. From that point on, the conversation never lagged. Veronica did the talking,

Linus the listening.

She said she was the daughter of an Italian diplomat, which meant she probably *was* living a novel-worthy existence. And though she tried to monopolize his attention Linus was more interested in the extraordinary scene unfolding at the far end of the salon. Melisandre, enthroned in a high-backed chair of maroon and gold brocade, was holding court. Jules was stationed dutifully by her side. And the devotees came and went all evening. Veronica seemed to know them all. They'd say hello then get onto the reception line leading to Melisandre.

Some of them arrived singly, others came in pairs. There was a fairly even mix of men and women and they were all ages. Linus could only manage to overhear a few disconnected words. One of them, which came up more than once, was "*Novangelis*".

Yet, though their conversations were muted their deference was obvious, even from across the big room. Linus couldn't remember when he'd seen so much hand kissing, bowing and scraping. Most had their audience with Melisandre then lingered a bit at the buffet – where food was kept in abundance by the dedicated wait-staff. And they all bore gifts. Remarkable items. A dignified gentleman in an impeccable blue suit brought bolts of silks wrapped in brown tissue. The equally impeccable woman with him presented several dozen boxed gloves in different fabrics and leather.

Another man brought shoes, many pairs, all colors and styles.

The vintner, a broad-shouldered man with a panhandle jaw, clutching a case of wine in his big, rugged hands, was the most physically impressive. The most *unusual* – and best smelling – was the scent maker and ointment mixer. She seemed a fey flower child of twenty-six though Veronica said that she was actually a registered pharmacist and freelance 'scent consultant' from Quebec, sought after by the world's biggest perfumers.

The simplest gesture came from a young couple who brought a case of orchids, which Melisandre shared with the guests. To a person they were content to wait on line with their offerings – sometimes so copious that the wait-staff had to help – then join the others for the banquet. And Jules, ever the diplomat, was never far from Melisandre's side, shuttling the guests to and fro and inventorying the bounty. Towards the end of the evening, after most of the guests had come and gone, Linus was still sitting in the same spot. Vera had moved onto the table and sat cross-legged like Dietrich, reveling in her life's exploits. Linus saw no signs at all that he was overstaying his welcome and probably wouldn't have cared if he was. The day had given rise to a thousand questions and this evening, a thousand more. And more than ever he was convinced that Gervan, the old shop keep, had directed him to this *soirée*, though he was still at a loss for a reason.

But now at least he had a strong hunch – that Melisandre was the key to why he was there.

The Escort

The clock struck midnight. Everyone had gone and the original four were back together. Melisandre was in the sitting area chatting quietly with Jules.

"Half an hour," were her last words to him, then the two stood up to join Linus and Veronica, who was again suggesting episodes for a novel about herself.

"Why did you leave the embassy party," Linus asked her.

"When you date diplomats, they get called away," she observed dryly. "I ask you, really ... what affairs of State could *possibly* be more important ...?" she said with smile.

"None that *I* can think of," Linus affirmed. Melisandre and Jules came to the table. She seemed different from the talkie barfly he had met earlier. Now there was a special calmness about her and a bearing which exuded confidence and leadership. Jules's face was pretty much a blank page. He was polite enough but Linus sensed that Jules was a very tough nut to crack.

"I'm sorry I abandoned you both. Did you enjoy yourself?" Melisandre asked Linus.

"Very much. *Danke schön*," he said. Jules reached out his hand and with his deep pulpit voice said,

"Bon nuit, monsieur." Linus shook hands and responded in kind. Veronica stood up and straightened her dress.

"I'm leaving, too," she said, grabbing her cape and handing it to Linus who helped her as she and Melisandre exchanged amused smirks. "Thank you *signor* Linus. I had a lovely evening," she said as she spread her veil over her hair and, in an act which struck Linus as very sisterly, Melisandre arranged it to hang gracefully over the shoulder. Veronica bade Linus *"Buona fortuna"*, said goodnight and left the room with Jules in tow. Linus and Melisandre were finally alone.

"She's very ... *captivating*," he said.

"She held you captive," Melisandre said with a smile. "Because she likes you."

"She must like me *very much*," he noted. "Any word on you friend from the shop?" he asked. The question put a wrinkle in her confidence and she seemed genuinely crestfallen.

"No. Nothing," she said but that was all. Clearly, anything more was out of bounds and Linus wondered why. He looked at the mountain of presents in the corner and asked,

"Your birthday?" Melisandre glanced over her shoulder.

"Sort of," she said as she walked toward the gift corner. "I'm a co-founder and spokeswoman for a rights group. This is our anniversary and these gifts are tokens of larger contributions," she explained.

"What type of rights?"

"Human rights. Nothing terribly radical, though I'm sure we intimidate a few people from time to time," she said, though without a hint as to who those intimidated souls might be. Then she checked her watch. It was Linus's cue.

"Can I drop you someplace?" he asked, assuming he'd get them a cab. She said,

"Yes, but actually it's just around the corner if you wouldn't mind walking me home?"

They got their coats, said good night to the hostess – who was stationed like a sentry on a chair just outside the salon – and left through the *Blauer Apfel*'s front door. The bartender locked up after them. Linus was surprised when Melisandre latched onto his arm as they strolled.

"I always thought journalism would be rewarding and exciting," she observed.

"It ain't all it's cracked up to be," he said. "Most of the time it's very plodding, one-foot-ahead-of-the-other type stuff."

"Why did you get into it?"

"Idealism I suppose. I wanted to go someplace where I could make a difference."

"And you don't feel as though you have?"

"Are you kidding?" he huffed. Melisandre just shrugged. The dampness was gone from the air and the July night was cool. A few blocks from the restaurant Melisandre led them into a pedestrian mall lined with gray stucco townhouses. They stopped at the weathered front door to one of the buildings. Like all the others in the neighborhood it was five stories high. She released his arm and stood at the bottom of the steps.

"So what about this rights group of yours?" he asked.

"We're advocates, really. Mostly for women's rights." she said. Again he waited for more but didn't get any.

"Would it be called *Novangelis* by any chance?" He had heard the word several times that night. She didn't seem surprised that he knew it and said,

"Yes. *Novangelis*. New Angels."

"Is there a religious affiliation?" he asked, since Jules the priest was so prominent.

"Not with a particular denomination, per se. But as I'm sure you've seen it does involve some clergy," she said. And just as he was thinking she was being secretive Melisandre blurted, "It's a good story. If you'd like to write it I'd be happy to meet you again." He wondered why she'd make *any* offer when she could have dropped it all right there. He considered three possibilities. The least likely –

though one he liked best – was that she liked him and wanted to know him better.

Then there was the possibility that maybe she *was* interested in getting some publicity for her cause – though that somehow seemed unlikely as well.

The third possibility, however, hinged on a darker motive. Perhaps her wish to keep him close had something to do with old man Gervan from the antiques shop, who's disappearance was something of obvious concern to her.

"I'm only in Berlin for a few more days," he said.

"I'm only here a few more days myself. How about tomorrow night at eight. At Paris Bar. Do you know it?" Linus nodded. It was a small out-of-the-way place where East German writers and thinkers gathered to meet their counterparts in the West.

"Then tomorrow at eight it is," he said, shook her hand, thanked her for the party and bid her good night. She started up the stairs.

Linus turned and walked away.

The Intrusion

It was half past one in the morning and all was quiet in the sleeping hotel. His steps were hushed on the carpeted stairs leading to the mezzanine with its gilded plaster grape vines framing the lush Arcadian landscapes painted on the vaulted ceiling. He took the mezzanine elevator to the sixth floor and went to his room, opened the door with his key card, stepped in and snapped on the light. Right away he noticed that the bed hadn't been turned down, though it usually was. And the vintage magazine he bought at the antiquarian shop was on the bed where he had left it. Or was it? The magazine was still on the bed, but something about how it was lying struck him, as though it had been moved.

As he closed the door and surveyed the room a strong feeling was gathering that something was out of place. Nothing drastic that he'd recognize immediately. It was more and overall impression, like *everything* was out of place – but only slightly.

The closet door wasn't completely closed and his suitcase was leaning against the wall, not upright on the floor as he remembered it. Suddenly it struck him that he might not be alone. His heart raced and he thought about getting out but instead grabbed the desk lamp and brandished it like a club. He whipped open the closet door and the hangers chimed in the wind. It was empty – though not undisturbed. His clothes, which had been spread out in the closet, were now bunched up. Maybe the maid had moved things when she tidied up, he thought. But if she had been there tidying up why hadn't she turned down the bed?

He moved to the bathroom. The shower curtain was drawn. He ripped it aside and braced for an attack. There was nothing but an empty tub. And there was no one under the bed, either. Suddenly he felt kind of silly. His heartbeat slowed. He was certainly alone in the room.

He took a quick inventory of his things, beginning with his carry-on bag. Nothing was missing but, again, everything seemed slightly out of place. His passport folder – an oversized brown leather wallet for carrying travel papers – was on the bottom when it should've been on the top where he had packed it. He opened the wallet. Everything was there but it wasn't arranged as neatly as before. Some of the cards and papers were crooked or not all the way into their slots.

He slid the passport out of the wallet. The blue cardboard cover was intact but the spine was flattened as though it had been bent open the way someone would spread it to copy it with a camera. An ominous realization tingled the back of his neck as his doubts vanished. His room had definitely been searched.

He thought about the shadowy figure in the back of the antique shop that afternoon, and the skinhead driver in the alley. Maybe they had followed him. It was chilling. A simple robbery would've been easier to shrug off because the thieves would never go back to the same room to rob again. But nothing was missing. It wasn't a robbery. It was someone being very nosy about who he was and what he was doing. And it was a gentle job – not a ransacking, but not quite subtle enough to escape detection. Maybe they were amateurs, he thought. Or they wanted him to know that they had been there.

But whoever they were, and for whatever reason, they apparently thought Linus had something they wanted or knew something they wanted to know. And maybe he did. All he had to do now was figure out what it was.

Chapter 5. PARIS BAR

July 23rd. Day 02.

Paris Bar was sparsely peopled when Linus arrived – just a few literati and some suits hanging at the bar – the lull between the after-work crowd and the evening crowd. He was twenty minutes early for his eight o'clock date with Melisandre, sitting at a small table in the front window. Waiting.

The small cafe filled up fast. By nine o'clock all the seats were taken – all except the one beside him. Melisandre's seat. Last night, as he laid awake wondering why his hotel room had been searched and by whom, he couldn't escape the feeling that his meeting Melisandre was no mistake and that the it was somehow related to the search. And his suspicions grew stronger with each tick of the clock. It was almost 9:30. He wanted to tell his story about the intruders in his room and gauge her reaction, but it was clear that she wasn't coming and he wouldn't have that chance tonight.

The waiter came by and offered another drink. Linus declined but asked if there had been a message. The waiter polled the other waiters and bartenders and asked the manager and the hostess. No one had taken a call. Linus checked at his hotel, too. There was only one message, from *Dark Star*, his photo agency in New York, screaming for the Jamie Richards photos – which he hadn't sent. But that was it. Linus paid his tab and left.

As he stood in the glow of the pink neon *Paris Bar* sign, scanning the street and holding one last hope of catching a glimpse of Melisandre, a cab pulled up to the curb. Four people got out and went inside. Linus held the door open, had a last look around, then leaned in and asked,

"Sind Sie frei?" The driver looked over his shoulder and grunted,

"Ja," Linus hopped in.

"Berliner Ensemble, bitte," he said. The driver re-set the meter and drove off across the city. Linus's thoughts of a pleasant evening and frank conversation – maybe even a bond – evaporated, replaced with a strong sense of betrayal. He reminded himself that there might be a logical excuse for Melisandre's absence and he didn't know for sure what had happened to her. But he *did* know where to look for her... or so he thought.

New Angels

The two cars were identical, inconspicuous sedans with dark tinted windows – hardened against bullets and small bombs, purchased within a week of learning that an organization in Paris had secretly proclaimed a successor. After centuries of intrigue, murder and usurpation, there was no reason to believe that the present would be any different from the past. Security was essential. This was a time for vigilance and no one knew that better than the leadership of *Novangelis* – the New Angels.

Beginning precisely at nine p.m. the New Angels began to arrive. Their arrival schedule was staggered to be unobtrusive. But the rendezvous – in an outlying Berlin warehouse where the group secreted their physical assets – was well beyond the public gaze.

By ten o'clock the team of seven was assembled. The weapons officer issued tasers and black batons. Two of the guards were given guns loaded with rubber bullets. Despite their belief that the danger was potentially mortal, *Novangelis* had a strict prohibition on lethal weapons – for now at least.

They were not in uniform but they were all dressed in black. Other things connected them – the variations on the yellow scarf, and the gold bees pinned to their jackets or blouses. And the cropped hair. Together they were unmistakably a team, a unit. Apart they would look like any other citizen. They drilled and operated with military precision. Each knew their job and didn't need to be told. Some of them were recruits from the general population. Some of them were rescued from hellish lives. And some had aristocratic lineage claims of their own.

But all were fiercely devoted.

At eleven o'clock they began the ten-minute drive to a safe house where Melisandre and two more bodyguards were waiting. Just as no one had seen them coming, no one saw them go. Indeed few people knew that *Novangelis* existed. And even fewer knew their true intent.

Ghost House

Linus paid his cab fare then stood beside a thick-trunked tree, watching the door of the townhouse that Melisandre said was hers. The walking paths that crisscrossed through the leafy mall were empty and the buildings lining both sides were all the same – a basement, four floors and an attic above. There was only one difference – the one she said was hers, the one she left him at last night, was totally dark. Not a single light in any window.

He waited and watched but the only sign of life was a thimble-shaped woman in a housedress and apron who shuffled past without noticing him. When she was gone the mall was again empty and quiet. But nothing had changed at the house. Linus decided he had waited long enough.

He jogged up the stairs and pressed the bell. Nothing happened – no bell nor buzzer. He rapped lightly on the door and listened. Again, nothing. No stirring. No approaching footsteps.

He retreated to the sidewalk and checked up and down the mall. As far as he could tell he was still alone. He rounded the corner into a slim alley between the buildings and found a side entrance – five narrow steps leading down to a small basement door. He descended the stairs and crouched in the deep shadow at the bottom. The solid wood door was locked and dead-bolted. But there was one chance of getting in – the three frosted glass panes of the door's window.

He tapped the glass with his fingernail. It was very thick – breaking it would be too noisy. So he took out his keys and began scraping away the dried putty around the pane nearest the door knob. When enough was cut away he checked for alarm wires – there were none – then began prying until he was able to wedge his fingers in and pull it free, then reach in and unlock the door. He checked the alley again then ducked into the dark basement.

The room stank of coal oil and the blackness turned woolly gray as his eyes adjusted. The shadowy form of a staircase appeared – stairs leading up into the house. But there was no noise at all. If anyone was home they were either being very still or sleeping. And even though this wasn't the first time he'd pulled this kind of stunt, the thought of stumbling into a snoozy resident gave him pause. Breaking and entering in the nighttime was bad enough – even riskier in a foreign country.

On the other hand, he thought maybe Melisandre *was* there and in trouble. Maybe that's why she didn't keep her date. Maybe she was sick or injured – or worse. Maybe he had an obligation to find out why she had vanished. Thin rationale perhaps, but at the moment it was enough. Besides, someone had done the same to *his* space, his hotel room. Thin vindication, he knew. But again enough.

He climbed the stairs three at a time, pausing between steps so he wouldn't create a pattern of sounds. At the top he turned the glass knob and cracked open the door. The lights were off but ambient light brightened the room. It was a kitchen, but the glass-doored cabinets were curiously empty.

He stepped up and checked a few drawers and they were empty, too – not a single utensil. There was a stove, but no refrigerator. This kitchen had been idle for some time. Likewise the dining room – no furniture, no curtains, no decorations. It was all adding up to one thing – this was a vacant house. And judging from the dust it had been vacant for a while. Still, he wouldn't take any chances.

He shucked his shoes, crossed the hardwood hallway and started up the winding front staircase, expecting someone to leap at him from every shadow. But each floor and every room was the same as the one before – stark and vacant. Except for one. It was in the attic and at the rear of the house. A folded cot with no coverings was pushed against one of the walls. There was a small wooden table near it and a tall chair in the middle of the room which faced a bare, shade-less window. There was a ball of white paper – a sandwich wrapper – and a squashed paper bag on the table. Linus knew what he was seeing – a dormant stake-out.

He shaved along the wall toward the window and peeked out. At first there was nothing remarkable to see – the backs of some smaller buildings directly below, a quiet street with a few parked cars just beyond. Then it struck him. He was looking at Gervan's antiquarian shop, a clear view of both the front and back entrances. The events of the past twenty-four hours took on an added dimension as he realized that not only had he been seen going into the antiquarian shop yesterday afternoon, he was probably photographed as well. And probably by someone who had shown the picture to Melisandre. And that, he figured, was why she materialized out of no where at the *Blauer Apfel* restaurant.

But where was she now? Why did she ditch him? Was she satisfied that he didn't know anything – which, as far as he knew, he didn't – and that he was no longer any use? Did she think that his appearance at *Blauer Apfel* last night was merely coincidence?

Probably all of the above.

Melisandre apparently hadn't concluded that old man Gervan and his cryptic note – about which she knew nothing – was actually responsible for their meeting, and not – as she must've assumed – her initiative.

In any case, Linus knew that someone out there might still think he has something they wanted. If so he'd be hearing from them, and probably soon. He also realized that *they* probably didn't know what they were looking for, either. It was the oddest possibility of all but the one with the most solid supporting evidence. His hotel room was searched in a way that the average, unsuspicious person wouldn't notice. But if the searchers knew what they were looking for they would've ripped through his stuff, knowing full well they'd recognize what they wanted when they saw it. Yet someone who was unsure and hoping to make a discovery would be gentler. Because if they didn't make a discovery they'd have to rely on Linus to lead them to something, and they wouldn't want to tip him off.

Unfortunately for them Linus had discovered their ruse. Ironically, he had no clue what they wanted, and couldn't lead them anywhere. But of one thing Linus was sure... that the antique shop and old man Gervan were at the center of some sort of intrigue, and that Melisandre was the key to discovering what it was.

He left the attic and was descending the last few steps to the first floor when he noticed a business card atop the bottom post. It was for a company called *Immobilien Berlin*, a real estate company. It made perfect sense – vacant townhouse being shown to prospective lessees or buyers, the agent's business card left behind. But whoever was showing the townhouse must've known about the stake-out in the attic, and maybe the Immobilien Berlin office would yield some leads.

He hurried back through the kitchen, into the basement and out the side door. He approached the end of the alley and looked around the corner. The mall was empty in both directions. He stepped out of the shadows and went hunting... first for a rental car, then for a real estate office called *Immobilien Berlin*.

The Tail of the Peacock

It was just after 10:30 and the *Immobilien Berlin* office was closed – as he knew a real estate office would be at this hour. But he figured he could at least find it and have a look. Maybe the location would hold some type of clue. Maybe he'd recognize a face or a name in the neighborhood.

The office was on Margaretenstrasse, a narrow street lined with four-story modern buildings made of light brown brick. The ground floors were shops and offices with apartments above. And the street lighting was subdued – more residential than business, which tended to be less bright. He drove past at a crawl. Muted light, probably a nightlight, was showing through the slats of the vertical blinds in the front window, but the office otherwise seemed dead. Linus decided to pay a visit the next morning, posing as a potential client.

But before he left he had an impulse to check if the office hours were posted at the entrance. He parked across the street, opened his door and had his left foot on the pavement when the dim light in the office went out. He pulled in his foot and closed the door. A woman came out and locked up. Her dark coat flowed open revealing long, shapely legs and an exquisite dress. She hurried into a silver BMW at the curb. The brake lights flashed. The engine started. The headlights came on. The car pulled out and she gunned it down the street. As she passed, Linus got a clean look at her face. It was Veronica Franco – Melisandre's friend Vera. Linus moved quickly and followed.

The BMW wove aggressively through the city as Linus struggled to keep up in his mid-size rental. Away from the congestion of Berlin he worried that she'd notice him so he hung back even farther. They got onto an autobahn then, about ten miles outside of Berlin Zentrum, they exited onto a dark, narrow road cutting through patches of forest and across open fields. Luckily there was other traffic so Linus blended in easily.

But after about twenty miles the traffic had thinned to nothing. The BMW kept a steady, fast pace with Linus trailing about a quarter of a mile behind. They passed through more open fields and into a thick black forest with streams and small lakes that shone like mercury in the moonlight. At every corner, when the BMW disappeared ahead, Linus slowed down. The last thing he wanted was to go screaming around a corner and find the BMW stopped on the other side. But each time, at each corner, the tail lights would be up ahead, moving right along in front of him as he made the curve.

But this time they were gone.

He rode his foot down hard on the brake and began scanning the woods on both sides of the road, watching for red and yellow taillights, looking for a spot in the tall arrowhead pines where the

BMW might have turned off. To his right he could see a sliver of lake through the trees but nothing else. Then something caught his eye – a tiny fleck of red taillight cutting through the woods. He was sure it was the BMW, heading toward the lake.

He stepped on the gas and pulled forward, scanning for a place to hide his car. Just ahead there was an opening where a hiking trail crossed the road and he pulled in. The brush scratched along the windows and doors as he maneuvered onto the path and into the thicket then doused the lights and stopped the engine. He reached overhead, popped the plastic cover off the dome light and pulled out the bulb, then walked along the road to where the BMW had turned off. It was a dirt driveway flanked by two stone pillars, meaning it was probably a private drive and not just a picnic area or boat launch.

Linus passed through the pillars and headed into the dark woods.

Ritual at Midnight

He walked along the tire-rutted road sloping toward the lake, careful not to twist an ankle in the dark. The woods were so dense that he couldn't see more than a few yards in any direction. He came upon a sharp turn and looked around the corner. A long wooden building like a meeting hall was about fifty yards away. Light spilled out of a long row of windows, partially hidden by bushy hemlocks that ran along its side.

He moved into the cover of the forest and headed toward the building, a cushion of pine needles hushing his steps. From his crouch behind a big tree he could see a tin-pan shade over the door casting a cone of light on two sentries. Both wore dark form-fitting clothes, and both were women. In unison they turned and looked down the road. Linus heard the sizzle of tires on dewy pavement – a car was approaching on the main highway. It turned onto the dirt road and headed his way.

He ducked deeper into the woods, rubbed his hands on some wet bark then smeared his face with the black mossy goo. An oversized

Mercedes sedan with heavily tinted windows braked to a stop at the hall's front door. One of the sentries spoke to someone inside the building and two well-dressed women, one middle-aged and the other younger, came out to greet the car. The younger woman opened the door and the visiting dignitary emerged from the back seat.

It was Melisandre.

Everyone bowed their heads as she passed and went into the meeting. It was all very ceremonial and deferential – like last night's scene at the *Blauer Apfel* – though this time with a distinct militaristic air.

Linus slid deeper into the woods and moved in a wide arc until he was behind the building. He rubbed more dirt on his face so no one would see his shiny white forehead. And just as he was about to sprint to a window between two thick hemlocks, the hall lights went out. Flickering shadows replaced the brightness. For some reason they had switched to candle power. Instinctively he checked his watch. It was midnight on the button.

Whatever they were doing had begun. And the chance that he'd be caught playing *Peeping Tom* had just dropped dramatically. He ducked into the hemlocks beneath an open window then took out his Blackberry, opened an audio file and started recording.

At first there was nothing to hear save for the distant laugh of a loon echoing from someplace up the lake. He rose up, his face pressed close to the side of the building, and leaned out sideways for a peek inside. Thirty to forty women were seated in rows facing a stage at the far end of the room. From their shapes and styles he guessed that they were mostly in their fifties though a few looked slightly younger and a few considerably older. Melisandre was seated front-row-center. Her long hair was again gathered and hanging down her back. Her friend Vera, whom Linus had followed here, was at her side.

Before them, on a low platform stage, two groups of six young women were dressed in hooded white robes with gold bands at the cuffs and necklines. Each held a lighted white candle. A woman in a gold robe came down the center aisle from the back of the hall, walking slowly and swinging a smoldering censer. The audience was attentive though animated as they savored the aroma and spoke quietly among themselves.

The incense bearer ascended the stage, turned toward the audience and spread more aroma. Then she opened a door at the back of the stage and two women wrapped in haircloth blankets stepped out, followed by two more women in the white robes like the others. The two in blankets stepped forward, arms crossed, blankets tightly closed. Both were fuzz bald. The robed escorts placed their hands on their shoulders and removed the blankets to reveal the women's naked bodies. A murmur arose as the audience craned for a better view.

The naked women were astonishingly fit – not overly buffed like body builders but perfectly sculpted and sinewed. They stood with their arms hanging straight, hands against their sides and eyes never lifting from the floor, as the escorts rotated them – one slow, full circle – to show off their exquisite forms.

Then one of Melisandre's greeters rose from her seat and helped each of the naked women into a white and gold robe like the others. Once clothed they raised their eyes and beamed as the audience burst into enthusiastic applause. The others onstage gathered around, offering their welcome and congratulations. Linus knew that an induction had just taken place. Finally Melisandre rose. The commotion subsided.

As she stepped onto the stage, all of the robed women dropped to one knee. Melisandre moved among them, touching their elbows and drawing them up. She smiled and shook hands with the two inductees. Veronica handed her two gold silk scarves, which Melisandre draped around each inductee's neck. Then she turned to address the audience. Linus pressed closer to hear.

"To meet the many challenges we will face we must continue to grow our numbers," she began. She was speaking in English, which probably meant the audience was a mix of nationalities. "Recently we have received intelligence from Paris that the *Priory of Sion* has secretly named a successor.

"We also hear that we may have fallen under the surveillance of a rival, perhaps the Priory, perhaps someone else. It is presently unclear.

"While we are certain that our activities and our coming pronouncements are well secreted, we must never underestimate the treachery of others.

"Over the centuries, forces ranging from the mayors of the palaces and self-proclaimed dauphins, to misguided treasure hunters and obsessed tyrants, have usurped our privilege and power. We must be on guard but we must be on the offensive as well.

"As our mission proceeds we will undoubtedly make many new friends. But we will continue to make enemies of the sex slavers, the Islamic fascists, and all those who chose to oppress. To succeed we must be prepared to embrace our friends and converts, and to destroy our enemies.

"So tonight we welcome into our ranks two more sentinels. We bid them good fortune in their service to our great and just cause.

"Through them, and the many individuals and groups under the aegis of *Novangelis*, may the hope held out to oppressed persons the world over never dim."

It was a rousing speech. The group stood and applauded and an impromptu reception line formed. Linus wanted to stay and see what happened next but figured he'd already seen the most substantive part of this powwow in the pines, and it looked like the group was about to break. In a few minutes everyone would be outside. Now was the time to start moving – especially if he wanted to follow Melisandre when she left.

He crawled away from the building, back into the cover of the forest and headed toward his hidden car. He knew there was a chance that Melisandre wouldn't be in the sedan with the dark windows when it left. But that was her ride, he reasoned, and it was waiting, not stored for the night. The odds were in his favor, so it was a chance he'd take.

He sat in his car and watched, trying to clean some of the pine pitch camouflage off his face and hands. After about ten minutes

Veronica's BMW pulled out onto the road and sped off back the way it had come. Linus waited. A few minutes later the sedan emerged and headed in the same direction.

Linus raced off in pursuit.

Chapter 6. HEADQUARTERS: BERLIN

July 24th. Day 03.

Melisandre's two-car convoy drove deep into the old East Berlin through complexes of squat cement apartment buildings, rusty chain-link cordoned rail yards and soot-blackened factories.

The sedans turned a corner and passed a couple of women in tight micro-skirts and stiletto heels who were hanging out, smoking cigarettes. It stopped in front of a dark stone building. Linus passed by without making the turn then pulled over and hurried back on foot. The two women gawked at him but didn't speak. Odd street for hookers, he thought.

He stepped into a doorway and watched but no one was getting out of the stopped cars. Finally the door of the building opened. Two women in plain black clothes came out and surveyed the street. They nodded to the drivers and the cars opened up. The drivers stayed put but the sentinels cordoned a path from the cars into the building. A path for Melisandre.

His hunch was right. Melisandre had indeed returned from the ritual at the lake. She hurried up the stairs and disappeared into the building, followed by the plainclothes women who then secured the door behind them. The sentinels got back in their cars and departed and the street was again quiet and lifeless. Almost.

Linus stepped out of his shadow for a closer look. He noticed that Veronica's silver BMW was parked a few spaces down from the house, which was a tired looking place but not dilapidated. Its heavy wood door looked new, of course – Linus figured it was newly-installed security. And all of the windows were protected by decorative wrought iron bars. The first two floors were dark but warm interior light projected onto the curtains of the upper two floors. He checked the time – it was just after 1 a.m. In the corner of his eye he noticed the two hookers coming toward him and he tried to walk away.

"Wer ist da, bitte?" one of them called out. He pretended not to hear.

"Wait a minute baby," the other said, her English heavily accented. If she spoke English, he thought, maybe she could tell him something about the house. So he stopped and let them catch up.

"You speak English?" he asked as the women sidled up, one on each side.

"I speak very good," the taller one said. "I'm Afra. *Und zis* is Pelagia," she said. The names seemed odd. *"Was ist du namen,* honey?" Afra asked.

"Louis. It's Louis," He said. He looked at Melisandre's building. "I think I know someone who lives there ..." Then he noticed something sticking in his side.

"It's a taser. Fifty thousand volts," Afra whispered in his ear. Linus didn't move.

"You want my money?" he asked with a hearty laugh. Then he noticed that the one called Pelagia was on a phone. She said "Ja" then hung up. And the two women escorted him to the Melisandre's door. One of the plainclothes women inside let him in and up to the second floor. She then pointed to the door to the third floor apartment, which was opening. It was Melisandre.

"Linus. What are you *doing* here?" she asked softly though with detectable dismay.

"Where were you?" he asked.

"I called," she said. Linus wasn't ready to take her word for it. He knew that his sudden appearance was a major lapse of security, and though she seemed calm she must've been angry. But if she wanted to know how he found her she'd have to let him in. Which she did.

The interior was in far better condition than the outside and the apartment was freshly renovated and bright. Veronica was coming down the hall from another room, a leather briefcase slung over her shoulder. She tucked it behind her with her elbow then smiled and shook Linus's hand.

"*Signor* Mercator. We meet again," she said. Linus nodded and said hello.

"He didn't get my message about breaking our date," Melisandre said.

"What message?" Linus wondered.

"The one I left at Paris Bar. I was called away at the last minute. I'm sorry but it was urgent," she said though Linus was sure that the ritual in the pines hadn't just popped up at the last minute and no one at Paris Bar knew anything about any message.

"I waited there from seven-thirty to nine-thirty. There was no message," he said. Veronica put her hand on Melisandre's shoulder.

"I'll leave you to your bickering," she said and again shook Linus's hand. This time she noted how dirty it was – still smeared with pine pitch from his earlier romp in the woods.

"Flat tire," Linus apologized, wiping it on his pants.

"I'm sure you'll recover," she smiled and added. "*Buonanotte.*"

"I'll see you out," Melisandre said. Linus figured they needed a few private minutes. He held out his pine-pitched hands and asked, "May I ... ?"

"Down the hall on the left," Melisandre said.

The bathroom was large and had another full sized door inside. It was locked from the opposite side but didn't seem too formidable. He took out a credit card and managed to push the latch bolt away from the strike. The door clicked open.

The other room was dark but the spill from the bathroom was enough for a quick look – very quick. It was an office or a study. The notebook computer on the desk was open but not booted. Beside it there was a large zippered leather portfolio. He opened it flat on the desk. It was a case of maps in plastic sleeves. He paged through until he found one that had been marked. It covered two pages and was of Europe and the Middle East. Locations were marked with small round stickers and some of the place names were written onto the map by hand. The biggest cluster was in Europe, with France having the most – spread throughout the country, from Paris to the *Ardennes* to the Languedoc and Spanish border in the south.

Only a few places outside of France were marked – two in England, one each in Germany, Spain and Italy. He was surprised to find two locations as far away as India. One was in a village called Mari. The words *Pindi Point* were written in red beside it. The other was in a place called *Srinagar* and the words *Rauza Bal* were written there. Linus didn't know why – yet – but it all looked important. And too good to pass up. He decided to take a chance.

He snapped the desk lamp on and copied it all with his phone. When he finished he listened. There was still no sign that Melisandre had returned. He zipped the case closed then leafed through a couple of books beside the laptop. One was called *The Pistis Sophia*. The other was called *Les Rois Perdus*. It was written in French – his understanding of which was limited to common conversation, road signs, menu items and Paris metro maps. But he knew plenty of people who could help him read it.

The third book was titled *Art for the Ages*. Yellow post-it notes marked two pages – on 252, a plate of a painting called *Les Bergers d'Arcadie* by Nicolas Poussin, a 17th-century French classicist, and on page 375, a plate of a naked, modestly shadowed young woman lying on her stomach, her head resting in her hand, reading from a book. It was titled *Penitent in her Grotto*, and was by an unknown 16th-century artist. It reminded him of the painting on the wall at the *Blauer Apfel* restaurant. Linus photographed it all.

As he reached to the file drawer he heard the apartment door closing – Melisandre was returning. Oddly there were only four files in the drawer. One said *Mercator, LP* – Melisandre had started a file on him. It didn't look too thick. Another said *Kohlhertz, Wolfgang*. The only thing in it was a report from a genetic fingerprinting lab. Linus quickly copied it. The footsteps were coming closer. Another file said *Lawrence, L.*, and the last, *Codex Brucianus*. He photographed them as well. The footsteps were already at the top of the stairs, then in the apartment. He hurried back into the bathroom. Melisandre was rapping on the door when he got there.

"Would you like a fresh towel?" she asked. He looked around. All the towels – a large stack of them in fact – were fresh.

"Plenty here, thanks," he replied. And the footsteps walked away. Linus washed up and toweled off. He fished his Blackberry out, set it to record an audio file, and put it back in his breast pocket. Then he went to join Melisandre.

Justice and Other Dirty Deeds

The room was strewn with pens and empty cups that Linus figured were left over from some sort of meeting – maybe a briefing before the ceremony in the pines. More and more, Melisandre's moves were looking like precision clockwork.

"Sit here," she said, offering a spot on the couch. Linus sat on the edge of the cushion. Melisandre, more relaxed, sat across from him in an upholstered chair. Her eyes were gas-flame blue. Linus remembered having a similar thought last night. Except last night they were green. Maybe it was the light, he figured, or maybe he was just mistaken.

"How did you manage to find me?" she asked. Linus had been waiting for this one. He drew a deep breath.

"Well, last night I was more interested in charming you than I was in your story." Melisandre was amused but obviously not fooled. He tried another tack. "All right, truthfully, the more I thought about the odd collection of people at your dinner party the more intrigued I was. You said they were supporters of your woman's rights group?"

"Mostly."

"But you never said what your group was doing, exactly. I started wondering what could possibly attract such a cast of characters and figured maybe there *was* a story to take back to the States. Something like," he shrugged, "local woman making a difference globally.

"Then you vanished. And that made me *more* curious," he added. It was all innocuous enough and – in a way at least – it was the truth, though he was actually more *suspicious* than curious. "Is this your apartment?" he asked.

"Yes. Well, one of them. I travel a lot."

"Are those two hookers ... "

"Former hookers."

"Are those two *former* hookers working for you?"

"They are members of our group."

"*Novangelis*," he noted, and she said,

"Yes. *Novangelis*."

"What exactly is your mission?" he quizzed, though he was convinced he wouldn't hear anything like the truth about the secretive society.

"We don't restrict ourselves to any specific area but we're generally a woman's rights group."

"Rights?"

"Yes, as in a woman's right to be clean and sober, free of the streets, to not be beaten by a drunken boyfriend, husband or pimp, to not be abandoned or excluded. To speak and think freely. To have un-mutilated genitals. To choose her own mate. Those kinds of rights."

"That's ... comprehensive. Sounds like dirty work."

"How so?" she wondered.

"Well for one thing rescuing prostitutes involves other nasties, like boozers and druggies. And I also know that most batterers and pimps don't go away easily. Nor do the Islamo-fascists. They go down very hard as a matter of fact."

"All that matters is that they do go down," she said.

"So you do whatever it takes?" he wondered. Her para-military bodyguards sure looked like they were up to delivering a few bashings.

"Out philosophy is reclaim, restore, and redeem," Melisandre explained. "There are many places in the world where that is a dangerous mission. It requires varying levels of security. Providing safe houses and secure lives through the critical stages of a woman's comeback isn't always easy," she acknowledged.

"I bet. But exactly how far do you go?" he persisted, looking more for a reaction than a truthful answer. But what she said next surprised him.

"Off the record?" she asked. Linus nodded – though he'd broken such promises in the past. "We operate a modest level of proactive crisis intervention. Within certain acceptable limits of course," she admitted.

"Hit men? Or should I say, hit *women*?" he said half-jokingly.

"No, no. But if we interrupt a beating or an FGM in progress, or if some predator should be imprudent enough to follow someone to our safe house, someone is likely to go away with a changed physical condition," she said. Linus chuckled. It was bastard dashing at its best and it sounded great to a guy who had met his share of scumbags that deserved just such a pounding.

"Instant results always impress me," he said, though he wondered how much of what she was saying was a thinly-veiled warning aimed at him.

"Justice delayed is justice denied," she opined then added, "It's our motto."

"Has anyone been ... ?"

"No Linus, we haven't killed anyone. And we won't."

"Do you think any of it will really make a difference?" he asked, his cynicism bubbling to the surface – though these days it was never too deep.

"To the ones who dry out and get out of the stews, or who don't have to be a punching bag anymore? Absolutely."

"Well there's a lot of 'em. You'll need a bigger army," he said. "Are you faith based?"

"Not *per se*. We're an independent philanthropic organization but we don't exclude people who are members of organized religions."

"Like Jules the priest?" Melisandre nodded. Linus sensed forbidden territory.

"He's not part of our organization, actually, but he's a great help sometimes."

"Ya? Well he looks like a major player," Linus remarked, knowing that the priest was far more than Melisandre wanted him to believe. Jules was no casual volunteer and had been very prominent at last night's *soirée* at the *Blauer Apfel*. But why was she minimizing him? "What denomination is he anyway?"

"I don't know. Catholic, I believe."

"Not like any Catholic priest *I've* ever seen," he muttered. Melisandre didn't respond. Linus decided not to push it – for now. His interrogation was vexing her, anyway – as it did *everyone* who had something to hide. And that's how Melisandre was looking – like someone with something to hide. Judging from her entourage, the fealty and the armed bodyguards, great pains were being taken to conceal her movements and affairs. "I suppose I'll have to talk to the priest myself," he said in an offhanded manner. Melisandre's silence told him that she didn't think it would happen. Linus, however, thought otherwise.

"By the way, you never told me your full name," he said, hoping to get back on a more amicable track.

"That's true," she replied, smiling as though she wasn't going to tell him now either.

Melisandre's Tale of Woe

"I am Melisandre Cortona," she announced, but only after a long dramatic pause.

"Spanish?"

"Italian,"

"So rescuing distressed women isn't something you just wake up one day and decide to make your life's work. Or is it?"

"No it isn't," she replied, drawing a deep breath as she began her story.

She said she was born in Winchester, a wealthy suburb of Boston, though not to wealthy parents. Her father was a construction laborer and her mother took in ironing and cleaned houses. She was an only child and her mother died when she was twelve. Since her father was still a fairly young man, he remarried two years after her mother died.

"Unfortunately he chose a woman who needed constant attention," Melisandre continued. "She resented me deeply and never missed a chance to drive me and my father apart.

"He *did* try to mediate things but I guess the constant complaining just wore him down. He usually ended up siding with my step-monster," she said. "I suppose he thought that, being a woman, she knew what was best for a young girl."

She said that as soon as she turned eighteen she left home and moved in with a group of runaways living in Kenmore Square, Boston, waitressing and doing other odd jobs, barely getting by. And that's when she got to know some girls who started having sex for money.

"I thought about it because it looked pretty easy and was always available. And it paid more than waiting tables, that's for sure.

"But then one of the girls was badly beaten up. Her nose and her jaw were broken. Her arm. It was horrible. Suddenly having sex for money didn't look so great. So I did more waitressing, six nights a week, sometimes seven, and got a decent place to live. Then on one of my rare nights off I ran into this guy from my hometown. At a nightclub, in Harvard Square. His name was James. He was two years older and he remembered me from high school.

"I remembered him, too. His family was rich and he had a new car and a beautiful house in the country," she said then, shrugging, added, "I was just swept away."

They started dating, she said, and within a few months were living together on an estate in Vermont, an old farm that had been passed down through generations of his family. James was good to her and gave her everything she wanted, but his family considered her beneath them and he was threatened with ostracism if they married.

"He said he didn't care about the fortune and wanted to marry me but I turned him down. I didn't want to be the cause of something like that. Besides, we had everything a married couple would have – more, really – even if we didn't have the blessings and friendship of family.

"So we lived secretly. The relatives thought I was gone. They never came around, anyway, so it wasn't difficult to fool them. We lived blissfully in the country, raising horses, dogs, and cats.

"Then one day James went out riding. Four hours later our golden retrievers came back alone, barking and very agitated, then ran off into the woods again. I took the jeep and chased them.

"About a mile away I found James's horse grazing in a field. Then I found James dead under an oak tree. Shot through the heart."

The death was ruled a hunting accident, she said, but no one ever came forward to take responsibility. And when the family realized she was still around, the murder accusations started. She packed her things, closed the house and left just ahead of the eviction notice. The family tried to ban her from the funeral, too. She was twenty-two, homeless again, and broke.

She said she couldn't go to her father for help – he never forgave her for running away – but it turned out that help came to her.

Melisandre said that James's widowed aunt, who wasn't of the original bloodline but had married into the family, thought she was being treated badly and was sympathetic.

"She took me under her wing and opened her home to me. Shortly afterward she was diagnosed with breast cancer. I took care of her for three years while she fought for her life then buried her when she died.

"She didn't have any children and I guess my hard-luck story moved her, especially the part about my girlfriend who was badly beaten. I always knew she was okay financially. I just never knew that she was enormously wealthy. Her will established a trust foundation to benefit women's causes. And I was named the sole trustee."

Melisandre's story of woe had softened Linus's skepticism and aroused his empathy – exactly as she had hoped. She knew she'd have to gain his friendship and trust if she was going to get rid of him. Intentionally or not, Linus had inserted himself in her affairs. Now, one way or another, he had to go.

"You still haven't said how you found me," she noted. He was hoping she had forgotten. Now he had a decision to make. Should he tell her? Or should he lie? He decided that the truth – a version of it at least – would best serve his purpose.

"When you didn't show at Paris Bar, I went to the apartment, from last night. No one answered. So I broke in." Melisandre was annoyed though secretly amused by his bravado.

"Maybe I just wasn't home. Ever think of that?" she asked.

"I was *worried*," he countered, though he knew it was lame.

"Taking a big chance, aren't you?"

"I don't think so."

"What makes you so sure I won't have you arrested?" she asked. Linus took a deep breath and looked down at his folded hands.

"Two very simple things," he said. "First, you'd have a tough time proving it." Then he looked up at her face. "Secondly, I believe that you'd prefer not to publicize tonight's little nude-fest in the forest." Melisandre was surprised. "I saw the whole ceremony," he said.

"It was nothing illegal," she insisted.

"I'm sure. But it would still make a great story. Your speech was inspiring."

"Burglary *and* blackmail. I knew journalism had devolved but this is even lower than I imagined," she disdained.

"You ain't' seen nothin'" he said.

"Have you *any* scruples, Linus?"

"Plenty Melisandre. And you?" What's the big secret? Why are you lying about some things?"

"It's a safety issue. It's not easy getting women off the streets.

The two you saw tonight ..."

"The two inductees."

"... yes, the inductees. They pledge their support and we offer a sense of belonging, the promise of anonymity and security. No past. Just a brighter future. It takes years to establish that kind of trust. A ham-fisted expose by an overzealous journalist could be devastating."

"Now I'm ham-fisted and overzealous? Weren't you singing my praises just last night?"

"Last night you weren't blackmailing me."

"Last night I didn't know you were lying to me."

"What exactly *do* you want Linus?"

"Simple honest answers Melisandre. That vacant apartment was a stakeout. Who was being spied on and why?"

"I had nothing to do with that and I know nothing about it," she insisted.

"Then why did you say you lived there?"

"Why should I tell you, a stranger, where I live? Or anything at all, for that matter?"

"No shit. But why did you pick *that* house?"

"This is absurd. Because a friend of mine is the real estate agent showing it. That's how I knew it was vacant." Linus knew she had him. It was, after all, the *Immobilien Berlin* business card which led him to Vera, and the ritual by the lake.

"What happened to the old man who ran the antiquarian shop?" he quizzed.

"How did you know he was an old man?" she asked. He had never said he was there but, because of the stake-out and likelihood that he'd been photographed, he figured she already knew, anyway.

"I was there," he admitted.

"For *what*?"

"Now *you're* being absurd. I was a *customer* for cripes sake. Can't I go into a shop?" Melisandre didn't answer. "So what happened to the old man?" She hesitated. Now it was her turn to make a decision. By tracking her down, Linus had been much more resourceful – and much luckier – than she had expected. She hadn't anticipated this inquisition. And he already knew more than she would've liked.

On the other hand she didn't perceive him as a natural enemy and realized that he was a bigger threat if he was left to discover things on his own. Making him think he was being brought into the circle was safer. So she decided to trust him – ostensibly, at least.

"The old man, his name is Gervan. He was working on something for us and had just called to tell me he had made an important discovery and that I should come to the shop right away. When I got there the door was locked and Gervan was missing. The fire alarms went off about a hour later," she said. Linus was finally believing her.

"And he's still missing," Linus conjectured. Melisandre nodded. And despite all else, he knew that her worry for old man Gervan was genuine.

"You were there? Yesterday afternoon?" she asked. Of course she already knew that – thanks to Jules and his attic stake-out.

"Late. About four, I think."

"What happened?"

"There was someone in the back room, I don't know who, and a car and driver in the alley behind the shop. The old man seemed nervous. He sold me some worthless junk then hurried me out the door."

"Did he say anything?"

"Just that I was getting a good deal. And that I should enjoy my purchases."

"Did he give you anything else?" she asked. Linus shook "no". His intuition told him to hold back the part about Gervan slipping him a note – at least until he had to time to test her on one more thing.

"Apparently someone else is interested in my travels," he said. "My hotel room was searched." Melisandre feigned surprise.

"Are you sure?" she asked. He nodded. "Robbery at the Grand Hotel. Hmmm."

"No. Not robbery. Snooping. Nothing was missing," he corrected. But nothing Melisandre was saying or doing diluted his suspicion and he couldn't shake the feeling that she was involved right up to her pretty chin. She never once mentioned the police, or asked if he reported the intrusion, what the police had to say about it. Those would've been natural questions for her to ask. Oddly she didn't.

But he didn't want to send her running for cover so he let it drop. And he decided he'd said enough. She checked her watch – standard hint that the guest had worn out his welcome – and yawned.

"I'm glad you weren't hurt," she said then, "You're leaving Berlin tomorrow," recalling what he had said last night.

"Yes. Maybe we'll meet again. In Boston," he said though in truth he planned to cancel his ticket and extend his European stay.

"I'm there most of the time," she said. "What's your phone number?" Linus learned long ago that listed phone numbers and addresses were an occupational hazard.

"They change a lot but my e-mail stays the same," he said and he wrote it down. Then Melisandre showed him to the door.

"I know it all seems strange but there's nothing too dramatic going on," she assured, and Linus thought,

'sure, nothing *too* dramatic – except an old shop keeper's disappearance, an arson fire, a secret stakeout in an abandoned house, a strange ritual in the woods with two naked women paraded before a secret meeting of a militant woman's organization...' He could hardly hide his derision.

"I suppose you're right," he agreed. "Anyway, I won't be around long enough to find out." His lies – like hers – were piling up. She pressed a buzzer and one of the plainclothes sentinels came to see Linus out.

"I'll be in the States in about a month. I'll get in touch," she said.

"I look forward to it," he replied, sensing he'd be seeing her a lot sooner than that. Outside, Linus looked at his watch as he walked to his car. It was three a.m. – the end of a long day, but one which yielded a recorded speech, a file full of photographed clues, and a head full of questions. Now it was time to put them all to bed.

But tomorrow morning the digging would begin in earnest.

Chapter 7. ACCUSED!

The first message on Linus's Blackberry wasn't surprising. It was from Dark Star, his photo agency in New York, *pleading* for the Jamie Richards pictures. The bids had reached half a million.

But the second message was a shocker. It was Jamie Richards herself. The fact that she got his number – his private line at that – was a surprise. Then he remembered that old pal Massimo, his paparazzo rival, had the number. Jamie Richards was certainly rich enough to buy Massimo. And she was apparently also rich enough to leave a message saying she'd match any offer for Linus's shots.

Linus chafed at the thought of being bought off.

But he didn't send the picture files to Dark Star either. Right now he had other things on his mind, like the list of cities and towns on the map he copied last night at Melisandre's. So far it was a long trail to nowhere.

He downed the last tepid swallow of his second coffee. It was already nine o'clock. The morning was slipping away. He had managed to log about five hours of shallow sleep before the churn of questions and events in his mind dragged him back to his laptop, uploading images, adding and amending his notes.

The *Blauer Apfel* dinner party was still a vivid image. The curious mix of guests looked like the cast of a parlor mystery, though the plot was missing.

But they did have *some* things in common, like their homage to Melisandre and the exquisite gifts they gave her. Linus didn't find blind devotion in humans so uncommon but he wondered what it was about silks, gloves, shoes, wines, perfumes, and flowers that connected the devotees.

Next, he listed and abstracted the three major players. One was

Veronica Franco, beautiful and swank daughter of an Italian diplomat. She played the part of a jet-set party girl but Linus sensed she was more like an international lobbyist, possibly for *Novangelis*, Melisandre's "charitable organization" – which was looking more like an army of women than a charity.

Jules the priest was on his shortlist, too. Melisandre said "sometimes he helps out". Linus was sure it went well beyond that. His full name was Jules Doinel, supposedly Catholic. If so he would be listed someplace and might even be searchable through the Vatican web site. Linus figured he'd know soon enough.

But at the top of the list was Melisandre. Last name Cortona, it turns out – always well-dressed, remarkably fragrant, smothered with flowers and fawning acolytes. Said she was the spokesperson for a "woman's rights group". But no spokesperson he'd ever seen was handled with such care and treated with such reverence.

She said she grew up in a suburb of Boston – easily confirmed through things like birth certificates, voting records and driver's licenses. But if Melisandre was *anybody* at all or had ever done anything even remotely notable, her name would be listed someplace. Maybe in one of the "*Who's Who*" compilations. If she'd ever been written about or mentioned in the press, any internet search engine would cough it up.

In any case a few quick internet searches might get things going in the right direction. But rather than rack-up a lot of wireless charges and leaving a trail, he decided he'd use a public access computer at the American Library.

He ran under a quick shower, dressed and headed out. The first opening for an internet-capable computer was at 10:30 - 45 minutes away. He put his name on the list then found an empty table. He spread his map of Europe then fired-up his laptop and began locating places from the image he made of Melisandre's map. France had the most locations – Paris, Arques, Aix-en-Provence, Besançon, Bayeux, Verdun, Rheims, LeMans, Vezelay and Stenay. Rennes-le-Château, Bellevault and the Forest of Woevres were also in France but not on his detail-challenged road map. But a library atlas gave him the missing locations as well as the two mountain peaks, *Montsegur* and *Bezu*, which were near Rennes-le-Château in the foothills of the Pyrenees. He also located the Forest of Woevres, which was in the *Ardennes* near Stenay. He transferred them all to his road map.

Next he turned to England. There was Exeter on the southeastern shore and a hamlet called Wiggenhall, which also wasn't on his road map. He marked them both.

In Spain he marked the northern city of Oviedo. And in Italy, Venice.

One of the locations in India was called Mari and it was written onto Melisandre's map by hand. It was probably a village, Linus figured, and it was noted as the location of something called Pindi Point. The other location in India was Srinagar, a small city in Kashmir. Like on Melisandre's map, Linus wrote the words "Rauza Bal" beside it.

He pushed some hair off his forehead and straightened up for an overall view. He tried squinting his eyes, looking for a visual clue, like a connect-the-dots shape – though it seemed too corny. Then he tried alphabetizing the places frontward and backward, looking for an anagram. But all he could conclude was that the places were randomly scattered.

Suddenly something struck him. Tiny red crosses. Crucifixes. One near or at almost every location – all but three in France and the two in India. It was the symbol for a Christian church, abbey, or cathedral. He checked Exeter in England then Oviedo in Spain and Venice. Each had at least one red cross. Venice of course had many. Something was happening or was going to happen involving churches.

He went back to his laptop notes and put stars beside the places without churches then clicked on the clock icon. It was 4:30 a.m. Boston time; 10:30 a.m. in Berlin. He gathered his things and moved to a small office with a single internet terminal, set-up his laptop and inserted a blank CD in the library's computer for downloading. His first search was on "Melisandre Cortona". Two hits came back – both for hotels and villa rentals in Tuscany.

Next he tried just "Cortona" and got over two thousand hits!

He scrolled down through the first few dozen. They were all about *places* named Cortona but none were about *people* named Cortona. So he moved off the search page and onto the official website for the State of Massachusetts, looking for a Melisandre Cortona. Nothing hit. No birth records, no driver's license, press mentions, nor business involvements. Melisandre Cortona didn't exist – at least not in Massachusetts.

The name didn't surface in the national phone book either. He went back to the search page and typed "m AND cortona". The hit list was shorter. One summary was titled Saints Lives / L thru R. It was a link to an encyclopedia of saints with short bios which some university student had compiled. He clicked it and an entry for *Saint Margaret of Cortona* opened. Linus began reading:

St. Margaret of Cortona / 1247 - 1297
Margaret was born into a poor peasant family of Laviano, in Tuscany, Italy. Her mother died when she was seven. Two years later her father remarried ...

After only two sentences Linus knew what was happening. He read on and discovered that young saint Margaret was fleeing a harsh and unsympathetic stepmother when she ran away with a young nobleman at age seventeen. She was his mistress for nine years and they had a son. Then one day the nobleman went out riding with his dog. Later the dog came home alone, barking and agitated, and led Margaret to his murdered body in the forest.

It was Melisandre's life story! The one she told him last night. Plagiarized from a saint, the whole woeful tale ... wicked stepmother, class struggle, mysterious death of the young, wealthy lover. Even the damn dog had the same role in both stories. And there was more.

Like Melisandre, who said she was tossed off the family estate and lost everything , the aggrieved Saint Margaret shucked all her worldly possessions – giving everything to charity – then took her son and returned home, only to be rejected by her father and stepmother.

She ended up in the sanctuary of two matrons – like Melisandre's surrogate aunt.

"Serves me right for not being religious," he muttered to himself. He was impressed that Melisandre could concoct such a charade on such short notice.

But Margaret had founded a hospital, counseled penitents and organized a confraternity to help prisoners – all things Melisandre's organization might do, he thought. So maybe Margaret was their model and her life story their standard red herring. He wondered who else had been treated to the same canard.

His next search subject was "Jules Doinel". Only six entries came up. One was all he needed. It was titled *Gnostic Scriptures and The Gnostic Church*, written by someone named Stephan A. Hoeller, who listed himself as: *Bishop, Ecclesia Gnostica.*

" ... One of these incidents of emergence occurred in the late 19th Century, when Jules-Benoit Doinel du Val Michel (Tau Valentin II), inspired by spiritual influences that appeared to have been of Cathar origin, founded the French Gnostic Church, which by way of its various branches and under several names has functioned ever since."

He checked names in the news, the Vatican website and various Christian websites all over the world. None yielded anything about a contemporary Jules Doinel. So Jules the priest was probably lying about *his* name, too – but perhaps not about his persona. He plucked the words 'Cathar origin' from the paragraph and delved deeper.

The Cathars were a heretical Christian sect that flourished in western Europe in the 12th and 13th centuries, mostly in France's Languedoc. They denied the validity of any official or ordained intercessors between man and God – i.e. the church – and insisted on direct mystical experiences called "gnosis." Cathars conducted services in open air, barns, houses, halls, etc., eschewing churches. They meditated and were strict vegetarians – though they did eat fish. Some scholars allude to evidence that Cathars practiced birth control and abortion. Some also called them an early version of the sixties "free love" society. They lived somewhat reclusively, abhorred opulent religiosity and worldly possessions, and they also believed in reincarnation. Indeed the Cathars – like Jules the priest with his silk cassock and playboy mien – were rather unconventional Christians.

But most intriguing was the Cathar recognition of the feminine principle, especially in their religion. Cathar priests, preachers and teachers could be – and often were – women. In that single fact Linus found a solid link between Jules the priest and Melisandre... women's rights and women's rights in religion.

Naturally the Vatican took offense to the Cathars' views. In 1209 thirty thousand Christian knights and soldiers descended upon the foothills of the Pyrenees. And in what was perhaps the first case of genocide in Europe, they wiped out the Cathars. It was known as the *Albigensian Crusade*.

He copied the Cathar related text to CD and turned to his next search – Veronica Franco. Only one hit turned up – a review of a movie starring Catherine McCormick titled *"Veronica Franco The Courtesan."* It was about Veronica Franco, a renowned courtesan – from Venice of course. He was amused that she struck him as a lobbyist and she was named after a prostitute – arguably similar professions. He saved it all to disk and went back to the map.

One by one Linus searched each location using the Boolean expression 'AND church'. The results were dismal. They had churches but none of any particular eminence. None except Vezelay.

Vezelay, in central France, returned a hit under the title *Images of Medieval Art and Architecture - France*. The town boasted an architectural landmark – the Benedictine Abbey Church of Sainte-Marie-Madeleine. Linus repeated the name in a whisper. "Sainte-Marie-Madeleine. Mary Magdalene." His catechism was rusty but he remembered Mary Magdalene as the reformed prostitute who washed Christ's feet with her hair. Her long hair. Prostitutes and hair seemed to be gaining significance. Melisandre's hair was unusually long. Her *"New Angels"* – at least the militant ones – mostly wore theirs cropped. Some were reformed prostitutes – protecting and reforming other prostitutes. Even the paintings he'd seen – on the wall at *Blauer Apfel* restaurant and the plates from *Art Through The Ages*, the book in Melisandre's study – featured extra long hair.

He finished saving it all to disk then shut down. His time slot was up and the next user was lingering outside the office. He was already planning his next stop – another surprise visit to Melisandre's apartment or, more accurately, her Berlin headquarters. But there was one more important chore to do before leaving.

He found a copy of today's *Berliner Zeitung* and scanned for a news story about old man Gervan, the missing antiquarian, or the fire at his shop. Indeed, he found the name and a picture of the shop. And much more. There was a grip-and-grin photo of old man Gervan receiving some type of award. Another distinguished looking man, slightly younger with a cropped gray beard, was handing him a plaque. The other guy wasn't identified but the name Gervan was in the caption.

Then came the real stunner. There was a second picture just below the first – a grainy, poorly focused shot of a man going into the antiquarian shop. His face was obscured, but the clothes were unmistakable. It was him! Linus's German wasn't bad but he wanted to be sure. So he took the paper to a frail-looking, pink-skinned woman at the reference desk and said, *"Bitte."* She looked up, her face a bit gaunt but nonetheless pleasant. "Could you help me translate something?" he asked, motioning to the newspaper. She smiled.

"Mein Englisch ist nicht gut, but I will look and see," she agreed. She took the paper and Linus pointed out the article. "A fire at, er, shop, here in Berlin. Shop full with smoke from a book left on a hot stove. Damage minimum," she explained.

"What does it say about the owner?" he asked. Her eyes narrowed as she got down to the part about old man Gervan.

"Gerhardt Gervan, seventy-one years, er... well-known, former professor, *mit* Humboldt University, was not... not at *der* shop." She continued reading then looked up at Linus. "Did you know zis man?" Linus shook 'no'. "I'm afraid he is dead. In Landwehr Kanal."

Gervan's body had been found floating in a canal. The cause of death was officially pending but Linus's gut told him it was from foul play. "Police are wanting zis man, for questions," she continued, pointing to the picture of him going into the shop. "Maybe American," she added. Not only was he being sought for questioning in Gervan's death, they also knew that he was probably an American.

He thanked her and went back to the newspaper rack, convinced that Melisandre and her playmates had set him up... almost. If they really wanted to finger him they would've provided his name or at least a good picture. Apparently they had done neither. They probably did it as an anonymous tip to avoid a lot of questions. In any case they didn't want to frame him. They just wanted to send him into hiding, maybe scare him off. Linus was angry and piqued, but not scared.

They knew he had nothing to do with Gervan's disappearance but he also had a feeling that they actually *did* know – or had a strong suspicion at least – who the real abductors were.

But if they knew who it was, why not just turn them in?

There were two more key players in this mystery – the shadowy figure in the back room and his wiseguy minding the car in the alley. Whoever had taken the picture of him must've photographed them as well. Did the police know about them? Did *they* get ratted out, too? Were *they* the kidnappers?

He folded the newspaper and replaced it on the rack. What began as simple curiosity was growing into a story, with Gervan's suspicious death at its core. And it was personal now. Someone had fingered him as a suspect and someone had to answer for it.

Melisandre would be first.

Accosted

The soft gray daylight did little to improve the gloominess of the neighborhood but at least the factories didn't seem as sinister to him as they had last night in the midnight shadows. He parked across from the entrance to Melisandre's headquarters. A guy in green coveralls was unloading bundles of clothes from a van and piling them on the sidewalk. He took one bundle and carried it up the steps. Linus hurried across the street and followed him in.

They reached the apartment together and were met by a 50-ish woman in a white doctor's coat. The guy with the bundle went right in but the woman blocked Linus's path.

"Kann ich Ihnen behilflich sein?" she asked. Linus looked past her to the interior. There was a pile of clothes in the middle of the room, and two women were sorting them into smaller piles. Another in a white doctor's jacket was holding a woman's head in her hands and pressing an ice pack to her face.

"I'm looking for Melisandre. She lives here," Linus replied, looking everywhere except at the woman's face.

"There is no one here by that name," she responded in lightly accented English. Linus craned for a better look into the room. She pulled the door tighter to block his view.

"Melisandre Cortona?" he tried again.

"I'm sorry," she said then added, "Excuse me," as she tried to close the door in his face. Linus held it open with his foot.

"Wait. Please. I may have the name wrong. She's about so tall," he began, his hand hovering before his face, "very attractive, late-thirties, early forties, very long, brown hair." Her pasty expression hardened. She wasn't going to budge. Linus was losing patience, tired of hearing all these lies. Yet the scene he was witnessing – the sorting of what looked like donated clothes, the medical assistance to the battered woman – all fit with Melisandre's story. Certainly she had misled him but her lies also had a smattering of truth.

"I'm sorry. Now, if you'll excuse us," the woman said and she began closing the door. Linus didn't move. The two sorters stopped to see what was happening. They were young, with very short hair. And yellow scarves. Melisandre's marauders, he thought.

"Look, I met her here last night and I know I'm not crazy," he argued. The sorters stood and began moving toward him, one of them dangling an andiron by her side, ready to take his head off. It was time to make a move.

"I'm afraid you'll have to go. The police are coming." It was as though she knew that mention of the cops would send him hopping. And she was right.

"You know exactly what's happening here," he snapped. No one bothered to deny that. He could already hear a siren's wail. He turned on his heels and split.

A few hot sun rays punched through the broken clouds as he jogged to his car. In his rear-view mirror he saw a police car turn onto the street and stop in front of the apartment. An ambulance was right behind it. The woman wasn't bluffing. Thinking that Melisandre's minions still might set the cops on him he made a series of quick turns to cover his tracks. No one followed so he eased up on the panic button and mixed into the city swirl. The day – indeed the week – was assuming a surreal quality. No one he had met lately was *who* or *what* they claimed. And at least one of them was dead. Even some of their places – like Melisandre's headquarters and the vacant apartment – weren't what they appeared to be. He didn't know *who* these people were. And more troubling he didn't know *where* they were .

But he *did* know that they had him running in a circle. And in a few minutes that circle would close – at *Blauer Apfel*. And that's where he headed. The dinner party she hosted would be hard to deny, particularly by people he had seen while he was with her. Melisandre Cortona – or whatever her name – definitely existed. And someone would have to admit it.

But actually locating her, he knew, would be a different matter.

Assaulted

The square-jawed man in jump boots and black tunic followed Linus into the *Blauer Apfel* restaurant and took a seat near him at the bar. He looked about mid to late thirties, with a flat-top haircut and a long ponytail. Linus knew the chiseled profile – it was the guy he had seen lurking in the back of Gervan's shop. In his starched white tunic, wide black belt, big silver buckle and black pants he looked like the guru of some pagan cult. He was Linus's height, maybe a few inches taller, with broad shoulders and a pumped-up chest which inflated his presence.

When Linus and the bartender made eye contact they recognized each other from Melisandre's party. The bartender retreated to the kitchen – no doubt to alert someone. A minute later he returned. Linus – and the stranger – ordered a beer.

"I was here a few nights ago with a woman," Linus began. The barkeep stared blankly, filling a glass. "She hosted a dinner party in the back dining room that night. I was ..."

"I'll check with the manager," the barkeep said and again disappeared into the kitchen. The stranger down the bar looked at Linus.

"An American woman by any chance?" he asked. The humble-helpful stranger routine didn't fit well with the black jump boots and bitten look on his face. "I don't mean to pry," he began – the standard disclaimer of someone who is about to pry into your affairs. "But I saw her. I'm sure of it," he said. His accent was unmistakably American.

"Really," Linus responded. "Did you get her name?" The stranger leaned forward and lowered his voice even further.

"She was with a *priest,* " he whispered as though it were too taboo to say aloud. "I think he called her Melissa. I met them in a book shop just around the corner. I'm a collector and I was having a piece appraised. Now the shop is closed and I'd like to get my property back," he explained.

"What was she doing there with the priest?" The stranger shrugged.

"Beats me. You a collector, too?"

"Journalist."

"Writing about *her*?" Linus shook 'no'.

"Don't tell me. It's the oldest trick in the book. She treated you like a king all night then slipped you a fake phone number. I hate when they do that," he sympathized. Linus knew it was the voice of experience talking. The stranger gulped half a pint of dark beer. "I wouldn't mind finding her myself," he continued, wiping his mouth with the back of his hand. "I'll bet she knows where the shop owner went with my piece," he groused then, leaning closer, added softly, "I think the fucker ripped me off!"

The bartender returned. Naturally the manager wasn't available and no one knew anything about a woman or a party. The stranger heard it all and said, "Surprise, surprise. Nobody knows fuckin' nothin'. These krauts hate Americans, anyway." Linus grunted. It sounded harsh but it was indeed a tough time to be American in Europe.

And he knew the stranger was right about another thing – it was hard to believe that no one at *Blauer Apfel* had ever seen Melisandre. He noticed that the kitchen door was filled with large aproned men.

"Did you know that before unification you could get arrested here just for having an American flag?" the stranger said, eyeing the human roadblock warily.

"No kidding," Linus said. He left his tab on the bar and turned to leave but the stranger latched onto his sleeve.

"I know another place to look. Here in Berlin," he said. Linus removed the stranger's pinch and said,

"No, thanks."

"There's an apartment over in a part of town that's just a lot of fucked-up people doing a lot of fucked-up things," the stranger persisted. Linus knew he meant Melisandre's headquarters and said,

"Not interested. Thanks anyway." He pivoted and walked out the door. The stranger waited until Linus was on the street then slipped a cell phone from his pants pocket. He put it to his ear and said "east." A call had been connected the whole time. Their chat had been bugged with an open cell phone. Now someone was out there, somewhere, waiting for Linus. And the stranger was not far behind.

Linus strode toward the vacant townhouse where he had found the stake-out, thinking that maybe it was active again. As he approached the brick arch into the pedestrian mall leading to the doorway he looked around to see if he had been tailed. He wasn't surprised by what he saw. The stranger, his rugged boots gripping the paving stones on the sidewalk, was half a block away. He waved at Linus to flag him down then jogged to catch up.

"I'm glad I caught you," he said as he approached. Linus kept his back to the wall for protection. Just on the other side of that wall a stout, darkly dressed man with a grim expression eavesdropped on the ensuing exchange. "I haven't been completely truthful," the stranger said as he flashed an Interpol ID. "I'm working with the Berlin police on this missing person case. The old man from the shop. So why don't you be smart and talk to me here and I won't have to haul you in for an official questioning." But Linus had been around the cops some, and the police ID wasn't intimidating.

"I don't know anything about the shop or the owner," Linus claimed. The stranger's face hardened. A block away the dark sedan that Linus had seen behind Gervan's shop sped around the corner and raced toward them. The stranger stepped closer. Linus heard the snap of an opening switchblade as the car skidded to a halt beside them. The driver jumped out. Linus grabbed the stranger's hand as he tried to push the knife up to his neck. A tattooed ink blotch and the letters *MD* on the stranger's wrist were at his nose. Their feet slipped on the paving stones as Linus fought to break free. The driver pulled a pistol and placed the muzzle against Linus's chin. The fighting subsided. Linus, sandwiched between his two muscular foes, was trapped.

"We'll see how fucking brave you are," the stranger hissed between gulps for air. The gunsel smirked. As they moved toward the car the dark grim-faced man on the other side of the wall stepped out and pressed the muzzle of a pistol against the stranger's temple.

"Move again *Monsieur* Kohlhertz and I will put air vents in your head," he said with a French accent. Linus couldn't see who was speaking but now he had a name for his attacker. It was Kohlhertz, probably Wolfgang Kohlhertz, because that was the name he saw on one of Melisandre's files. "Drop the weapons," the newcomer intoned, his voice sounding more familiar. But Kohlhertz and his sidekick weren't moving fast enough. The newcomer jammed the muzzle hard against Kohlhertz's head and clicked back the hammer. "You will be first *Monsieur*!" he sneered as the gun dented into

Kohlhertz's temple. Kohlhertz nodded. He and the driver dropped their weapons. Linus turned to see his rescuer.

It was Jules the priest! Wearing his black cassock and white collar, wielding a 9mm Glock!

Jules reached out and clenched Kohlhertz's long blonde ponytail, jerked his head down low then shoved him across the sidewalk onto the hood of his car. Linus collected the surrendered knife and gun. Kohlhertz recovered his balance.

"Well if it isn't God boy," he japed. "So this guy's one of yours," he said, nodding at Linus. Jules just shook 'no'.

"And I recommend you forget about him."

"What was he doing at Gervan's shop the other day?"

"I was a *customer*, dammit," Linus said.

"He knows nothing. And that's how it's going to stay," Jules said. Kohlhertz adjusted his tunic. The driver stood by stiffly, hands at his sides.

"Look at you, priest!" Kohlhertz sneered. "You haven't got the balls to pull that trigger!" he said as he moved toward Jules. Linus stepped up as he cocked the hammer of his captured pistol and said,

"You that sure about *me*?" Kohlhertz stopped in his tracks and looked at the gun, then at Linus. The answer was no. He backed down again.

"I'm warning you *priest*," he hissed. "Fuck with me and you'll regret it." Then he pointed at Linus. "Same goes for you fuckhead. Puke like you means *nothing* to me." Kohlhertz and his gunsel got in their car and raced away. Linus turned to Jules.

"What the hell is going on around here?" he demanded, still trembling from the adrenaline rush. Jules was in no mood for interrogation.

"It doesn't concern you," he said. "Be smart, *Monsieur*. Go home." He turned and started to walk but Linus seized his arm and spun him back. A young man in dark clothes at the end of the street started to jog their way. Jules waved him off then pulled his arm out of Linus's grip.

"You're the one who has the stake-out here," Linus said,

pointing toward the vacant house.

"This is dangerous business. Stay out of it."

"Where's Melisandre, or whatever her name is?"

"She doesn't want to see you."

"I don't give a damn *what* she wants! I want some truth or I swear I'll go right to the police."

"Go ahead. They're looking for you anyway," Jules challenged, referring to the picture of the "unidentified American" that was published in the newspaper with the story about Gervan's disappearance.

"You know damn well I had nothing to do with that. Why did you set me up?"

"What gives you the right to be snooping and following people? Who do you think you are?"

"I was dragged into this by Melisandre."

"Well she apologizes. Now drag yourself out."

"Not until I get a few answers."

"I just saved your life. Consider yourself lucky and leave it at that. Go home while you still can," Jules implored though plainly this little episode wasn't enough to frighten Linus off. "Kohlhertz is the leader of a group that uses crime to support their activities. I am investigating church thefts and I think he is involved. That is all I can tell you."

"So it's a crime story. What's the big secret?"

"The story cannot break until the appropriate time *Monsieur* Mercator. And perhaps you are the one to break it. But not now. You will just drive him deeper and we'll never get enough on him to ... "

"Old man Gervan is missing. I can place him at the scene. What more do you need?"

"It is not enough. I have reasons," Jules said. He signaled to the young guy at the corner who in turn signaled as well. A blue Saab collected him then hurried down the street and pulled up beside Linus and Jules. Jules moved to get in but Linus grabbed him. He then got the biggest surprise of the week. Jules spun around and landed a vicious kick squarely on his *solo plexus*. Linus crumbled, wind totally gone, gasping for breath. Jules frisked the pistol out of Linus's pocket, jumped into the waiting car and sped away.

PART TWO

"Not all are maidens that wear fair hair..."

Chapter 8. The FLEEING PROFESSOR

July 25th. Berlin, Germany. Day 04.

Ervin Fischer clutched the newspaper in his armpit as he fumbled the key into his apartment door. Time was short. Maybe they were on their way to his house right now. Or maybe they didn't make any connection. There was no way to be sure. So he had to escape.

He turned the key and shoved the door. It banged open against the inside wall and Fischer slammed it shut as he hurried inside and went straight to the phone. His nervous fingers could hardly cull out the numbers. The phone started ringing and a woman answered.

"It's me!" the old man said. "Have you seen the paper?" he added, choking back tears – unusual emotion for the tall stoical academician. Apparently she hadn't seen the papers.

"Don't look!" he cautioned. "Just come. Immediately. We must get to someplace safe." The woman on the line objected and wanted to know what was wrong. "I'll tell you when you get here!" he shouted. "Come now. There is no time!"

Fischer hung up. His hands trembled as he stood in the center of the room and began a mental checklist: large suitcase from the attic; clothes; briefcase and all the papers relevant to the case, especially the copy of the scroll. He could cancel classes from the road. Everything else would have to wait. He tossed the newspaper on the desk and began stuffing his files into a big leather briefcase. The newspaper was folded open to a picture – two professors on the dais, one handing an award to the other. The recipient was Gervan, the dead antiquarian. The presenter was his colleague, Ervin Fischer, the fleeing professor.

Linus stepped out of the shower, wrapped a towel around his waist and sat on the bed drying his hair and checking his messages. One was form his agent in New York, screaming "Where are the Jamie Richards pictures?! They're throwing money. Let's go Lines. Move it or lose it."

Then there was Jamie Richards herself, definitely *not* screaming. "Mister Mercator? This is Jamie Richards again," she began then repeated her offer to match the market price – though this time she added ten percent. Like his postponed trip home to Boston, Jamie would have to wait. His instincts told him he was onto something more explosive or scandalous, something involving the church, good or bad. Something of great value. Something that had cost people their lives. the suspicious circumstances of Gervan's death and Linus's tussle with Jules the priest and Kohlhertz the kidnapper made it clear that murder could happen, and Kohlhertz could kill.

But Jules the priest was no push-over either. The tall, solid, middle-aged guy with the leathery face carried a gun and kicked like a mule – as Linus's bruised ribs would attest. Not your standard skills and equipment for your standard priest – if indeed he *was* a priest. Unlike Kohlhertz – whose mien was patently outlaw – Jules's character and motives weren't so clear. He said he was sort of a priest-detective investigating church thefts, a function which no doubt bore great conflict for a clergyman. Luckily those conflicts didn't prevent him from stepping forward to save Linus from Kohlhertz otherwise Linus could have been going for a long unpleasant ride – maybe like the ride Gervan took.

In return for being the hero Jules expected Linus to "Go home," as he put it bluntly. But going home wasn't under consideration for any time soon. So Linus bailed out of the too-visible Grand Hotel and checked into a small four-star place tucked into a leafy square in *Friedrichshain*, formerly east Berlin. He knew that he had lost track of *them* and now they had surely lost track of *him*. He hoped they'd think he went home. Whichever the case, Linus had no intention of being *anyone's* victim – momma didn't raise no rubes or fools.

Ironically his confrontation with Jules presented another mystery which only made him more curious. Gervan was dead. Kohlhertz, the prime suspect, was positively placed at the crime scene – maybe even photographed by Jules from his attic stake-out. Suddenly the number one suspect – Kohlhertz – ends up helpless in the pistol sights of the number one accuser – Jules Doinel the priest. And Jules lets him go! Nowhere is there a single law enforcement official to be found. The lawguys are all off on the wrong path, maybe chasing Linus, and no one intends to put them right.

Obviously Jules needed Kohlhertz free for some reason, at least to track him. But by saving Linus, Jules blew his cover *and* his strategy. Kohlhertz now had the advantage of knowing Jules *was* following him but wouldn't – or couldn't – dime him to the police. So everyone now knew that each needed the other. Linus kept coming back to a thought he had on the night he discovered that his room at the Grand Hotel was searched: everyone was looking for something, but nobody knew what the hell it was!

But there was *one* known object of common desire, and that was Melisandre. Surely she was deep underground thanks to Linus finding her at that odd ceremony where the two women were stripped naked and displayed. One night she was the queen of the ball and the next night no one knew anyone fitting her description, let alone calling herself Melisandre Cortona. In any case, keeping tabs on each other had just gotten a lot harder.

He shed the wet towel and sat at the desk. Morning air streaming through a sunny window cooled his damp skin as he weighed his leads. They were dwindling. The three people he wanted to question most – Jules the priest, Kohlhertz and the enigmatic Melisandre – were for all intents and purposes gone.

Yet he had one new lead to follow, one more loose end that he hoped could tie up. He opened his laptop and brought up an image from Gervan's obituary and studied the picture – Gervan getting an award from a smiling colleague, the name *Humboldt University*,

Berlin, on the podium. Right now *that* as his best lead. Gervan must've talked to *someone* about what he was doing for Kohlhertz, or Jules, or Melisandre. Maybe it was *this* guy. He enlarged and enhanced the photo then dumped it onto his Blackberry. Someone at the University would know the nameless guy, he figured. And that would be a start.

But like all good leads it came with a nervous question: Who else might have discovered it? Who else was looking for the guy on the dais with Gervan? What would happen if *they* found him first? He threw on a shirt and jeans then headed out.

The neighborhood – like the hotel – was small and quiet, as yet unknown to the hoards of "westies" who were still discovering the other half of Berlin. He asked for his car at the desk then waited for it on the sidewalk. It was just after eight a.m. The summer morning was warm and sunny. People on the street seemed sleepy. Parked cars still outnumbered moving cars and baking scents, as yet unmingled with bus fumes, lingered on the sidewalks and in the cafes.

Another day in Berlin was just getting underway.

Fischer Found

Linus hung around the grassy quadrangle in front of Humboldt University's main building showing passers-by the picture of Gervan and the other man at the podium. But the best he got was directions to the University personnel office. So he decided to change tactics and moved off campus to the local cafes where he found four student types a few blocks away in a news shop. They were standing at a coffee and pastry counter at the back of the shop, holding white ceramic cups and talking. Each had a knapsack full of books slung over their shoulder or on the floor at their feet.

He showed them his press card and said he came to Berlin to meet Gervan, who had died suddenly. So now he wanted to interview the other man – whoever he was.

"American?" one of the students asked. Linus nodded. These

days you never knew what that would bring. He held out his Blackberry and showed them the photo on the screen. The two young women looked at it then at each other. Linus knew he had struck pay dirt.

"He is Professor Fischer," one of them said. Linus began writing in the margins of his newspaper.

"Do you know his first name?"

"Ervin," she replied. "Professor Ervin Fischer, specialist in ancient literature. He lives someplace near *Zionkirchplatz*." Linus looked questioningly – he didn't know *Zionkirchplatz*.

"It is just there," a young man said, pointing over his shoulder. "Very close."

"Zion ... ." Linus said as he wrote.

" ... kirchplatz. Zionkirchplatz," the student said and he produced his own pen and wrote in the margin of Linus's newspaper. "You can walk. *Fünfzehn minuten*. Fifteen *minuten*."

Linus thanked them, paid for his paper and began walking in the direction that the student pointed. About a block away he found a telephone booth and a Berlin directory. He fanned the thin pages until he reached the *Fs*, then the *Fischers*. There were many – none named Ervin, but many with the first initial *E*.

He turned to the street maps and found Zionkirchplatz where the students said Fischer lived. There was a *Fischer, E.* listed on *Veteranenstrasse*, one of the streets which enclosed the Zionkirchplatz square. It was about six blocks away in the *Prenzlauerberg* section of the city.

He strode through neighborhoods of five- and six-story apartment buildings. Every third or fourth building was recently renovated – the new Berlin replacing the old. He found the address he wanted – two-twenty-four Veteranenstrasse – across from a sandy playground filled with sunning parents and shrieking kids. The building for which Zionkirchplatz was named – a looming beaten-down red brick church wrapped in an apron of mildew stains and tangled undergrowth – was just beyond.

He stepped into the entry of 224 – a medium sized building with four apartments – and found *E. Fischer* listed in 401. It was only 9:15 a.m. so he figured there was a 50/50 chance he'd find Professor Fischer at home. He thought about buzzing but considering the good professor's colleague had just turned up dead in a canal Linus didn't think the Fischer would open up for a stranger. He'd need a better plan. And right on cue that better plan punched into the back of his knee. His leg buckled and he turned to see the snout of a big black Labrador with a long pink tongue lolling over his jaw. A young woman was at the other end of his leash. Linus scratched the dog between the ears. The dog smiled. The woman smiled. Linus stepped aside as the smiling pair went in.

And Linus elbowed the door to keep it from latching closed.

The woman and dog went into a first floor apartment. Linus slipped into the foyer and sprinted up to the first landing. The faint voice of a radio or TV announcer drifted in the bright stairwell. He started upstairs, reminding himself that someone might have found Fischer before him – like a police detective. Or a gun-toting priest. Or maybe old man Gervan's abductor. Suddenly he wished he had a weapon. He took a deep breath and continued to the landing beneath Fischer's apartment. The sounds of locks turning and clicking stopped him short. Fischer's door was being opened from inside.

He ducked, ready to bolt downstairs if he had to. Someone wearing moccasins and baggy chinos came out. Linus could see the feet. He backed down, expecting the feet to come his way.

But the feet went upward out of sight, probably to the roof or an attic. A few moments later the feet returned to the apartment door. Linus hurried up the stairs and confronted an older guy, about late sixties, carrying a big brown suitcase and going into the apartment. He was tall and narrow-shouldered, wearing khaki chinos, a white shirt and a straw hat shaped like a pith helmet. It had to be Fischer. The old man saw him coming and a look of horror overtook his face. He tried to close the door but Linus was too quick.

"*Bitte*. Excuse me," he said, jamming the door with his foot. The old man pushed harder but Linus leaned into it with his shoulder. "Professor Fischer. I'm a friend," he appealed. Fischer wasn't interested. But Linus was too strong. Fischer quit the struggle and backed into the room. "Professor Fischer. It's okay... " Linus said as the old man retreated to a bowl of fruit and began pelting Linus with apples and oranges. Then he grabbed the big cruciform sword hanging over the mantle and charged. "Don't!" Linus exclaimed as the heavy sword swung, spinning Fischer with it as it decapitated a floor lamp then flew out of his hands and crashed on the coffee table. Linus grabbed him in a bear hug from behind and covered his mouth.

"Professor Fischer. I'm not one of them," he said – not knowing for sure who "them" really was. The old man struggled valiantly for half a minute or so then succumbed. Nonetheless, Linus held on tightly. "I know why you're afraid of me. We need to talk," he said. "Do you understand me?" The old man nodded. "I think it would be prudent if I let you go and we close and lock the door. Do you agree?" Again Fischer nodded. As soon as Linus released him Fischer bolted and armed himself with a floor lamp.

"Why should I trust someone who forces their way into my home!" he sneered.

"Would you have let me in otherwise?" Linus asked. Fischer brandished the lamp like a lance.

"We have nothing to talk about," he insisted.

"I know what happened to your colleague Gervan and I'm sure his killer wouldn't mind getting his hands on anyone Gervan might've talked to. They may be on the way here right now," Linus explained. But Fischer's fearful look was proof enough that he had already figured that out. And the clothes scattered around the room, the open suitcase, added up to one thing: Fischer was taking a powder.

"What the hell do you think I'm doing here?" he said as he dropped the lamp and continued packing.

"I want to know about Gervan."

"It's a police matter. Ask *them*."

"Wasn't he your friend? Wouldn't you like to see his killers, caught?" Linus pressed. The papers said nothing about kidnapping or murder but, like Linus, Fischer knew Gervan's death was no accident.

He stepped closer and glared.

"More than you know," he said. Linus saw it as a sign that Fischer was in up to his ears. He was a hot target – for some reason – and he had to move fast.

"What was he doing with the woman and the priest?" Linus quizzed. Fischer grew more angry. "I also believe they know it was murder and that a guy called Kohlhertz did it, but they won't come forward. I need to know why." Now Fischer was enraged. His hands shook as he loaded small items into a shoulder bag.

"*I* know who killed him. *They* killed him," he sneered. "They dragged him into their schemes and got him killed. *They* did it! This Kohlhertz fool is only part of it."

"What schemes? What was he working on?"

"I want nothing more to do with it. Go and leave me alone," Fischer insisted, retrieving his dented straw helmet.

"Who's Kohlhertz? What's he up to?" Linus persisted. Fischer gripped his bag and headed for the door. Linus stopped him and took the heavy suitcase out of his hand.

"I can arrange a safe place for you, a safe house, in exchange for your cooperation. I'm a journalist," he said. Fischer aimed his sunken brown eyes directly into Linus's.

"Journalist? Keyhole peeper? Garbage can sifter? No thanks. I can take care of myself!"

"Please Professor."

"What do you care about me or my friends?"

"It's a story."

"Write a book, make a million dollars, move to Hollywood leaving a trail of broken lives. Isn't that what you American journalists are all about?"

"Some. Not all," Linus admitted – the commercial possibilities were definitely a big part of his interest. "Look. In the past week I've been ditched, mugged, and threatened all because I stopped into an antiquarian shop. Wouldn't you be at least *curious* if you were me?" Fischer's defenses were deflating. The appeal to his intellect was working.

"Those people you mentioned, the woman and the priest. You should be questioning *them.*"

"Sure. But who are they? *Where* are they?" The old prof didn't answer though Linus sensed he would. He helped him again with his bag and followed him down to the sidewalk where Fischer scanned up and down the street. A silver Mercedes convertible pulled up with a classy fifty-ish woman at the wheel. Fischer loaded his luggage and got in beside her as Linus watched from the curb. He was losing his last source – didn't know where Fischer was going and hadn't learned any more than he already knew. Then the cagey old professor threw him a bone.

"There is an ancient abbey in a small town about an hour from here," he said. "It's some sort of convalescent home now called *Das Giudecca.* I suggest you look for your chums there."

"How about a phone call when you feel safer?" Linus asked. Fischer wrote something on a small white card and held it out the window.

"The abbey is in a town called Lindow. Let me know what you find," he said. Linus took the card. It was an e-mail address. Nothing more. Screen name: *Anfortas.*

The Mercedes pulled out and sped away.

Chapter 9. The SECRETS of LINDOW ABBEY

Linus smoothed the map on his knee and traced a route to
Lindow, a small town about forty miles north of Berlin. Just an hour
ago Ervin Fischer, the dead man Gervan's nervous colleague, gave
him a cryptic instruction. "Go look for your chums there," he said,
meaning Melisandre and Jules. He didn't know why the old professor
said it but Fischer was a frightened man – panicked as only a man
hiding a dangerous secret could be. So Linus decided to follow the
lead.

As he drove through the tall green rye fields and dense rolling
forest Linus had a strong sense that he was covering some of the same
ground he did on the night he followed Melisandre's friend Veronica
to that strange induction ceremony by the lake. This Lindow Abbey
was in the same neck of the woods.

It was just after noon when he arrived in Lindow, a small, sleepy
village of stone houses and shops. At the center of town where the
roads forked a small piece of wood was bolted onto a sign post. The
words *"Das Giudecca"* were painted on it above a right-pointing
arrow. Fischer said that the abbey had been converted into a
convalescent home. *Das Giudecca* was the place.

He eased off the gas and steered to the right. About a quarter
mile away he came across another *Das Giudecca* sign nailed to a tree
beside a dirt road. He didn't want to barge down the road on a cloud
of dust so he passed by, parked near a small house behind a high
hedge, then walked back. The dirt road cut through the thick woods to
the sunny shore of a large placid lake, then ran along a high stone
wall until it reached an old – possibly ancient – gateway. The words
Das Giudecca were carved into a weathered wooden plaque affixed to
the pillar.

The light from the lakeside faded beneath the leafy canopy but bits of sun spiked through the trees and cast bright yellow dots in the underbrush all around him. Ahead he saw a primitive stone structure or at least what was left of one. It was the ancient ruined abbey. Out of caution he stepped over the runoff ditch beside the road and followed a path into the cover of the woods. The thick brush swept his legs and invisible insect silks streaked across his face.

On the other side of a massive tumbled-down wall a big shaft of light cored through the canopy and split the forestial shadow. He climbed atop the wall and viewed an old courtyard on the other side. Eight large tablets in evenly spaced rows were lying flat on the ground. A peaked stone wall, shaped like an arrowhead with a cruciform window near its apex, stood high over the small yard. Though the sides were fallen in and there was no roof, it clearly had once been a church. Linus climbed down for a closer look.

The tablets were about the size of a small human and each bore an inscription. Linus knew that they were the lids of ancient sarcophagi but he couldn't quite make out what was carved on the stones. The ancient characters were weathered and shallow and he didn't recognized the language. But the numerals were clear enough – a series of X's, I's and V's enumerating dates. All were from the 11th and 12th century.

He noticed that the tablets were circled by freshly trodden dirt and wondered why the ancient site seemed to be so active. Then he discovered the reason. He bent down and examined the fresh white scrapes and pry marks on the pocked, stained stone. The vaults had been opened recently. His first thought was the most obvious – grave robbers. Or maybe archeologists. Perhaps the contents had been moved for safe-keeping. Jules the priest claimed he was sleuthing *"Sacré Furtá"* – sacred thefts. If so, it would fit and provide some hint as to why Fischer sent him here.

He left the burial yard and entered the big debris field that was once the abbey. At the far end there was a restored chapel which looked like it had once been part of the original church. In the distance he could see bright red patches of terra cotta through the trees. It was the roof of a large building, probably the rehab center or convalescent home that Fischer said was here.

He tugged the iron handle of the chapel's arched wooden door but it was locked. The chapel was built on a slope and Linus found a small barred basement window on the side, conveniently hidden in the brush. Dried streaks of pollen on the glass clouded the view and wiping it didn't help much. He blocked the glare with his hand and moved his face closer. The inside came into focus. He could see objects scattered across a long wooden table. One looked like a large marble pestle and mortar. He could also see what looked like a corner of a book. But the rest was in darkness.

He knew he had to get inside. He peeked around the rear corner and saw a basement door with a long stone staircase leading away from it – down the hill and into the gravel parking lot of the red-roofed building he had seen through the trees. It was a three-story institutional-looking place with small windows and a stucco facade. A white van with a yellow French number plate was parked at the front door. Linus pulled out his camera, zoomed in and shot the van and the plate.

But the chapel would have to wait. The basement door was too out-in-the-open, and breaking in through the window was also too risky – at least for now. But maybe not after dark, he thought. Suddenly he heard the low whine of an engine. A car was coming. He made his way into the woods and found a perch with a view of the road. A silver Audi passed beneath him. He looked into the window at the passenger – a woman with bright auburn hair. At that instant, almost as though she sensed his presence, she looked up and saw him. Her unnatural azure-colored eyes seemed to glow.

She turned away as they passed. Linus climbed down onto the road as the car stopped, the tail lights flashed, and the doors flew open. The woman bolted through the abbey graveyard and down a path into the woods. All he saw of her was her brown jersey and black leather pants.

He jogged ahead to get a look at her face but her driver, his brown sport coat spread wide over his broad shoulders and flapping against his sharply creased black pants, strode in front of him and blocked his path. It was Jules Doinel, the priest.

"*Monsieur* Mercator," he said loudly but calmly. Linus's eyes were affixed to the fleeing passenger. "You are tenacious. But I find your judgment to be questionable," he said. His face was ashen – like he hadn't been sleeping much lately. The woman disappeared into the woods. Linus looked Jules straight in the face.

"We all have our strengths and weaknesses, Jules. What are yours?"

"Many. But gullibility is not among them. You are not here by chance. Who sent you here, *Monsieur*?"

"An historic site. I came to see the chapel."

"Access to the chapel would be impossible. It has been abandoned for a very long time and it is unsafe," Jules said. From what he had seen through the basement window Linus knew he was lying.

"Too bad," he replied. "Maybe you could tell me something about the tombs."

"They are old."

"No shit. Why have they been opened recently?"

"Thieves and vandals."

"Then you're here to investigate sacred thefts," Linus presumed. Jules didn't comment. "I did a bit of research and found another Jules Doinel, leader of a Cathar revival in the nineteenth century. Is it your real name?"

"I am distantly related to the man of whom you speak," Jules confirmed, being surprisingly candid. But perhaps not so surprising after all. His notable ancestry would've made him notable himself. Hiding his identity was impractical – though he could still hide his affairs.

"Who is Melisandre Cortona? What's her real name?" Linus asked. Jules gave him an inscrutable look.

"I know her only as Melisandre Cortona."

"That tragic story of forbidden love was heart-wrenching. And she's a long lost relative of Saint Margaret of Cortona, no doubt," he said sarcastically.

"Anything more than what she has already told you will have to come from her, *Monsieur*."

"Alright. And she would be where?"

"I'm sorry, I do not know."

"I'm sure you don't. Well thanks Jules. I'm glad we had this little talk. See you around." Linus began to sidestep Jules in the direction of the woman's escape but the muscular Frenchman stepped right with him.

"I'm afraid this is private property, *Monsieur*, and I am instructed to evict you by any means necessary," he stated.

"Instructed by whom?"

"The authorities."

"And by any means necessary. You know for a priest you talk and act a lot like a gangster."

"That would be *your* specialty, *Monsieur*, not mine."

"Exactly what kind of priest are you anyway?"

"One bound to protect the confidences of his flock. Surely as a reporter with sources you can understand *that,*" Jules lectured. "You will be leaving now, *Monsieur*?" Linus decided to be prudent.

"Yes, I'll be leaving," he said and the tension siphoned off. Jules ushered him down the road away from the abbey. If he thought he'd get answers, Linus would've asked Jules why he let Kohlhertz get away and who owns this so-called "private property", and what was taken from the tombs? What was Gervan working on? But the answers, like the graves in the abbey burial plot, would require more digging. They got to the outer gate and Linus asked, "Who was the woman?" Jules's reaction was a surprise. He could've shrugged her off as "a friend." Instead he got testy.

"Asking questions can be a cumbersome burden, *monsieur*. I strongly recommend that you cease talking and begin listening before you find yourself with deep regrets." Linus stepped up and got right in Jules's face.

"I'll shut up when I want to shut up and not a second sooner," he asserted.

"I'd prefer there to be no need for us to speak at all," Jules assured.

"Withholding evidence in a capital crime is a serious offense," Linus warned, gambling on his hunch that Jules knew more about Gervan's abduction and death than he was revealing.

"Before you start making threats you had better take inventory of your own liabilities. You news people are nothing more than cockroaches scratching for crumbs," Jules retorted as he reached his hand into his jacket pocket. Linus lunged forward and grabbed Jules's arm. They stumbled off the road into the brush. Linus pinned him backward over a fallen tree.

"You won't need that gun of yours," he said as he jammed his fist hard against Jules's jaw. "And I haven't forgotten that kick in the gut."

"I should've shot you!" Jules croaked as Linus pushed harder against his throat. "It's not a gun! Get your hands off of me!" Linus pushed off and stood back. Jules got to his feet and pulled out his hand. Linus jumped. It was a cell phone.

"You fool. You'll regret this." Jules asserted as he thrashed to free himself from the brambles. Linus didn't wait around. He turned and beat tracks back to his car. There was nothing more to be learned right here and now. If he wanted a closer look inside the Lindow Abbey chapel he'd have to come back at night – tonight, before they had a chance to sanitize the place, which they would certainly do.

Linus was gambling that they wouldn't expect him to come back so soon.

Playing with the Patsy

"He's a menace," Jules said. "I want to get rid of him right away." He was sitting on the lakeside patio picking thorns out of his socks.

"What do you propose?" asked the woman with the azure eyes and auburn hair, sipping from a *demitasse*.

"We go back to the original plan. Turn him over to police. Our contacts can hold him for questioning, revoke his visa and have him deported."

"That'll cost us. It's a big favor. And a potential scandal."

"Yes. Especially if they give him a beating in the process," the gruff Frenchman said, then muttered, "It wouldn't upset me." The woman smirked as she took his foot in her lap and continued plucking the nettles. Jules leaned back in his chair and relaxed.

"If he gets hurt I want us to be miles away from it," she said.

"That may not be possible unless we get rid of him."

"It's not the 'getting rid' that bothers me Jules. But it's better for everyone if he loses interest on his own."

"He won't."

"Maybe not. But he's also a person of interest to Kohlhertz. It wouldn't hurt to know why."

"*I* know why. Because Kohlhertz didn't get what he wanted from Gervan. He knows nothing and he's desperate to find someone who does."

"And he thinks that someone is Linus Mercator. Do you?" she asked. Jules sipped his *espresso*.

"No. I think Mercator is a treasure hunter just like the rest," he said. "He sensed something was going on at the shop when he was there. He's after a story to sell."

"I'm not so sure. You think his appearance at *Blauer Apfel* for the feast was a coincidence?"

"I do. But not his being in the area. He was returning to the shop. When he saw there was a fire he went into the restaurant for supper. That's all."

"So Gervan didn't ... "

"No. Gervan wouldn't ... a total stranger? No, I say we'll find it elsewhere, whatever it was that Gervan discovered and wanted to tell you. But not with Mercator."

"Possibly. But I say we have to look *everywhere* so it might not be a bad idea to keep an eye on him. And Kohlhertz will be watching him so it'll help us keep an eye on *him*, too. If we string Mercator along we can direct him to where we want Kohlhertz to follow," she said and Jules muttered,

"Siberia would be nice."

"But we'll be prudent and keep our distance. He may not be as mercenary as you think, and people driven by their ideals can be reckless," she said, knowing that Linus was once so driven. Jules huffed.

"Ideals? He's a *paparazzo*. Not even a legitimate journalist. And they are all bloodsuckers and cockroaches anyway."

"Just stand back and let him do some leg work for us. We'll fiddle behind the curtain while he and Kohlhertz dance," she instructed, and Jules agreed.

Chapel of Bones

Linus sat in the brush watching the roads leading to both Lindow Abbey and the nearby red-roofed building called *Das Giudecca*. The last light of day was disappearing and the big spider web hanging above him was doing the same. A few more minutes and it would be dark enough to prowl.

After his afternoon scuffle with Jules, Linus left the village and lay low. It was nearly seven when he got back. He ditched his car in a field of tall rye then snuck back into the woods, found a spot where he could watch the Abbey and the other building, and waited. Now, after two hours, the wait was about to end.

Jules's silver Audi was gone – of course there was no way of knowing who was in it when it left. The white panel truck with the French number plate was gone too – maybe filled with the contents of the chapel basement, maybe replaced by someone waiting inside to bushwhack him.

The rhythmic evening cicada overlaid his thoughts as he plotted his entry and checked his equipment – especially the long-handled flashlight which could be used as a club. And he had the car's tire iron with him, too – but more for prying locks and latches than for use as a weapon.

The last of the gloaming was leaving the lake. All was quiet. Not a soul came or went the whole time he was there. A few lights shone in a few windows of the red-roofed building but no people were shadowed on the shades. Linus decided to make his move. He found his way out of the black woods, took a wide arc around the burial plot and climbed through the crumbled-down walls of the old abbey. He knew he had to hurry – the rising full moon was still low but the sharp silhouette of the chapel's peak was already stabbing a shadow into the ruins.

He leaned against the stone foundation next to the basement window. No lights were on inside. It looked like no one was there. He slipped around the corner to the back door. It was made of thick wood and looked old. There was no keyhole, only a hasp and padlock which were new and no doubt added recently. He pushed the wedged end of the tire iron into place, checked over his shoulder then pulled upward. The metal bent. The hasp loosened. He checked around again then pried from a different angle and the hasp broke free. Linus pushed the door open and slipped inside.

It was as dark as a cave. He drew the heavy flashlight and gripped the steel handle, his heart pulsing in his throat as if someone had already come at him out of the darkness. A slight acrid odor soured the dry air. Moonlight sliced through the window grate and cast bars of shadow onto the opposite wall. Soon he could see enough to know that he was alone. The question was ... for how long?

But no one had heard him. No one was coming. He covered the window with his jacket then turned on the flashlight but filtered the light through his fingers. The room was about the size of a one-car garage. There was a desk against one wall and two benches in the middle.

On the desk, Linus found a small stack of books and a cardboard box filled with papers. Most of the books were written in French. His smattering of French, along with the textbook design and illustrations, was enough to know they were about chemistry and biology. The title of one was a man's name – *Nicholas Flammel*. It appeared to be a biography. Linus entered it into his Blackberry then turned the flashlight into the file box.

Most of the documents were internet printouts and most written in English. One set of papers – a US Department of Energy publication – was titled *Human Genome Project*. There were also several copies of a newsletter called *Human Genome News* published by the US National Institute of Health and the US DOE. Someone had genetics on their mind.

There was also a three-ring binder labeled *Online Mendelian Inheritance in Man Database* – Gregor Mendel, the Austrian father of genetics, had done so well with his pea plants that he now had a database in his name. The binder's contents were from Johns Hopkins University, co-founder of the GDB – Genome Data Base. A line on the title page described the Mendelian database as "a catalog of inherited human traits and diseases". Someone wasn't just interested in genetics. They were interested in mutations as well.

He leafed through dozens of pages of bar-code representations of human gene sequences. Each was numbered: cluster 131, cluster 772, and so on, but they appeared to be in random order. In the back pages Linus found a lot of text about something called *aniridia*, which was defined as "an inherited semi-dominant ocular disorder of variable expressivity characterized by iris hypoplasia (disturbed development of the iris)." Dozens of technical notes and case histories followed.

But time was running short. His uneasiness was growing. He couldn't leaf through them all. He entered "aniridia" in his notes and moved on. In a file titled "receipts" he found a printout from a German company he didn't know. It was mostly stock numbers with no description. Their prices however told a different tale.

On the last page he was surprised that they totaled half a million euros – over six hundred thousand dollars. There was nothing in the basement which looked like it was worth anywhere near that amount.

Yet the shipping destination of everything was "Lindow Abbey, Lindow, Germany." It was an ancient ruin and couldn't be a legitimate address, Linus thought. He leafed back through the pages, looking for a clue as to what it all was. Suddenly his ear captured a faint sound. There was a car on the road. He doused the flashlight then listened – it was going to the red-roofed building. He peeked out the door and saw it stop. It was the small white van with the French plates. Two people got out and went into the building.

He scanned the shipping lists – numbers, numbers, and more numbers. Then he found a named item – ten gallons of something called "agarose." At less than three hundred dollars it was the cheapest item on the list. He didn't know why "agarose" sounded familiar. He entered it in his notes then went to the benches for a quick look before he ran.

A large well-dripped candle was on one bench, along with an old marble mortar with matching pestle. There was also a clear glass dish, sooty and burned on one side with irregular reddish stains on the other. It had a long wooden handle for holding it over a flame.

Something draped with a black cloth was on the other bench. It was about the same length as the slabs in the abbey burial plot and Linus thought it might be a coffin. But it was a clear plastic container with a blue lid. There were four containers in all, side by side. Each filled with human bones. They must've come from the disturbed graves in the abbey plot, he thought. He shined the light closer. In one the top of a skull was rolled towards him. There were three holes in it – where no holes should be.

Then he heard faint talking.

He doused the light and covered the boxes then grabbed his jacket off the window and went to the door. A man and a woman were crossing the parking lot, walking toward the abbey. Linus knew it was time to run. He crouched low and slipped out the door, hustled back up through the ruins and into the dark woods. In a few minutes they'd discover the broken lock on the door to the chapel basement and they'd be looking for who did it. He felt his way along the ground with his hands, holding his head down to protect his eyes from low branches. Ahead through the trees he saw a pair of passing headlights and knew he had made it to the main road. His car was in a rye field just on the other side.

He dashed across the road into the rye field and got into his car.

His tires spun in the dirt and the car bumped up onto the paved road. He imagined the white van from *Das Giudecca* pulling out of the abbey road and cutting off his escape. But it didn't happen. No one was in front of him. No one was behind him. He'd made it out safely.

And as he sped past the abbey road he switched on the headlights and bolted out of town.

Chapter 10. ACCESSING ANFORTAS

July 26th. Berlin, Germany. Day 05.

Linus was a half hour away from Lindow Abbey when his pulse finally slowed. His escape was clean. If someone hadn't shown up in his rear-view mirror by now they weren't coming. It was midnight and the hotel was quiet when he got back to Berlin. He went straight to his room and e-mailed Fischer, the fleeing professor – a.k.a. Anfortas.

> TO: Anfortas
> FM: LP-Merc
> SUBJECT: Lindow Abbey
>
> Located abbey. Several ancient graves in abbey burial ground recently disturbed. In basement of nearby chapel containers of human skeletal remains presumably from disturbed graves though no proof of their origin yet. Also found primitive implements, possibly for crude experimentation or ritual (?); books on biology and chemistry. ALSO: printouts from Human Genome Project and Online Mendelian Inheritance in Man database indicating serious interest in genetics. Other discoveries as well. Did indeed encounter (unfriendly) priest Jules Doinel w/unidentified woman. Need your input. Suggest a meeting at earliest opportunity. L.P. Mercator.

Linus wondered how Fischer knew he'd find Jules at the abbey. It was one of many things he wanted to quiz him about. He sent the e-mail then went searching the internet. First he found that Fischer's screen name – Anfortas – was the legendary Fisher King – keeper of the Holy Grail, lord of the Grail Castle. Fischer's choice of his on-line handle seemed simple – Ervin Fischer, Fisher King. Yet Linus wondered if it meant that Fischer was the keeper of some important secret?

Next he checked out the name Nicholas Flammel, which was the title of the only book he had found at the abbey chapel which wasn't about biology or chemistry. He discovered that Flammel was a famous medieval alchemist. Linus had always thought of alchemists as cabalists and sorcerers, purveyors of hocus-pocus trickery, best known for their futile efforts to manufacture gold. But were those efforts really futile? It was an intriguing thought – that there actually *was* a formula for making gold and now someone had discovered it. It made him shiver. Such a formula would be highly coveted, to put it mildly – definitely worth a few small murders to keep it secret. It was pretty far-fetched, but truth was often stranger than fiction. He didn't rule it out.

Flammel was also the Grand Master of something called the *Prieure de Sion* – the *Priory of Sion* – a secret Paris-based society whose members claim to be descendants of a usurped royal line, seeking to restore their rightful place on the French throne. He checked his notes from the strange ritual in the pines and, sure enough, Melisandre had mentioned the Priory in her speech. "Recently we have received intelligence from Paris that the *Priory of Sion* has secretly named a successor," she had said. Why Melisandre should be concerned with the French throne was a mystery.

The word aniridia was also in his notes from the abbey. It came from a page that originated at a database called the *Online Mendelian Inheritance in Man*, at Johns Hopkins University in Baltimore. And that's where Linus found the definition:

Aniridia – a congenital abnormality. Aniridia is a semi-dominant disorder in which development of the iris, lens, cornea and/or retina is disturbed. Mutations in the human aniridia (PAX6) gene have now been identified, and there is a large pedigree in which visual acuity of affected members is nearly normal.

It was an interesting condition, one that was expressed as a defective iris – which was an observable defect – but which didn't necessarily diminish vision of the affected person. But why would Jules be interested in genetics at all let alone in aniridia, a condition also described as "extremely rare"? He then searched for Agarose, the named item on the shipping list he found, and discovered that it was "a jelly-like product made from seaweed used in a process called electrophoresis", which was the second of six steps to DNA fingerprinting. Genetic fingerprinting. And that was the binding tie.

It seemed almost certain that someone was making genetic fingerprints and that the numbered items on the shipping invoice were pieces of lab equipment. Yet there was nothing as sophisticated as that at Lindow Abbey. Obviously genetic fingerprinting wasn't something you cooked up over a big candle. If there *was* a lab, it was someplace else, like in the red-roofed building called *Das Giudecca*. That was his next web search. *Das Giudecca*.

Unfortunately it came back "no results". So he dropped the German *Das* and typed *Giudecca*, and got this: *"A small island near Venice which, in the 1540s, was a refuge for reformed prostitutes. A monastery, dedicated to Mary Magdalene, was built there in 1551, and later converted into its current use as a woman's penitentiary."*

The pieces began to fit. *Das Giudecca* in Lindow, Germany, was probably a house for women, possibly former prostitutes or others in crisis, connected to *Novangelis*, Melisandre's woman's rights group. And Vera, Melisandre's friend, said her name was Veronica Franco, which he'd already discovered was an alias taken from Veronica Franco, a famous courtesan – *from ancient Venice*. If not evidence of an emerging theme, per se, at least their choice of fake names was consistent.

It was just after one in the morning – an hour since he had e-mailed Fischer – and his eyelids were getting heavy. As he was about to quit for the night his mailbox pinged and the flag icon went up. Fischer had replied.

TO: LP-Merc
FM: Anfortas
SUBJECT: Input
Call 30-65-2938481 at precisely 10 am, from telephone outside metro entrance at Marx-Engels Platz.

Fischer wanted him to call a specific number from a specific phone at ten this morning. He still had time to rack up a full night's sleep – which he needed. As he shut down the laptop and the screen went black he closed his tired eyes and yawned. It felt good. It had been a long day.

The Brains of the Bode

People were coming towards him from all directions across the wide stone-paved plaza, converging on the metro stop, driven from the sidewalks by the intermittent rain. It was a gray morning in Berlin. Low clouds hung like smoke over the city. Linus stood beside the stairs going down into the metro at Marx-Engels Platz. He checked his watch – it was exactly ten o'clock – then dialed the number Fischer had e-mailed. It rang twice then it was answered... a pre-recorded ad for a canal boat excursion!

Thinking he'd misdialed Linus tried again. The same thing happened. He listened for a hidden message but stopped listening and hung up when he spotted a guy in a cloth hat and wrinkled trench-coat coming across the square. It was Professor Fischer, his stare fixed on the phone booth. Linus set his Blackberry to begin recording.

"*Guten Morgen Herr* Mercator," Fischer said. Linus nodded. "The canal boats are very pleasant. I highly recommend it," he said, then added, "Walk with me."

Fischer moved quickly for an older guy and Linus had to catch up. They dodged the chaotic traffic on *Unter den Linden* then crossed over a bridge to *"Museum Island"* – a group of museums surrounded by canals. At the Bode Museum, a large granite building faced by classical columns, Fischer mumbled "this way." But they passed the main entrance and went instead to a side door with a keypad – Fischer had the code – then down into a dark basement passageway. The air was stale and numbered steel doors of storage vaults lined both sides of the long corridor.

Near the end, the aroma of brewed coffee replaced the flat air. They entered a small office where a fit looking fifty-ish woman with black-framed glasses and pinned blonde hair was sitting at a wooden desk, arranging papers beneath the green shade of a banker's lamp – the only light in the room.

"My colleague, Ute, curator, conservator, and woman of expertise on many subjects," Fischer said. Ute nodded, her smile restrained. Linus recognized her as Fischer's getaway driver from yesterday afternoon. Fischer dumped his trench coat over the back of his chair then extracted a pipe pouch from its pocket. "Some interesting finds at the Abbey?" he asked.

"Odd anyway," Linus replied. "An unusual interest in a genetic disease called Aniridia. And there was a shipping list which may be for genetic fingerprinting equipment," he said. Ute took notes. "Before I go any farther would it be fair of me to ask what, exactly, was Gervan's part in all of this?" he said. Fischer dragged a wooden match on the tile floor then puffed up a cloud of soft smelling blue smoke from his pipe.

"My understanding," he began, "is that the priest, Jules, investigates thefts of artifacts. Presumably church artifacts. Gervan, as an expert antiquarian, would help verify recovered items from time to time."

"Then how does he hook up with this Kohlhertz character?"

"Simple. Kohlhertz had an object that needed study. He took it to an expert."

"Then Gervan got suspicious and alerted Jules," Linus surmised.

"As I'm sure any reasonable person would do, *Herr* Linus."

"But it was more than an alert, wasn't it. They were working this Kohlhertz guy, stringing him along. But Kohlhertz figured it out. And Gervan got chopped," Linus said. From their faces, he wished he'd chosen a better word. "What did Kohlhertz have that needed study?"

he asked quietly.

"A document," Fischer said. "The question is, *what type*? Most of the important ancient documents are of religious origin, like the finds at Qumran," he said. Linus knew he meant the *Dead Sea Scrolls*.

"But Kohlhertz? He doesn't strike me as the archeological type. It'd have to be stolen."

"Not necessarily. Many ancient documents have surfaced in strange ways," Fischer said. "In 1945 an Egyptian peasant near Nag Hammadi plowed up thirteen scrolls dating back sixteen centuries, some of which he used to stoke his home fires before someone realized the magnitude of his discovery."

And there were others, he went on: a Gnostic text called the *Codex Brucianus* – same name on one of Melisandre's office files – was found by the Scots adventurer James Bruce in 1769. "Some documents," he continued, "no one knows *how* they were discovered." As an example he cited the 1785 sale to the British Museum of the *Pistis Sophia* – origin unknown – by Doctor Anthony Askew. "The circumstances were similar for the *Gospel of Mary*, Mary Magdalene, which surfaced in Cairo in eighteen-ninety-six."

"So another manuscript of questionable origin is surfacing via Kohlhertz. Or so it would appear," Linus observed. Fischer nodded his tentative agreement. The Kohlhertz parchment was tested and dated at roughly two thousand years old, he said, and added that it made many references to the *Lapsis Elixir*, the Philosopher's Stone of Alchemy. "It appears to be more like an alchemist's cookbook than a Gnostic gospel," he said.

"A formula for making gold," Linus said. Alchemists, though probably the precursors of modern scientists, were best known to the modern world for their futile efforts to manufacture gold – though no one could say for sure that such a formula *didn't* exist. Fischer, though obviously amused, shrugged it off.

"Unfortunately that is all Gervan revealed to me," he said.

"Jules must've known at least that much. I found a book about Nicholas Flammel at the abbey," Linus noted, referring to the renowned medieval alchemist. Linus produced his Blackberry and opened the pertinent files. "And these locations are from a map that I found in the Melisandre woman's office," he said as he viewed the image he made. Ute plotted them in an atlas as Linus read them out. "In France ... Paris, Arques, Aix-en-Provence, Besançon, Bayeux, Verdun, Rheims, LeMans, Vezelay, Stenay, Rennes-le-Château, Bellevault, the Forest of Woevres. In England: Exeter and Wiggenhall. In Spain: Oviedo. Italy: Venice. Then in India, a village called Mari, and one in Kashmir called Srinagar. The words Pindi Point were written beside the former, and Rauza Bal beside the latter," he said.

"Finally, there are a couple of mountains near the *Pyrenées* called *Montsegur* and Bezu," Linus finished. He looked up from his notes and said, "Maybe they're searching for something?" Fischer freed his pipe from his clamped jaw.

"The ruins of a Cathar citadel sit atop *Montsegur*, in the Pyrenées," he noted. The Cathars were a catholic sect, he said, but were declared heretical by Rome in 1242. "Thirty thousand knights were sent to the Languedoc to eradicate them. It was called the *Albigensian Crusade*. But a number of Cathar parfaits, or priests, held out under siege at *Montsegur*.

"When the siege ended, two hundred chose mass immolation in a wood-filled barn over recanting their Cathar beliefs. But twelve escaped by rappelling down the cliffs one night, supposedly with the Cathar treasure which many believe included the Holy Grail."

Linus told them that Jules claimed to be descended from another Jules Doinel, a neo-Cathar from the nineteenth century. "I read that many Cathar priests and teachers were women," he said, then he told them about Melisandre's group, *Novangelis*, which appeared to be a militant woman's organization, and he suggested the possibility that the group had Cathar roots as well. Ute wrote it all down. Fischer chewed his pipe.

"The village of Rennes-le-Château has hidden a fabulous mystery for many centuries," Fischer continued, citing a name on Linus's list. The seasoned teacher was in his element and enjoying his dissertation.

He said that in 1891, Beringer Saunière, the *curé* of the village abbey, was renovating his little church and discovered four parchments in a hollow pedestal. The priest was suddenly wealthy beyond his lot, he said, waving an arm for effect. "And perhaps a bit crazy as well," he added. Saunière went on a building spree beginning with an elegant stone tower, the *Tour Magdala*, at the abbey. He also commissioned a series of grotesque Satanic stations of the cross which still hang on the walls of the abbey today.

"The source of this fortune was never discovered," Fischer said, adding that everything from the lost Cathar treasure and the Holy Grail to the vanished Knights Templar treasure and extortion from the Pope has been suggested.

"The Grail *is* the Templar treasure, eh Anfortas?" Linus asked, calling Fischer by his screen name, Anfortas – name of the Templar who was charged with the Grail's defense.

"Perhaps only a small part," Fischer stated. The Templars were first and foremost the *Knights of the Temple of Solomon*, and they swore allegiance to the Pope alone, he said. "They've also been called the *Warrior Monks of Outremer,* and *Storm Troopers of the Holy Land.*"

"You know just as I was entering Gervan's shop I heard someone, him I think, say something about the Temple of Solomon. But I'm not sure what," Linus recalled.

"Could be important. We'll have to see," Fischer observed dryly. His lecture continued. Early in the 12th century, he said, a small group led by French nobleman Huges de Payan presented itself to Baudouin I, King of Jerusalem, as protectors of the Temple of Solomon. Hence the name *Knights Templar*. "But there is solid evidence that the Knights spent the next decade digging in the stables beneath the temple. It's theorized that they were sent by European powers, perhaps to find the body of Christ. No one knows if anything was ever found.

"Yet their power and wealth grew immensely over the next two centuries, which some say proves that they did indeed make a potent discovery," he said, adding that at their apex the Templars had strong alliances with foreign potentates as well as with the *Hashishim*, their Islamic counterparts who were infamous assassins. And that they also were responsible for establishing the first system of international money transfer by *cheque*.

"So what was their potent discovery or secret?" Linus asked.

"Well," Fischer began skeptically, "some scholars make *appealing* arguments that Christ did not die on the cross, that he was removed before he succumbed, revived and spirited away."

One theory, Fischer said, has Christ living to the ripe old age of eighty then dying during the siege of Masada. Yet another says he and his mother went into exile in India and died there, at Srinagar, another of the places on Linus's map list. "This is what Muslims believe," Fischer said, noting that Christ is considered a prophet in Islam.

"In fact, there is some vague reference to a counterfeit crucifixion theory in the Sura al-Nisa, a book of the Koran," he said, adding that most of these theories also assert that Jesus was married and had children, and that his bloodline still exists.

"So the Knights Templar had proof that the crucifixion was a scam?"

"A covert operation," Fischer corrected, adding that because of it the Templars became more estranged from the church and the church's version of the crucifixion. And by the late 13th century the Templars were uncontrollable, even by the Pope, and confined their recruiting to excommunicated knights.

Then, Fischer continued, in 1306 King Philippe IV of France perceived them as a threat. "Of course the fact that he owed them a fortune and was once refused membership didn't help their cause," he said. It was Philippe who ordered the murder of Pope Boniface VIII and he was also believed behind the poisoning of Benedict XI – all to get his man, Clement V, into the papacy, Fischer explained.

"Under the circumstances Clement was happy to endorse an inquisition against the wayward Knights," he said, adding that the Templars were accused of heresy and Satanism and were said to engage in the pagan worship of a severed head, the *Caput Mortem*.

"Who's head is unclear, though most accounts say they were in possession of a *woman's* head."

But the end for the Templars was imminent, Fischer noted. At dawn on Friday, October 13th, 1307, Philippe's agents rounded up the Templars and sacked their preceptories. "Most were tortured, tried, imprisoned and executed," he said. "But some were warned in advance and managed to slip away. Legend has it that they loaded their money and documents into three galleys from their private navy and vanished."

"Along with the Temple of Solomon treasure," Linus stated. "So what's that got to do with Rennes-le-Château?"

"There are several possibilities," Fischer said. He explained that the parchments from Rennes-le-Château may have located the lost Cathar treasure, which supposedly included the Grail and maybe the Temple treasure as well. "During the uprising in Palestine in 70 AD the Romans destroyed Jerusalem, sacked the Temple of Solomon and removed their plunder to Rome.

"Then almost 350 years later the Visigoths sacked Rome and removed *their* plunder – said to include the Grail *and* the Ark of the Covenant – to southern France, presumably to the Languedoc region near Rennes-le-Château which was a Visigoth stronghold at the time."

Then in 1156, Fischer said, the Templars imported German-speaking miners, segregated them and said they were working area gold mines – which had been played out by the Romans nearly 1000 years earlier. "Engineers and geologists at the site in the seventeenth century said the evidence pointed to a treasure hunt but definitely not to mining," he said, and added that treasure hunters have been searching around Rennes-le-Château for centuries. "The Nazis sent archeologists during World War Two, digging holes and searching caves. You probably know that Hitler was obsessed with religious icons," he said.

"But how could a dozen or so Cathar priests escaping *Montsegur* by rappelling down the mountain carry a treasure?"

"Precisely, *Herr* Linus. That is why some say that the Cathar treasure was no more than a valuable secret, which Saunière used to extort huge sums of money from the Church."

"Like proof of a fraudulent crucifixion," Linus noted, and Fischer replied,

"For one example."

"So where are the Rennes-le-Château parchments now?" Linus asked. Ute stood up and began searching through the bookcases on the wall behind her desk.

"I believe ... " Fischer began, squinting to recall, " ... there were four parchments, all of which went missing. However two were copied and studied but with varying results. The other two are still missing. No one alive today has ever seen the originals but parts of the copies contained some sort of code. There was a translation circulating in the early seventies. I think it included a French phrase... *Il Est Là Mort*. It means 'he is there dead'," Fischer said. By now Ute had selected a book. She turned toward the men, held it open and read.

"To Dagobert the second, King, belongs this treasure, and he is there dead," she recited.

"Yes. That's it. It supposedly refers to the location of the Christ grave as well as the treasure," Fischer recalled. Then, to Ute, he said, "There was another translation..." Ute nodded and again consulted her book.

"By the cross and this horse of God I destroy the demon of the guardian at noon blue apples," she read. The sentence made no sense but the last two words – blue apples – jumped out.

"The restaurant in Berlin, the *Blauer Apfel*, or Blue Apple. Where I met Melisandre and Jules. Kohlhertz too, for that matter," Linus observed.

"No one knows what is meant by Blue Apples. Archeologists have reported seeing a bright blue image at the bottom of cave shafts which was actually the blue sky above projected like in a pin-hole camera," Fischer said.

"And why Dagobert the second?" Linus asked. This time it was Ute's turn.

"He was a king in the Merovingian dynasty," she said. "He married Giselle de Razes, niece of the Visigoth king. The wedding was at the church of Saint Madeline in the town of Rhedae, which was the name of Rennes-le-Château at the time,"

"But if Kohlhertz's scroll is based in alchemy it seems unlikely that it is a treasure map," Linus said. And Fischer agreed.

"But let us remember that it was *partially* based in alchemy. Gervan believed it to be a piece of a larger work. So anything is possible."

Fischer had talked so much that his pipe was out. He struck another match and puffed as Linus shifted the conversation from history to current events. He told them about being stood-up by Melisandre at Paris Bar and about the empty house with the attic stake-out. "An observation post," Linus explained, "with a full view of Gervan's shop."

"That fuzzy picture in the newspaper with the story about Gervan was you," Fischer deduced. Linus nodded.

"Who was using this stake-out thing?" Ute asked.

"Jules the priest," Linus speculated. "He was watching Kohlhertz. I also found a business card," Linus continued. He told them about *Immobilien Berlin*, the realtor, and about trailing Melisandre's friend Veronica Franco to a lakeside camp guarded by female sentries where he witnessed a ritual performed by white-robed inductors on naked inductees. Fischer smiled broadly and said, "Veronica..."

"I know. It's the name of a famous Venetian courtesan," Linus interrupted. "Anyway, turns out Lindow Abbey is just the other side of the lake from this ritual camp," he said. "Melisandre was the guest of honor. In fact she made a speech. I have an audio file on my laptop. I'll send it." Ute looked at Fischer.

"Weissfrauen?" she wondered aloud.

"There is a German group called *Weissfrauen*, dedicated to establishing women's rights in religion, specifically Christianity," Fischer explained. "They are also known as *Dames Blanches*, because of their white robes," he said. "Their objective is the ordination of women."

"Women priests. Like the Cathars," Linus said, noting another possible connection between Jules's Catharism and Melisandre's *Novangelis*.

"There is also a group called *Revealers*. Nakedness is the symbolic shedding of worldly values and materialism, like a vow of poverty," Ute added. But Linus said,

"Everything I've seen points away from poverty," explaining that, on the night he met her at *Blauer Apfel* Melisandre was showered with exquisite gifts. He paged his notes and read the list. "Leather gloves and matching shoes, scents and perfumes, bottles of wine, bolts of fabric and silks, orchids."

"Charitable donations," Ute surmised, but Linus said he thought they looked like personal gifts even though the quantities were large. He also told them about his encounter with Kohlhertz and how Jules intervened with his gun. "Gervan didn't reveal enough to Kohlhertz. That's why he tried to abduct me. He saw me at Gervan's shop that day and he has to make sure I don't know anything."

"Or that you are silenced," Ute observed. Linus was skeptical.

"He had ample opportunity to assassinate me. I think he wanted to make me talk."

"*Then* he would've killed you," Fischer asserted. It was a chilling thought. Linus couldn't disagree.

"I also think that if Gervan did indeed discover something, he never got to tell it to Jules," Linus said. "Jules had Kohlhertz under the gun and let him go, probably so he could tail him. He needs to know where Kohlhertz goes and what Kohlhertz knows.

"The same is true of Kohlhertz, who doesn't know how much Gervan told Jules and Melisandre or whether they know more than him," he said. "It's crazy. Everyone thinks everyone else knows something, and no one know anything. And I think it will drive Kohlhertz to try something bold."

"Such as ... ?" Fischer wondered.

"Don't know. Kidnapping and extortion seems likely. Grab someone then ransom them for information."

"You," Fischer suggested.

"Nah. He'll try Jules or Melisandre. Someone worth ransoming."

"Nonetheless you had better watch yourself, *Herr* Linus."

"You too, *Herr* Professor. If *I* found you someone else can find you, too." Fischer agreed.

"So first we'll study the list from the map for some connection," Ute said.

"And the ritual in the woods, and who sponsored it, which groups were present," Linus suggested.

"And I will research the alchemy references in the scroll," Fischer volunteered.

"Good. Then you have a copy of the scroll," Linus observed. Fischer puffed his pipe but didn't answer, instead asked,

"And you, *Herr* Linus? What is your assignment?"

"Well, as I see it, find one and you'll find the others, since they're all trying to follow each other. I'd like to be a distant observer for awhile," he said.

"You won't find them anyplace you've already been," Fischer advised. Linus agreed.

"I've got a new lead," he said and he told them about the van at the Abbey with the French plates. "Zero-five-two-three-two-seven-nine-nine-X."

"This zero five is from the Languedoc," Ute said as she picked up the phone and dialed. Fischer looked at Linus.

"A friend at the motor vehicle department," he whispered as Ute spoke on the phone. "We will communicate at our current e-mail addresses, no?" he asked. Linus nodded.

"Jules and Kohlhertz are the most active, but I somehow think Melisandre is key."

"Are you certain your interest in her is professional, *Herr* Linus."

"Strictly professional. It's a story. Perhaps a big one," he said then asked, "And yours?"

"Gervan was our friend," Fischer said. "We want justice."

"As do I," Linus claimed. For now at least Fischer and Ute

seemed ready to take his word. The telephone rang. Ute took the call.

"The van is registered to *Ursa Industrie*, in Blanchefort, France," she said as she hung up and checked her map. "It is here, just minutes from Rennes-le-Château."

"*Voila*," Fischer said. "Then you will journey to the so-called *Village of Mystery*, Rennes-le-Château," he said. He rose from his chair, grabbed Linus's shoulder with his long, narrow hand and gave it an avuncular squeeze. He was strong for a man in his late sixties. "It will be a long trek, twenty four hours at least. But you can make it by tomorrow evening," he said. "But remember, I am convinced that at least one of them is a murderer," he warned. Linus nodded uneasily.

"Good luck," Ute said. Their sudden concern was giving Linus the uneasy feeling that there was something they weren't telling him, that he was walking into something more dangerous than he suspected. He made a mental note to watch his back and choose his friends carefully. But right now there was no time for second thoughts.

Chapter 11. The VILLAGE of MYSTERY

July 27th. The Languedoc, Southern France. Day 06.

Linus drove through the night, catnapping in tractor turnouts and petrol plazas along the way. It was an endless trek over monotonous autobahns and long deserted stretches of narrow roads through the mountains, farms and vineyards of Germany and France. The perfect five-day tour... done in 31 grueling hours.

The *Village of Mystery*, Rennes-le-Château, was only fifty miles from Spain in the foothills of the Pyrenées. He left Berlin at one in the afternoon and now, at a few minutes past eight the next evening, his highway-weary eyes were reading a sign – the turn for Rennes-le-Château was just minutes ahead.

He touched on the brakes as the road wound down the side of a hill then across a bridge over a rocky river. Heavy strokes of blue were filling the valleys but the sky was still bright atop the high hill where the tiny medieval village sat. Golden grass carpeted the hillside on both sides of the narrow road leading up to the village.

Near the top, Linus looked out over the valley to the silhouette of a ruined castle on a neighboring peak. This was Cathar country, as the historical signs had pointed out along the way. The cool evening air was reviving him so he decided to have a quick look around the village before finding a hotel. He stretched his face to loosen his pasty eyelids, pulled in a deep breath, then drove up into Rennes-le-Château.

The streets were shadowed and empty – mostly one-way and only wide enough for one car. He slowed to a roll and stopped in what looked like the village square – a few closed shops and a few stingy parking spaces at a bulge in the road. He got out and stretched in front of a shop window filled with pamphlets, picture books, paperbacks and postcards, all dedicated to some aspect of the *"Village of Mystery"*, thinking that the Abbot Saunière's parchment discovery had grown into quite a cottage industry.

One book in the window had a striking cover illustration right out of Marvel Comics. A priest was pictured – presumably Saunière – holding a lantern in the night, kneeling before an open tomb. Pale blue rays radiated from the grave and splayed across his horrified face. Above and behind, ominous black clouds churned around a church tower silhouetted against a full moon. Silly? Maybe. But creepy, too.

Linus figured the local phenomenon would be good cover as he snooped around asking questions. Now all he needed was someone to ask. He hadn't seen a soul since arriving in the sleepy village. He began walking uphill, guided by a small sign which read *"Tour Magdala – Abbey St. Marie Maddelena"*. As he wound through narrow streets of two-story stone houses, cooking scents filled the air. It was almost full dusk, and it was the supper hour. The streets were deserted. Almost.

A young woman on a bicycle rushed at him from around a corner, swerved at the last second to avoid him and sped away down the hill and out of sight. Linus turned but she never looked back.

He found the Abbey at the village's highest spot. An iron gate barred the entrance but he could see the wooden chapel door on the other side of a snarled garden. He passed by and entered the Abbey's small dirt parking area. It was on a bluff overlooking the entire valley. A tall, round, stone tower occupied the corner of the lot. It looked like a mini-castle, three stories high, complete with a parapet and separated from the parking area by a tangle of bushes and an ivy-covered iron fence. It was the *"Tour Magdala"*, erected by the mysterious priest, Saunière

A footpath led down into the brambles below the tower. Linus looked around – he was alone – then carefully negotiated the rocky path. The nettles pulled at his pants and sleeves and the stones underfoot became more unstable along the tower's apron. Daylight was fading – along with his ability to find his way safely. So he turned back before seeing enough to satisfy his curiosity but planned to come back the next day.

He stood at the rim of the parking lot watching the remnants of the day slip behind the horizon and the green and yellow crop patchwork in the valley disappear. This was a vista worthy of canvas, he thought. So he'd pick up an easel and supplies, some clothes to complete the disguise, then settle into a stake-out right here, posing as a landscape artist.

He plucked the last thorns from his pants then headed down the main road, which looped through the parking lot and back to the village center. On the way, he came upon a cafe. The lights were on, it was open, and there was a black bicycle leaning against the wall outside the door like the one that had almost run him down earlier.

But the sign over the door was much more interesting. In dark blue letters on powder blue background it read *"la Pomme Bleue"* – the Blue Apple! He wondered if it was the sister to the *Blauer Apfel* cafe back in Berlin. He entered and recognized the speedy bicycle woman. She was working the espresso bar and wearing a gold scarf like the scarves so common among Melisandre's *Novangelis* devotees. She was pouring a drink for a rough-sawn man with wiry black hair and coarse-looking clothes. He guessed them both to be in their late twenties. They seemed nonchalant when he walked up and asked for a Cointreau.

He took his drink to a table and sat facing away from them, sensing from their low voices that *he* was the topic of their conversation. Maybe his fatigue and paranoia was catching up with him, he thought. But he couldn't shake the feeling that they knew who he was. He decided to drink up and split. It was almost dark outside now. There were no street lights and very few house lights in the village. And the hamlet was too tiny for a hotel.

He got in his car and headed back down into the valley until he came to the *"Chambres"* sign he had noticed earlier. It was a small place, perhaps eight or ten rooms, but very tidy. The keeper was an older guy, short, stocky and pleasant. He gave Linus a key and directed him to a small walk-up on the second floor. It was toward the back, overlooking the river. Linus opened a window and took a deep breath of cool, clear air. The river was dark but he could hear the water splashing through the rocks as it rushed down into the valley.

He stood in the window and emptied his pockets onto the bureau. When he got to his Blackberry, he had an urge to e-mail Fischer with news that he had arrived in Rennes-le-Château. He was also anxious to know if Fischer or Ute had anything more on his clues from Lindow Abbey, the induction ceremony, or Melisandre's map.

But his strongest urge was to collapse on the bed. It was just before nine o'clock and Linus knew he could easily sleep until morning. But he wouldn't. He couldn't – not yet. He set his alarm for one hour, laid his head on the pillows and slipped into one of the power naps which had sustained him during the long drive. he had one more chore to do before granting himself the luxury of extended sleep.

A Roadside Drop

The motorcycle raced between the rows of trees on both sides of the road, its headlight blurring them by like pickets on a fence. Suddenly its tail light flashed and it disappeared onto a cart path cut through the thick brush surrounding a vineyard. The cyclist killed the engine and coasted to a stop. She took off her helmet and opened her jacket then sat silently in the night.

A dark sedan sped up the road from the other direction and also pulled onto the cart path, doused its lights and rolled toward the motorcycle. The cyclist took cover. The sedan stopped. The driver stepped out and scanned the area. It looked safe so she opened the back door for her passenger. As soon as the cyclist recognized her, she stepped forward and said, "Here, *Madame*." They met beside the car.

"Any trouble?" the passenger asked.

"No, *Madam*," the cyclist replied as she tugged a folded paper from a zippered pocket. "They have moved into a farm house, here," she said as she shined a pen light on the hand-drawn map. "It is very remote."

"You are sure?"

"*Oui, Madam.*"

"How many?"

"Four, perhaps five."

"They are there now?"

"One is always there. The others go away in daytime but return at night. Different times. Sometimes only one. Sometimes more," the cyclist reported, handing her the map.

"I'm glad you are safe," she said then, "*Bon. Merci.*" She and her driver got back in their car while the cyclist checked to see that the road was empty then signaled the driver to pull out. The sedan's tail lights disappeared down the road. The cyclist kicked-started her bike and rocketed off the way she had come.

Anfortas Checks In

Linus awoke to the dit-dit-dit-dit-dit of the alarm on his Blackberry. He fumbled and found the 'off' button then noticed that his e-mail flag was up. The first message was another e-mail from J.Richards – Jamie Richards, the actress that he and Massimo Ricci had ambushed back in Berlin.

"Please hold the photos you took. I will match any price plus fifteen percent," it said, followed by the details on how Linus could make the grab for the cash. The incentive had gone up from ten to fifteen percent above market price. He ignored it anyway.

There was also a message from Dark Star, his photo agency. Doubtless they were looking for the photos, too – since he hadn't got around to sending them. He deleted it without opening it and went straight to the message from Anfortas – a.k.a. Professor Fischer. It said that *Industrie Ursa*, the company to whom the van from Lindow

Abbey was registered, had the same address as a vineyard called *Domaine deBouillon*, which Fischer wrote was named for Godfroi de Bouillon.

Godfroi was a popular hero by dint of his capture of Jerusalem in 1099. It was Godfroi who inaugurated the *First Crusade*, who re-took Jerusalem from the Saracens, and thereby rescued Christ's sepulcher from 'the infidels'. He became the object of a cult that persisted long after his death.

Fischer wrote further that Godfroi may have been related to Dagobert II, the Merovingian king mentioned in the secret Rennes-le-Château parchments, but only through marriage. And since the Merovingians were usurped by the Church of Rome in favor of the Carolingians in the 8th century, Godfroi would have been one of the Merovingian *les rois perdus*, the lost kings. A king without a kingdom.

Which, Fischer continued, may explain why de Bouillon seized Palestine, the Holy Land, from the Saracens – to create a kingdom for himself, and the most precious kingdom in the world, at that. Of course it was also an exquisite means of exacting revenge on the Church that had betrayed his ancestors four centuries before.

Fischer signed off his message with a post script, noting that the bear – *Ursa* – was a potent symbol of the Merovingian Dynasty. As was the bee. Linus recalled having seen a gold bee on a chain hanging around Melisandre's neck.

Linus sent back a "thanks" e-mail along with the name of his hotel. He then checked the address for *Industrie Ursa* and *Domaine deBoullion*. As Fischer said, they were the same, located in the nearby village of Blanchefort. But the map he was using didn't show a Blanchefort.

It was 10:30 but the Innkeeper was still in the kitchen, preparing for the morning meal. Linus went to see him. He didn't speak much English so Linus wrote "Blanchefort" on a scrap of paper then held out his map. The old guy knew exactly what to do. He scoured the map then made an 'X' to locate the village. It was about five miles from Rennes-le-Château. Linus said *"Merci"* then wrote the words

"*Industrie Ursa*" and showed him that as well. The old man scratched his head a moment, his brow furrowed. Then his face lighted up and he said, "Ahhh," as he took a bottle of wine from a shelf and pointed his stubby finger at the words *Industrie Ursa*, Ltd. in fine print on the bottom of the label. The wine was from the vineyard called *Domaine deBouillon*. A gold bee was embossed at the top of the label. Linus asked to keep the bottle. The Innkeeper was more than happy to oblige.

Chapter 12. The DOMAINE of the BEE

Finding the road to *Domaine deBouillon* wasn't difficult. Linus followed along a river for a short distance to where the valley floor widened. Tall leafy trees lining the road shaded the moonlight that flooded into the endless rows of vines to his left and his right. He passed through the village of Blanchefort and pressed on several more miles until he saw a cluster of trees at the foot of a hill. It was a typical vineyard *Château* layout – a long, tree-lined drive leading to a lush oasis in the middle of the grapes. A large iron gate hanging from stone pillars blocked the driveway and there was no sign for *Industrie Ursa* or *Domaine deBouillon*.

But there was something just as telling – a golden bee about the size of a fist centering each panel of the iron gate. He checked it against the gold bee embossed on the wine label and it was the same. This had to be the entrance to *Domaine deBouillon*.

He ditched the car in a nearby field and started walking back. Near the gate he stepped into the brush, rounded one of the stone pillars and walked briskly down the gravel driveway toward the *Château*, staying near the side in case he needed to duck out of sight. Flashes of moonlight reflected on the blue slate roof of the *Château* at the end of the long driveway. Everything all around him was empty and still.

As he got closer he could see the face of a big stone house and the trickling fountain that centered the circular drive in front of it. Two lanterns hung on each side of the tall paneled doors in the middle of the house. Dim light was coming from the first floor windows on the left but the upstairs windows were dark. Then he heard hissing tires on asphalt pavement. He ducked into the trees and looked back toward the main road. A set of headlights was approaching. They slowed, turned and stopped to open the gate then came down the driveway. He tucked deeper into the brush as a dark sedan crunched past on the gravel driveway. A woman was driving, with another woman in the back seat. Linus couldn't see who they were.

It drove past the front doors and went left toward the back of the house. Linus crawled out of hiding and hustled past the *Château*. The car was waiting, red brake lights bright, as the automatic doors of a large detached carriage house swung open. The car pulled in. The doors closed. Linus crept closer. A few minutes later the chauffeur, followed by a woman with short auburn hair, came out through a side door. It was the woman he'd seen with Jules at Lindow Abbey.

They strode across the gravel parking area and into the *Château* through a service entrance. Linus held his ground until he was sure it was safe to move then went for a look inside the garage. He slipped in through the side door and froze, holding his breath in the pitch darkness. He could smell the warm engine but couldn't see the sedan until his eyes widened enough to utilize the few moon rays falling through a window someplace high up in the rafters. The car windows were open, thanks to the warm July night. Linus squinted for a look inside but it was just too dark.

He drew his penlight and muted the beam through his fingers. There was a newspaper on the front seat with an open, hand-drawn map on top of it. He leaned in, retrieved the map, then crouched beside the car to have a look. It was drawn in thick blue lines with circled route numbers – N26, E19 – and an "X" denoting something near where the two roads intersected. He lay the map on the floor and, holding the flashlight in his teeth, made a couple of images with his phone-cam. His heart leapt when he heard footsteps coming across the gravel. Someone was coming to the garage.

He tossed the map back on the front seat just as the garage door was opening. The only place to hide was under the car – not a good choice if someone were going to drive it. He flattened out on his chest and slid under the low sedan. A woman's legs appeared and circled around to the driver's side. She was wearing black pants and dressy shoes, and she had a flashlight. She opened the car door but, luckily for Linus, didn't get in. Instead she knelt on the seat, her toes dangling right in his face. Paper rustled, then the woman stood up, closed the car door, and began to leave.

Suddenly she stopped.

A piece of paper floated to the floor and landed practically on Linus's nose! It was the map, just inches away. Linus blew it gently and it moved to where she'd see it without bending down and looking under the car. The beam of the flashlight hit the ground and the reflection flared into his eyes. Her hand reached down and picked up the map. Then the light moved away toward the door and out of the garage. He was safe – but he waited a bit longer to be sure.

He crawled out and made his way back to the front of the *Château*. Shadows were moving across a curtained first floor window. He snuck across the driveway and took cover in the high flowering shrubs along the foundation of the house. The tall, lighted window was almost directly above him. He could hear talking – enough to tell that one voice was a woman and the other a man, and that the language they were speaking was French. He craned for a glimpse through the sheer curtains. A woman, her back to the window, was talking to someone out of view. She raised her arm and handed over the map he had just copied. A man's hand took it, examined it, then disappeared. Then the talking stopped, and the lights went out.

Linus crouched into the shrubs and waited. A moment later the lights at the front door went out, too. They were retiring for the night. This was his chance for a closer look into the room.

He stood up and looked in through the tall windows. In the dim light spilling in from the foyer he could see a large, lushly furnished salon with high ceilings. At first nothing seemed unusual – there was a fireplace at one end of the room above which hung a large oil painting of a reclining woman, reading a book by candlelight. Her nude body was partially veiled in a diaphanous wrap and her long, lush, golden hair flowed seductively over her bare breasts. But when he recognized the painted woman's face the hairs on the back of his neck tingled. It was Melisandre. The trip to Rennes-le-Château was bearing fruit indeed, he thought.

But his fatigue was catching up, so he made his way back to his car. It was almost midnight and there would be time tomorrow for finding whatever was marked by the "X" on the hand-drawn map. He had no clue what "X" was, but knew he'd know it when he found it.

July 28th.
The Languedoc, Southern France. Day 07.
Kohlhertz's lair

The old stone farmhouse looked like a pile of rocks with a roof, obscured by twisted fruit trees and overgrown weeds. Linus lay on his stomach, watching through a telephoto lens. Nothing was moving except a thin stream of smoke rising from the chimney. The map he copied last night at *Domaine deBouillon* had led him to the top of this hill, some thirty miles away from Rennes-le-Château. He had passed some ancient castle ruins less than a mile away yet something told him *this* – and not the ruins – was the place marked by the map's "X."

It was almost ten in the morning and thin fog clung to the dewy grass that had soaked his boots and pants. He scanned the dirt road to the farm from where it emerged from the tree line, crossed a field then dead-ended at the farmhouse. There were no vehicles or people in sight. So he waited, and watched.

After a quiet half hour things began to happen. A motorcycle emerged from the trees and parked outside the farmhouse door. The driver was dressed in blue jeans, a black leather jacket and knee-high black boots. He snapped down the kickstand, got off the bike and removed his helmet. It was a man in his early thirties but no one Linus recognized. He undid a brown paper grocery sack that was bungee-ed to the back of the bike and took it inside. Linus decided it was time to go knocking.

He galloped back down to get his car then drove ahead until he found where the farmhouse road was cut into the woods. The car shimmied and bounced as the craggy road wormed through the trees then broke into the field. He parked behind the parked motorcycle. The door was a dozen steps away. He grabbed an old ax handle leaning against a rain barrel and stepped up to the gray, cleaved-wood door. As he was about to rap with his knuckle he noticed that it was several inches ajar. He rapped gently. Once. Almost inaudibly. Then he listened. There was no sign of anyone coming to answer.

He leaned in closer and peeked through the opening. Heavy black boots were lying side-by-side on the floor just a few feet away. At first it seemed odd that someone would remove such boots and not store them upright. When one of the toes wiggled he knew why they were on their side... the owner was still wearing them!

He pushed the door open a few more inches. The feet were bound by duct tape, as were the legs. It was the motorcyclist, propped up against a wall, his bound hands hidden behind his back. More tape covered his mouth and a trickle of blood oozed from a large red lump on his forehead.

His eyes were charged with terror but he didn't make a sound. Linus gripped and raised the ax handle as he entered. The captive was motioning his eyes sideways, telling Linus that someone was in the other room. Linus held his breath and listened. He could hear rummaging just down the hall. He raised his brow and mimicked a pistol with his fingers. The captive shrugged – he didn't know if the intruder had a gun. A defining moment had arrived – run or rescue? Fischer's words of caution echoed in his brain as the desperate captive motioned, urging Linus to make his move. Linus heaved a deep breath, raised the ax handle like a home run king and started toward the noise in the other room.

Through the doorway he saw a tall, broad-shouldered man foraging through the room, shuffling papers, shoving some into an open briefcase and tossing the rest on the floor. Linus knew he had to get through the doorway or he wouldn't have enough space to swing the ax handle. But *how*? Quiet surprise attack? Or blitz? The intruder was engrossed in his pilfering and the ski mask covering his ears must've muffled his hearing. So a sneak attack seemed like the best bet. Linus zeroed in on a target for his club then started through the door.

Suddenly the intruder slammed the briefcase closed and turned to leave. Linus lunged and swung but the ax handle glanced the door jamb, softening the blow. The intruder shouted a muffled "*No!*" as the handle landed on his raised forearm, and he crashed into Linus with a body block. They tumbled backward into the kitchen, kicking and clawing on the floor. Linus was punching wildly, landing solid hits to the head as the intruder, his right arm damaged by the ax handle blow, tried to hold him at bay. He was failing fast and scrambling to get away. Linus tackled him, rolled him onto his back and pinned him. He grabbed a handful of hair through the ski mask. The intruder gripped Linus's wrist to keep him from pulling but Linus yanked hard and the mask came off.

It was Jules the priest!

"*You!*" Linus exclaimed, his fist poised over Jules's face.

"You *fool!*" Jules raged. Linus, astounded and panting, sat back on the floor. Jules stumbled to his feet. "Now what? *Kill* him?" he shouted, nodding to the tape-bound captive on the floor. "Let's have a photo, *Monsieur Paparazzo*, so he won't forget our faces!"

"How was I supposed to know?" Linus protested. He thought he was being brave, trying to save someone from a masked intruder. Jules began to calm down but grunted his displeasure as he walked on unsteady legs back into the other room. Linus followed. "I'm sorry. I had no idea it was you," he said. Jules patted the gash on his forehead and recovered quickly, reminding Linus of his un-clergy-like toughness.

"Why must you insist on invading my private affairs?" he hissed.

"Murder is hardly a private affair."

"No *Monsieur*. At least not my own. You have done your best to assure it will happen."

But Linus wasn't listening. He was looking at a large map of Europe on the wall. All the places from Melisandre's map were marked on this map, too. It made him wonder if Kohlhertz had stolen the info from Melisandre, or vice versa. There was also a pile of medieval history books – the Knights Templar, the Crusades, and

Cathars.

"This is Kohlhertz's place," he conjectured.

"*Très bon*. How astute," Jules confirmed sarcastically. Linus figured that Gervan *had* said something about the Temple of Solomon and its treasure to Kohlhertz, and the books meant that Kohlhertz was boning-up.

"Did you find the scroll?" Linus asked. Jules looked at him, surprised to hear that Linus had learned so much. "Yes I know about the scroll and your interest in genetics. *And* a few other things," he added. Jules winced and cradled his arm then bent down to retrieve his briefcase. "You should be convinced by now that I'm not going to just disappear. Why don't you level with me?" Linus persisted.

"Why? So you can get us all killed and sell a lot of books and newspapers?"

"That's not so. I don't do that."

"What makes *you* different?"

"Trust me and you'll see."

"Trust? I have learned much from trusting reporters, *Monsieur*," he said as he tucked the briefcase under his good arm and turned away.

"Where is Melisandre? Is she okay?"

"She is well, no thanks to you."

"Wait a minute, Jules. I didn't go looking for her. She came looking for me," he said, reminding him that Melisandre had made the first contact at the *Blauer Apfel* in Berlin.

"I'm sure she now regrets involving you in this matter," Jules said. "Please try to understand that she had no choice," he explained, his tone softening a bit.

"I want to see her," Linus said.

"She won't see you. It is too dangerous."

"What does she think I'm going to do?"

"Too dangerous for *you*, *Monsieur*. Not for her."

"Don't I have a say in that?"

"You do not."

"Who is she, Jules?"

"She is a very powerful person. Do not underestimate her determination, *Monsieur* Linus," Jules warned. It was the first time Jules had used his name. Linus saw it as an opening.

"We have to get out of here," he said and added, "I have a car."

The pair bolted out to the car. The tires spun in the dirt as they raced away from the farmhouse and through the woods. As they turned onto the main road Linus had to swerve to avoid a black sedan which was just turning onto the farmhouse road. The sedan screeched to a halt. Linus downshifted, fish-tailed around it and sped away.

"It's Kohlhertz," Jules said, staring into the sedan as they passed. "Quickly," he urged. Linus wound out the gears as Jules watched through the back window. Someone jumped out of the passenger side of Kohlhertz's sedan and ran into the woods toward the farmhouse. Then the sedan made a reckless turn and Jules said,

"He's chasing." Linus mashed the gas, shaving every curve perilously close, his tires rumbling from the pavement to the shoulder and back. The pursuing sedan appeared in his mirror then disappeared as he rounded each curve ahead of it. Jules held his injured arm close to his side and braced against the dashboard with the other. He looked back again. The sedan was obscured behind the last curve.

"There is an old road to the right at the next curve," he said. Linus's hand was poised on the stick shift. "*There!*" Jules shouted. Linus hit the brakes, downshifted, and cut the wheel hard. Both men bumped their heads on the roof as the car dropped into the brush. "*Quickly!*" Jules urged as Linus gassed it up a hill. "Here," Jules said, pointing left, and Linus cut in. They were in the ruins of the old castle he had seen earlier.

He wound his way through the large fallen stones, stopped behind a half-crumbled wall and killed the engine. Both men jumped out, crouched behind the wall and looked down at the main road. The sedan sped past. Linus started back for the car.

"Hurry. Before he comes back," he said. They reversed out of the stones, bounced back onto the main road and sped away in the direction from which they'd just come. Linus was driving too fast for the small, snaking road but somehow managed to maintain control of the car.

They rounded a curve onto a short straightaway and Linus uttered, "Ot oh." A motorcycle was coming right at them. "Is that a gun?" he said as they drew closer. The motorcyclist was slowing and aiming a pistol. "*Get down!*" Linus yelled as he ducked.

"*Go!*" Jules shouted as he seized the steering wheel and shoved it. A gunshot erupted as the car lurched left and clipped the motorcycle. The bike spun out of control, launching the rider into the trees.

"*Jesus Christ!*" Linus yelled as he yanked the wheel back and regained control of the swerving car. Sweat was pouring down his face. He looked in the rear view at the sparking motorcycle skimming along the pavement, then back at Jules. "Jesus *Christ*," he said again.

"Your prayers are welcome," Jules said. His face was grim and he was as calm as granite. "Quickly Linus," he urged again. They came to the intersection of N19 and E26. Jules pointed and calmly said,

"To the left."

Lex Talonis

Kohlhertz had his boot out the door before the sedan came to a complete stop. A cloud of dust engulfed the farmhouse. Another car arrived behind him with a mangled motorcycle – and a dead, mangled motorcyclist – in the half-open trunk.

"Dig a hole in the woods and dump him," he instructed as a pair of big-booted skin-heads clambered out of the second car. Then he and the driver went inside. The driver headed for the back room as Kohlhertz stood over the tape-bound guy on the floor. Long streaks of sweat darkened Kohlhertz's blousy white tunic and his black boots and pants were powdered with dust.

"You let them in," he said, looking straight into the floored guy's eyes. The bound guy got panicky and began shaking and grunting 'no'. The driver returned from the other room.

"It's been sacked. A lot of shit is missing," he said. Kohlhertz smirked with disgust.

"Lex Talonis," he muttered, staring at the hapless guy on the floor. The driver shrugged. "The law of retaliation. They paid us a visit. We'll pay them one in return," he said. Then he turned away and rinsed his hands in the sink. "Go out there and make sure those idiots dig deep so the boars don't have a picnic with him," he commanded and the driver hustled out the door. Then Kohlhertz dried his hands and used a damp towel to wipe his sterling belt buckle. There was a radio on the counter with a long chrome antenna. He snapped it off and sliced the air a few times to get the feel of the whip. Then he stood over the guy on the floor. "Lex Talonis," he said, then, mockingly, "You're having a bad day." And he tore into him with the antenna. His last stroke was across the face, opening a bad cut. The guy lay simpering, bound ankle and wrist, on the grimy floor.

Kohlhertz dropped his whip and left the house.

Chapter 13. A GRASSY KNOLL

The thick brush dragged along the car's fenders and doors as the road got narrow and became a footpath. Linus gently braked to a stop. Jules was cradling his hurt arm against the bumps. He lumbered out of the car and led the way through thick foliage and a grove of hardwood trees. Linus photographed everything with his phone and opened an audio file to secretly record their conversation.

They crossed a clearing, went over a trickling stream then up a small hill. At the top, a single large tree spread shade over an old mossy tomb. It was a coffin-like box of white marble that was pocked and stained black with age. And there were no other graves anywhere nearby. Jules brushed the pollen from the tomb's corner to reveal new striations in the pitted stone – marks of tampering, like the marks Linus saw on the tablets at Lindow Abbey.

"Kohlhertz?" he asked. Jules nodded. "This place seems familiar, but I don't know why," Linus said.

"It is the subject of several paintings," Jules noted and that made it click. Linus had seen a painting of just such a tomb in a book he found at Melisandre's Berlin headquarters. "The most famous is by Nicholas Poussin. *"Les Bergers D'Arcadie"* – The Arcadian shepherds," Jules added. Linus remembered that he had seen the name Poussin as well.

"The tomb had an inscription. Latin, I think," Linus recalled.

"*Oui. Et in Arcadia ego.* It means, And in Arcadia, I ... "

"I what?" Linus asked. Jules shrugged and said no one knew for sure.

"A man from Boston once owned this property. He opened the tomb in nineteen-twenty," he said.

"And ... ?"

"It was empty."

"Is it empty now?"

"Maybe yes, compliments of *Monsieur* Kohlhertz. The man from Boston interred his wife and mother-in-law here. Kohlhertz is too stupid to know that."

"What would he *think* was here?" Linus asked. Jules was looking out at the steep, blue-shaded cliffs and said.

"It is a beautiful place, *non*? It was once suspected to be the final resting place of Jesus," he revealed. Linus was surprised. If true, it would pretty much prove the fraudulent crucifixion theory. "But nothing has ever been found," Jules added.

"Which proves nothing, either way," Linus noted. Jules smiled faintly.

"Not all true things are to be said to all men, *monsieur*," he stated. "Some secrets survive for many centuries."

"And you're trying to discover one of those secrets."

"No. Nothing like that," Jules said as he leaned against the tomb and thought for a moment before going on. "Three years ago, I began to investigate a series of thefts in various parts of Europe."

"Church thefts?"

"Mostly, but not all. An organized gang was stealing religious artwork and artifacts and valuable furnishings, gold chalices, like that. I was charged with recovering objects and penetrating the ring." Linus knew it was pointless to ask who was backing him – anyone from the Insurers to the Vatican – because it was something Jules could never reveal. "I made many contacts with collectors and dealers and this is how I came to know Gerhardt Gervan," Jules continued, adding that Gervan helped him find and verify some of the items.

"And you think Kohlhertz has something related to the Rennes-le-Château parchments?"

"No. I am watching him for other reasons. He led me here. I don't know what he's doing down here," Jules claimed. Linus guessed that Jules was hoping to find out what the hell the Kohlhertz scroll meant, and if it's related to the mystery of Rennes-le-Château."

"Is there an active Cathar church right now? Are you a Cathar priest?" Linus asked.

"I am known to some as a man with strong Cathar heritage and sympathies. Though since I began my investigative work I suppose you could say that my priesthood has lapsed." Linus knew it meant that Jules wouldn't reveal his religious affiliation, either. And he wondered why Jules acted as though he had no specific interest in Kohlhertz's scroll – beyond the fact that he doubted Kohlhertz was the rightful owner. Likewise, Linus figured Kohlhertz had stolen the scroll from someone who had also stolen or got it illegitimately, and thus couldn't go to the police.

Yet he wasn't convinced that Jules's interest was as coincidental as he claimed. And Jules didn't deny that he knew part of the scroll message dealt with alchemy and part was regular text. But he said that Gervan never got a chance to tell him any more.

"Kohlhertz thinks everyone knows what it is but him," Linus observed. Jules agreed and said that he wanted it that way, so Kohlhertz would always stay close. "What do you make of the map on the wall?" Linus asked, though he didn't reveal that he'd seen the same plotting on a map in Melisandre's office.

"Unfortunately you jumped me before I could study it," Jules said, deflecting the question. Whether he knew something about it or not, he wasn't sharing. A breeze hissed through the trees and wafted pungent forest scents over the grassy knoll. Jules squeezed his eyes shut and turned his face up at the warming sun.

"What is your interest in genetics?" Linus asked, and Jules smiled knowingly. "Yes. It was me. I was the burglar at the chapel," Linus admitted.

"Many claims of ownership are dynastic, such as in an artwork which has been passed down through the centuries," Jules said. "As claimants come forward, particularly in the case of items which were looted during wars, there is often a need to confirm their identity. Genetic fingerprinting is one method of doing that," he explained.

"What about the eye mutation, aniridia? There were papers on it at the Abbey."

"Just a passing interest, something I stumbled upon in my

studies," Jules assured. It all seemed logical and true enough, and would also explain the shipping invoices Linus found. But setting up an entire genetic fingerprinting lab at the cost of over six hundred thousand dollars just to verify the occasional ownership claim seemed extreme. Linus was certain that someone had a much greater purpose in mind. And that someone, in his opinion, was Jules.

Jules held his wounded arm and sat down in some tall grass on the sunny side of the hill. "Someone should look at that arm," Linus suggested.

"I'm sure it's just badly bruised," he said, adding, "A short rest is all," as he lay back in the grass. The ground was warm and the grass, soft.

"Shouldn't we leave? If Kohlhertz knows about this place?"

"He's been here. He won't be back," Jules said with confidence. His eyes were already closed. "Rest, *Monsieur* Linus," Jules sighed. "It has been an adventurous day. Lie down. Contemplate the world and your place in it. Your future and your past. You'll be better for it. I promise," he said. In a way, it sounded like useless psycho-babble. But in a way, Linus envied Jules his sense of purpose amidst the chaos. It was more than he could say about himself.

He waited until Jules was asleep and made six more images of the tomb. Then he chose a patch of warm, soft grass, and heeded Jules's advice.

Kidnapped!

The two exhausted men dozed as the day faded away. It was dusk when they made the return trip to Rennes-le-Château. Linus guessed that Jules had been up all night, casing the farmhouse and planning his incursion. The mud on his boots and pants was evidence of a long night in the woods.

He dropped Jules at *la Pomme Bleue* cafe then drove away as though he was leaving town but left the car in a turnout just below the village, waited 10 minutes then walked back. From a dark doorway across the street he could see through the cafe's windows that the young woman who nearly ran him down with her bicycle yesterday was tending Jules's bruises and abrasions. After a few minutes, Jules came out alone and walked uphill toward the Abbey. Linus followed and watched from afar.

Jules opened the abbey gate and entered the grounds, then disappeared through the chapel door. It looked like he was in for the evening yet Linus decided to hang back at the cafe for awhile and see if Jules returned. The young woman who had nursed Jules's wounds – wearing the ever-present gold scarf – was again behind the bar. Her companion, the rugged looking guy, was there as well. Neither paid Linus much attention. Linus asked for *café au lait* then chose a spot with a street view and sat down.

Soon the woman brought his order, but before she could put the cup on the table the abbey bells began to ring. The waitress froze with the coffee mid-air. Linus checked his watch – it was nine-twenty. Unless his watch was wrong, or the bell keeper was mistaken, the ringing wasn't marking the time. The waitress just stood still, listening. Her companion came to her side. She looked at him and something struck them simultaneously.

"*La Maddelena,*" she uttered. The cup slipped from her grip and banged on the floor, and they both flew into the street. Linus was right behind them.

They raced up the hill, through the Abbey gates and into the small chapel. The woman ran up the aisle on one side and the man up the other. Linus was entering the chapel just as they disappeared into the anterooms behind the altar. He went straight up the middle aisle and found an elderly matron tied and gagged on the floor between two pews. She looked up at him with wide, disoriented eyes. A fresh bruise was blossoming on her cheek and she was clutching a scrap of paper. Linus took the note and helped her onto a bench.

As soon as her gag was off the matron began talking and pointing excitedly. Linus tried to focus on what she was saying but was distracted as he realized the hideousness of the chapel's demonic statuary and stations of the cross – grotesque gargoyle-like demons looking down upon him in the flickering candlelight. He quickly read the scribbled note – "*te diem de Maddelena. Conditions to follow. Keystone – T.Magdala.*" The first sentence was Latin and meant something like "the time of *Maddelena*". Linus also knew what a keystone was and assumed that the reference to "*T.Magdala*" meant the "Tour Magdala" at the abbey – the Magdalene Tower.

The woman from *la Pomme Bleue* was returning from behind the alter. Linus shoved the note into his pocket, unsure if she had seen him reading it. Her companion also returned and shook "no"... he hadn't found anything or anyone, either. As they converged on Linus the sound of screeching tires stopped them. The three ran out of the chapel to the edge of the parking lot and looked down at the foot of the bluff. Kohlhertz's car – the one Linus saw at the farmhouse that morning – was speeding away. No question Jules was in it. Linus figured they surprised Jules in the chapel then bundled him out the back and down the embankment. And Linus had his ransom note in his pocket.

"I'll have that note *monsieur*," the woman insisted, holding out her hand.

"Who the hell are *you*?" Linus demanded. Out of nowhere, the man's arm slung around his neck and clamped him in a choke hold. The young woman elbowed him hard in the gut then pulled the note from his pocket and bolted. The man released Linus, backed away, and ran after her. Linus let them go. He knew where they were going. He rubbed his bruised stomach and jogged to *la Pomme Bleue*.

The man and woman were inside – he at the bar and she nearby on the phone. Linus headed straight for the woman but the guy blocked the way and brandished a baton. Linus prudently stood back. The woman was speaking quietly and very fast but he was certain she said "Tour Magdala", then "*oui*." She hung up and stood face to face with Linus. Her features were bolder and more tense than before, and her eyes hard and fixed.

"Do not interfere," she warned, then hurried out the door. He tried to follow but her companion again blocked his path.

"*Monsieur, si'l vous plait*," he said, politely but sternly. There was no point in trying to be defiant. Linus nodded and said,

"My car is down the road."

"We will go there together," the man said and together they went to the car. And Linus drove back to his hotel.

The Counsel of Anfortas

The small inn was quiet when Linus got back from Rennes-le-Château that night. As he passed the front desk the innkeeper called after him from the kitchen and gave him a note. Fischer had called and left a phone number. Linus went to his room and returned the call with his Blackberry. Ute answered. Fischer was with her and she put him on.

"There is news from the medical examiner," he began somberly. He couldn't hide the quaking in his voice as he told Linus that his colleague, Gerhardt Gervan, had died from a heart attack. Linus had wondered why someone who wanted information from the old man – Kohlhertz, for instance – would kill him before he got it. Obviously things hadn't gone as planned and Gervan died during the interrogation.

"Poor old guy couldn't hold up under Kohlhertz's torment," Linus observed, and Fischer agreed.

"The police are saying he had a heart attack and fell into the canal. We think we should let it go at that for now," he said. Like Fischer and Ute, Linus knew it was murder. But blowing the whistle on Kohlhertz and the gang would only push them deeper underground. He also knew it meant that now, with him onboard for muscle, Fischer and Ute thought they had a chance of discovering the truth and nabbing the perpetrators on their own, without involving the police. "Our research on the locations you recorded from Melisandre's map reveals that they are not locations of sacred thefts," Fischer continued.

"You mean none that have been reported," Linus qualified.

"Yes, I suppose it is possible there have been *unreported*

incidents. But we believe we should look for something else."

"Any ideas?"

"Perhaps. With the exception of the two places in India and the two mountain peaks, all of the others have churches with very old histories. Most were consecrated in the eleventh and twelfth centuries. We will look to see if they are connected."

"I had a run-in with Jules the priest this morning at a farmhouse about thirty miles from here. Turns out it was Kohlhertz's place."

"Was Kohlhertz there?"

"He showed up when we were leaving but we shook him."

"What was the *priest* doing there?" Fischer asked.

"Ransacking the place. I'm not sure why. Kohlhertz has a wall map marked the same way as Melisandre's, by the way. I just wonder who had it first?"

"When we discover its importance we shall answer that as well," Fischer said.

"Since there are a lot of *old* churches, their interest may involve birth and death records, and burial places," Linus suggested, and he further reported that Jules said he sometimes used genetic information to verify ownership rights of restored artifacts.

"That seems believable, but surely most claimants only need to be traced one or two generations. One wouldn't need genetic forensics for *that*. I do not believe the priest to be completely honest. Did you see the van from Lindow Abbey?"

"No, but I found the *Domaine deBouillon* vineyard," Linus said. He told them about the wine bottle from the Innkeeper, and how he matched the gold bee on the label to the gold bee on the iron gate at the vineyard.

"Of course," Fischer said. "As I say, it is a symbol of Merovingian royalty. Like the bear. Industrie Ursa, as in Ursus, the bear. You remember that Godfroi de Bouillon, the crusader who took Jerusalem from the Saracens, was supposedly of Merovingian descent. Just one moment. I have more," he added. Linus could hear papers rustling in the background as Fischer began another of his briefings.

"The Merovingian period is considered to be the time of the Arthurian and Camelot legends, and many believe King Arthur was a Merovingian," he said. "Most of the so-called Grail romances, the Holy Grail legends, were set during this time as well. Unfortunately, the documentation from this period of history is thin – which is why it's known as the Dark Ages. The Merovingians were in power over most of what is now France and Germany from about the fifth to the eighth centuries. In fact, a few places on the marked map are ancient Merovingian strongholds," Fischer said.

"So they're trying to re-establish the Merovingian line, maybe to prove ownership of something, possibly Kohlhertz's scroll or, at least, of the treasure which it may reveal," Linus surmised.

"All fits neatly, doesn't it," Fischer observed, and Linus replied, "Too neatly if you ask me."

"Perhaps. However we must not allow our skepticism to obscure the obvious," Fischer cautioned. "At least now you have something with which to confront the priest."

"That could be a problem," Linus said, and he told them about dropping Jules at *la Pomme Bleue* and the chapel bells which began to ring for no apparent reason. "The waitress muttered something like "*la Maddelena*" then bolted to the abbey."

"And the priest was missing," Fischer presumed.

"You got it," Linus confirmed. "And Kohlhertz's car was racing down the mountain, no doubt with Jules trussed in the back." Fischer asked Ute the significance of the phrase "*La Maddelena*".

"Ute says that the bells were rung at executions during the Middle Ages were called the *Magdalen Bells*." That didn't bode well for Jules, Linus thought. He also told them about the phrase "*te diem de Maddelena*" in the ransom note. "It is a death imprecation. A curse, equivalent to 'may you burn in Hell'," Ute said – more bad news for Jules.

"He *has* to be worth more to them alive," Linus contended – hoped. Then he told them about the painting he saw at the vineyard *Château* – the reclining woman with Melisandre's face.

"It is called a donor figure," Fischer said, explaining that it was once fashionable among Renaissance aristocracy to commission depictions of themselves in heroic or divine settings. "Jeanne d'Arc leading the battle of Orleans was a favorite among noblewomen," he explained.

"It was more erotic than heroic," Linus opined. "She was reclining in a sheer gown, reading a book by a candle," he said, and he related how he came across the hand-drawn map to Kohlhertz's lair in Melisandre's car.

"So now that you know Kohlhertz will send instructions to the *Tour Magdala*, you will watch it. But others will be watching as well," Fischer cautioned. Linus told him of his plan to disguise himself as a landscape artist and camp out in the parking lot.

"Tonight? Should you be there now?"

"No. Kohlhertz has to give them time. And I think he'll parade one of his lackeys right through town in broad daylight, just to make a statement. He knows they won't call the cops," Linus stated. He paused a moment. "Ervin," he began. It was the first time he'd used his first name. "This whole Rennes-le-Château thing seems like a cartoon. I mean, missing parchments, cryptic messages. Do you really think there's substance to it?"

"Did you notice the chapel interior?" Fischer asked. Linus knew he meant the weird statues and stations of the cross. "The demon looking down upon you just inside the entrance is Asmodeus, the custodian of secrets, guardian of hidden treasures," he said, adding that Judaic legend has it that he was also the builder of Solomon's Temple.

Fischer also said that *Terribilis Est Locus Iste – This Place Is Terrible* – is inscribed in the lintel above the chapel entrance. Linus hadn't noticed.

"Well at least the characters in the latest travesty seem to be living up to their demonic potential," Linus derided.

"It is good for you to remember that at all times. You are taking too many chances, *Herr* Linus. Be more careful!" Fischer chided, then he hung up. Linus noticed that, lately, Fischer's last word was always one of caution.

He was beginning to think the cagey old professor really cared.

July 29th, 30th, & 31st.
Rennes-le-Château. *Days 08-09 &10.*
The Ransoming

Linus circled all around the Tour Magdala and found its keystone – a large wedge-shaped chunk of stone at the base. It was flanked on both sides by a decorative battle chase – a slot in the wall like a gun slot. One of these slots, Linus knew, was the kidnapper's mailbox. Unfortunately, the mail hadn't arrived, as both slots were empty.

Two days passed, from before dawn to after dusk, with Linus hiding behind an easel and a wide straw hat, spreading color on canvas and wiping brushes on his baggy shirt and pants to complete the ruse. Once in awhile he'd take a break beneath a chestnut tree, searching the village history on the web with his Blackberry. And though the mystery persisted, there was enough about the Abbey and its strange *curé*, Saunière – like the grotesque statuary and bizarre stations of the cross glaring down from the walls of the chapel – to intrigue anyone.

Even in death, Saunière was an enigma. Apparently he had transferred all of his wealth to his longtime housekeeper and confidant, Marie Denarnaud. Oddly – and despite pronouncements by the locals that Saunière was in excellent health at the time – Denarnaud signed a receipt for a coffin she ordered on January 12th, 1917. And five days later, Saunière, 65, has a sudden stroke. Reportedly, a priest was called who, after hearing Saunière's confession, is said to be visibly shaken and refuses to administer the last rites. And on January 22nd, despite a lifetime of inexplicable affluence, Saunière dies penniless.

But *Madame* Denarnaud lives on comfortably until the end of WWII. However, when the French government converted old francs to new, post-war francs, Denarnaud refuses to reveal the source of her wealth and supposedly burns all of her old francs, sells her house, and tells the new buyer that she will impart a secret which will bring immense wealth and power. Of course, before that happens, she dies – on January 29th, 1953.

But even if only half true, the strange events in the life of Beringer Saunière definitely indicated that *something* was going on at Rennes-le-Château, and that it involved a great deal of money, perhaps ill-gotten gains at that.

It was just past eight on the evening of the third day. Sunset was about an hour away and the sky was the color of a half-ripened peach. He loaded his art materials into the trunk of his car – he had swapped the other rental for one less recognizable – then got into the driver's seat, pushed the backrest down, and lay low to relax. By craning his neck he could just see over the dashboard and had a clear view of the road, the parking lot, and the Magdala tower.

It was almost dark when a big yellow cat stalked into the parking lot, mousing along the weeds at the edge of the abbey wall. Suddenly the cat stopped, jerked its head to look backward, then scurried into the brush with its ears pinned back. Someone was coming up the road.

Linus slid lower in the car. A young man dressed in black walked into the parking lot. Linus didn't recognize his face but his high black boots were the same as the ones Kohlhertz and his chums all wore.

He walked to the path leading along the apron of the tower. Linus knew this was it. He also knew that the path dead-ended at a cliff and there was only one way back. So he didn't try to follow. A few minutes later, the guy returned, bolted through the parking lot and down the road. Linus was about to get out of his car when the woman bartender from *la Pomme Bleue* stepped out from the Abbey garden where she had been hiding and watching. Linus had an urge to make a dash for the drop point and beat her there. But then he had a stroke of luck.

The woman, cell phone to her ear, didn't go after the ransom note but pursued the escaping courier instead. It could only mean one thing – someone else was making the pickup and he only had moments before that someone turned up.

He bolted from the car and ran down the path, scanning the ground to avoid the ankle-twisting rocks. At the keystone, he shoved his hand into the slot on the left, fluttering his fingers up one side and down the other, and feeling along the back. There was nothing. He reached into the other slot and found a small white box. A severed ear – presumably Jules's – was inside. The words "*Montsegur* – 21:30" were written on the inside of the box's cover. Linus put it back in the slot then headed back to his car.

But before he could get there, he heard the turbine-like whine of an approaching motorcycle. He slid down the side of the hill, off the trail, and hid behind some large rocks as a red and gold motorcycle stopped at the trail head. The driver, clad in a red leather biker suit, was a woman. She pulled off her helmet. Her short, unevenly-cut blonde hair stuck out in all directions.

She set off down the bramble trail. Linus ducked lower as she passed, then crawled up and chased. She was just opening the box when he caught up. She closed and zipped the box into her jacket pocket then turned to leave. Linus, in the middle of the thin path, cut her off. All he could say was,

"*You ... !*"

It was Melisandre!

Anger filled her eyes. The flowing chestnut hair was now short, golden blond. And the soft-style clothes were just as gone – but not the ever-present gold scarf. She was aiming an air taser stun gun at his chest. Linus put up his hands, stepped back and said,

"You'll never get close enough to Kohlhertz to use that thing. And it's no match for a bullet."

"I'll worry about that," she replied as she sidestepped him and bolted. Linus gave chase.

"Jules is a ploy. He wants *you*," he warned. Melisandre didn't respond. "Listen for a minute," he implored as he reached out and grabbed her arm. Melisandre turned and brandished the stun gun. *"No! Wait!"* Linus shrieked, shielding himself with his hands. "Just *listen*. He thinks you and Jules know something about the scroll. He wants to torture you both," he said. Melisandre lowered the gun. Clearly, it wasn't scaring him off. And it was just as clear that she didn't really want to zap him.

"I understand all of that," she said, calmer but still stern. "And that's why I'm the only one who can get close enough to do something."

"He won't be alone and he won't be unarmed," Linus insisted. Melisandre stepped closer, looked hard in his eyes and said,

"Neither will I."

That's when Linus knew that some broader strategy was afoot and nothing he could do or say would stop it. "He'll kill you both," he cautioned. "And you've done such a damn good job of keeping everything undercover and away from the cops that he'll probably get away with it."

"There is much of this you don't yet know," she said. "I can't explain right now. Please, if you want to help, leave me to finish this and I promise I'll explain everything. Just not *now*."

"What have your promises been worth so far?"

"For you, nothing. But for good reason," she said.

But Linus held his tongue. She was right about one thing – he had to let her execute her scheme. And he couldn't let on that he intercepted the ransom demands and knew about the exchange at *Montsegur* – the ancient, mountaintop citadel – scheduled to take place in one hour.

"Okay. I'll back off. But if you don't contact me at *le Pomme Bleue* within twenty-four hours I'm calling Interpol and going after Kohlhertz myself," Linus declared. Melisandre laid her palm on his shoulder and looked in his eyes. It was a gesture of thanks with perhaps the slightest hint of admiration – none of which made him any more confident in her ability to deal with someone as violent as Kohlhertz. She hopped on her motorcycle, pulled on the helmet with the full face shield, and sped away.

Linus ran to his car and headed for *Montsegur*.

The Martyr of Montsegur

High on the peak above him, the crumbling stone citadel of *Montsegur* cut an angular silhouette against the twilight sky – the perfect macabre setting for a ransomed exchange, Linus thought. He imagined the band of Cathar priests, rappelling down the jagged cliffs to escape Catholic holy warriors sent to exterminate them during the Albigensian Crusade, leaving behind two hundred "heretical" Cathars who were rounded up and burned alive in a wood-filled barn. And who still haunted the mountain's dark forests. Now, almost 750 years later, it looked like one more Cathar – Jules – was on the verge of being sacrificed to his convictions.

He pulled into a turnout and parked beside a steel signpost sticking out of the ground. The sign was gone but the worn foot path told him that he'd found the head of a trail, one which wound through a small stand of trees, crossed a clearing, then started rising at a steep incline. Linus grabbed his camera and looked up the trail to where it disappeared in the brush. The citadel loomed about thirty stories above. He tucked the camera then dashed across the clearing and started climbing.

The path was a never-ending stairway made of roots, rocks and timbers. Some of the steps were knee high and almost straight up like a ladder. Some stretches had to be climbed with hands pulling as well as feet pushing... and all while keeping a sharp eye for trouble up trail. The sweatier he got and the more his thighs burned from the climb, the more he worried that he was draining the strength he'd need to deal with whatever awaited him at the top. But he pressed on, and after about twenty minutes he reached the base of the citadel's massive stone wall – the south wall, as evidenced by the sun setting behind wispy clouds to his left. Linus moved from the trail to the brush and took a break.

He doubted that he was alone but he hadn't seen anyone and presumed that no one had seen him. But he didn't want to barge into the middle of the exchange so he bypassed the main steps and circled left, around the corner and along the apron of the ancient fort. The dusk was shaving out one last red sliver of sunset when Linus reached a large crack in the wall where some stones had fallen out, creating a narrow opening. He slid into the dark crevice then edged sideways towards the fort's interior. The massive wall was about ten feet thick at its base, but the crack went all the way through.

As he got deeper in he heard faint talking from someplace on the walls above. But it stopped as soon as he tried to listen. He slid in further. The interior of the citadel started to come into view. There were no interior walls, just the four walls around the perimeter. There was no roof, either. A long, narrow staircase of hewn rock led from the floor of the fortress to the top of the walls, and there were no railings on either the walls or stairs. When the talking began again, Linus could hear clearly *and* see the source. He took out his pocket camera, switched to video mode and began recording.

Melisandre was standing near the top of the stairs, face-to-face with Kohlhertz who – as Linus had warned – wasn't alone. A henchman was with him, holding a collared Jules on his knees at the end of a long handle. Jules's neck was bloody from the cut of the leather choker and from having had his ear hacked off to be sent with the ransom note. His wrists were bound to the collar so all he could do was bow on his elbows. He tried to rise up but was choked back down. His eyes were swollen closed and his right hand looked as though it had been punctured, like a Christ stigma. His bulging, twisted jaw was obviously broken. Poor Jules had taken a heartbreaking beating.

"Be reasonable," Kohlhertz urged in an unctuous tone. His wide stance was both powerful and intimidating. A light breeze twisted through the open bottom of his long black duster and twitched his blonde ponytail. "The money isn't important. Keep it. Just tell me what my scroll says and I'll let him go," he said. Melisandre didn't respond. "Is it treasure?" Kohlhertz continued. Still no response. "Maybe we can share," he suggested. Linus – and everyone else – knew he was lying. Even if he got what he wanted, Kohlhertz would rather kill them than share it. And if he *didn't* get any information, he'd kill them just to keep them from beating him to the secret.

"Let him go. We'll discuss it," Melisandre offered. Jules grunted a loud objection but Melisandre ignored him. Clearly she was willing to risk being taken in his place. As he surveyed the unfolding scene Linus realized that Kohlhertz had made a potentially fatal error – he let Melisandre get close enough to use her stun gun.

"Just tell me and you can *both* go," Kohlhertz offered. Jules raised up to sneer but was again choked down. Kohlhertz watched expressionlessly as Jules heaved for breath. Melisandre's angry eyes never left Kohlhertz's face.

"Let him go. When he's safely at the bottom, we'll discuss it," she repeated, upping the ante. Now she wanted him freed *and* safe at the bottom. Kohlhertz was nearing the end of his short fuse. His wide, square jaw hardened as he clenched his teeth.

"Make no mistake, I know exactly who you are and it doesn't make a shit's worth of difference to me. I could easily collect a nice fee for your assassination," he claimed.

"Don't be a fool," she warned. "You'd only be destroying yourself."

"Perhaps," Kohlhertz chortled. His eyes narrowed. "But it wouldn't make you any less dead," he said. Melisandre glared. "You see?" Kohlhertz asked. "It's exactly what I've been saying – we're all losers if you hold out, all winners if you give in."

"Just send him down the mountain and send your toady with him to make sure he gets there safely. Then you and I will conclude our business," she said, upping the ante again. Now she wanted both Jules and Kohlhertz's lackey out of the picture. Linus knew Kohlhertz would never go for it. But the suggestion made him wonder how Melisandre would know when Jules was at the bottom. She had to have backup somewhere, maybe hidden along the trail. Kohlhertz apparently concluded the same.

"So you didn't come alone," he said, shaking his head. Linus knew this was it. Kohlhertz would make his move and scram to save his own skin. Right on cue, Kohlhertz reached into his pocket for a weapon. Jules reared up and roared like a wounded beast. His handler was completely surprised as Jules lurched forward and shoved him hard, trying to push him into Kohlhertz and take them both over the edge. Kohlhertz sidestepped the lunge but the screaming henchman, the restraints wrapped tightly around his wrist, followed the diving Jules over the edge of the cliff.

For a split second Kohlhertz and Melisandre were stunned by what happened. Linus watched in horror, knowing it was hundreds of feet down to the bottom of the jagged cliff. He stared in disbelief – Jules had heroically sacrificed his life – *to save Melisandre!*

Suddenly there was scuffling. Kohlhertz was writhing on the ground at the top of the stairs, his hand still stuck in his coat pocket. Melisandre was standing over him holding her stun gun. She had managed to zap him – thanks to Jules's fatal diversion. She kept him covered and began backing down the stairs. Kohlhertz struggled to pull his gun. Melisandre zapped him again. A blue bolt of electricity shot through the air like lightening, no wires needed, and landed on his thigh. Kohlhertz convulsed. Melisandre quickened her retreat.

Linus began climbing out of his crevice to join her but stopped short as another of Kohlhertz's thugs came out of hiding and confronted Melisandre. She fired the taser but the weakened charge fell short. With Melisandre in his pistol sights, the thug moved toward the stairs, looking for his stung boss, turning his back on Linus in the process. It was Linus's chance – and a risky one at that. But he had to take that risk. Otherwise, Melisandre was dead. He slid out of his hiding place and began moving towards them. Melisandre saw him and distracted the thug.

"He'll live," she said of Kohlhertz. "He'll be back on his feet in ten minutes."

"Drop the taser and don't get any closer," the henchman ordered. Melisandre laid the taser at her feet. Linus was almost within striking distance. He picked up a grapefruit-sized stone, raised his arm and rushed forward.

But the gunman heard him coming. A gunshot popped. Linus felt it sting his arm as the rock crashed down on the base of the guy's skull. The gunman's eyes fluttered and his knees buckled. Melisandre leapt forward and kicked him in the gut to help put him out, then seized his pistol as he fell.

"Hurry," she urged, as she retrieved her taser and grabbed Linus's arm. Linus recoiled in pain. Melisandre looked at her blood-smeared hand.

"You're hit," she said.

"Doesn't seem too bad," he answered as he squeezed his wounded upper arm. Kohlhertz was beginning to recover from his tasing and the other guy was moaning and moving his legs.

"*Hurry*," Melisandre repeated, then they bolted.

They scrambled down the twisted, cascading trail, quickening their pace as the grade diminished near the bottom. A rugged-looking man dressed like a field worker and a statuesque black woman in a tight leather jumpsuit met them as they emerged onto the road. Their grim faces told Linus that they had seen Jules's plummet.

"He's hurt," Melisandre said, motioning toward Linus. The black woman disappeared into the woods and the man led the way to a large Mercedes sedan that was waiting, engine running, with a woman behind the wheel. He then took Linus's keys and hustled away as Linus and Melisandre got into the back of the sedan.

The car began moving even before the door was closed. The woman in leather sped out of the woods on Melisandre's motorcycle and took the point. The man in Linus's rental car fell in behind.

They sped down the mountain into the darkness of the valley. Melisandre said something in French and the driver placed a phone call. Linus understood enough to know that someone was being sent to rescue Jules. He glanced up at the citadel of *Montsegur*, a jagged black silhouette fading into the darkening sky, thinking that Jules might be out there someplace, suffering but alive. It was only a hope, and a weak hope, at that.

Deep down, Linus knew that no one could survive such a fall.

PART THREE

She standeth in the top of high places,
by the way in the places of the paths.
She crieth at the gates.

Chapter 14. REFUGE in the VINEYARD

Linus squeezed his bleeding arm as the big sedan sped through the night, away from *Montsegur*. Melisandre was beside him in the darkness of the back seat. She slipped out of her red leather jacket and yellow scarf.

"Let me see it," she said as she ripped his left sleeve open to the shoulder. The bullet had grazed his upper arm, leaving a deep gash. Linus's pulse pounded at the sight of it – bit more to the left and he would've been hit in the heart.

"Damned close," he muttered as Melisandre tied the scarf around the wound.

"You promised not to follow me," she said.

"Lucky I did. The gun that did this was aimed at *you*."

With steady, deft hands, Melisandre twisted the scarf tightly and knotted the ends, then tugged once more for tightness. Linus winced, then checked for sympathy. She showed none.

"I hope there's a good doctor wherever we're headed," he said, and Melisandre replied,

"You're with one already."

The car wound along the narrow roads, out of the mountains and into the moonlit vineyards of the valley. The woman on the motorcycle was setting the pace up ahead and the man in Linus's car was close behind. The motorcade buzzed between long rows of tangled trees then turned off to the left. Right away, Linus knew where they were – the long gravel drive leading to *Domaine deBouillon,* the vineyard estate.

The driver circled to the back of the big *Château* and stopped near the garage. Melisandre said, "Come in," as she got out, and Linus followed her to a first-aid room beside the pantry. He sat on a leather recliner as she collected supplies – tape, gauze, cotton, cleansing solution, forceps, suture pack, needle holder, syringe, and a small vial of lidocaine – laid everything out on the countertop then scrubbed-up at a small sink. "I think I can close it," she said as she removed the bloody scarf and gently washed the wound with betadine – an iodine solution which stained his skin dark yellow. Linus watched over his shoulder and the sight of the gaping tear gave him a queasy feeling. He'd been close to gunplay before but never hit. And this was *too damned close!*

"You'll have a nice scar for your efforts," Melisandre said as she tore open a package containing a sterile tray.

She opened the syringe, forceps, suture pack and needle holder, and dumped each on the tray without touching them. Though she was seething, Melisandre worked in silence. Linus knew that her worry for Jules was shoving all her other emotions aside. He couldn't shake the images of Jules, beaten and cowed, plummeting from the heights of *Montsegur*. The same images were doubtless playing in Melisandre's mind. She pushed her hands into some latex gloves, drew up some lidocaine in the syringe, then began injecting it around the wound to numb it up. Then she began stitching.

"What the hell were you going to do?" Linus asked as she leaned close to stitch.

"Save Jules," she murmured. Ironically, just the opposite had been achieved. Linus wasn't about to point that out that right now. She looped, tied, and cut another stitch.

"Kohlhertz isn't as stupid as everyone thinks. And a lot tougher, too," he observed.

"I don't know what would've happened if you didn't show up. Maybe nothing," she countered.

"Or maybe the worst," he said. She pulled a stitch extra tight and Linus winced. She finished and pushed away, her arms hanging limply at her sides. The emotional and physical fatigue was catching up – on them both.

"I'm sorry you became involved," she said, reminding Linus that she didn't know it was actually old man Gervan who drew him in, not her. He still hadn't told her about Gervan's note that sent him to the *Blauer Apfel*.

"It's not your fault," he said as he looked at the puckered, laced-up wound then asked, "How many?" Melisandre rolled her stool closer and began bandaging.

"Ten stitches inside and twelve outside. And that *will* hurt for a while," she answered. She tossed the gloves and added, "You should stay here tonight." Linus didn't react. "Or, I can get you a taxi, or have my driver drop you someplace." Linus wasn't convinced that staying was a good idea. Things had gotten pretty rough in the last few hours. But he *was* convinced that staying – if not necessarily the safest choice – was his best chance of learning more.

"Thanks, by the way," he said, holding out his bandaged arm. It was throbbing. "Maybe I *will* stay," he added. Melisandre seemed pleased.

She led him up the back stairs then to a bedroom at the front of the house. It had a private bath and a large window overlooking the driveway and lighted front fountain. As he sat on the bed and slipped off his shoes, Melisandre pointed out the bureau and closet filled with men's clothes. "Any of these should fit," she said, and added, "*Bonne nuit*" as she left and closed the door. Linus jumped up and leaned an ear close to the door. Melisandre crossed the hall and went into the opposite room. Then he heard nothing. The house was still. He pulled his camera from his pocket and shot the room, then set it beside him on the bed, turned out the light, and lay on his back.

August 1st.
A village in Southern France. Day 11.
A Hollow Condolence

Kohlhertz's hard-heeled boots thudded on the floorboards as he browsed the village florist shop. His henchman was speaking to the florist, who produced an album of the shop's arrangements and showed him a black eucalyptus funeral wreath. Kohlhertz leaned over and looked.

"But larger. We're not cheap," he said. The florist wrote down the wreath's destination – Jules's funeral at *Domaine deBouillon* – and they paid cash. Kohlhertz also gave the florist a sealed card to send with the wreath. It said, *"One that lives by other's breath, dieth also by his death"*.

But if Kohlhertz had guessed rightly, the line would have another meaning as well. A few months ago, a Frenchman calling himself a private investigator offered Kohlhertz money for a steady source of info on Jules, the dead priest, and Melisandre. He said he knew Kohlhertz was being investigated by Jules, and that meant he was well positioned to turn the tables and spy on them.

He didn't say why Jules and Melisandre were of interest, but Kohlhertz's discovered enough about the French agent – and the secret Paris society he represented – to form a theory of his own. And a simple line, from a certain poem, could be very telling. The card was initialed *"W.K."* – clear enough for them to know it was from *"Wolfgang Kohlhertz"*

"Make sure it gets there today," he ordered, then he and his flunky marched out.

Bearing the Pall

Linus awoke from a deep sleep to the sound of a car on the gravel driveway beneath his bedroom window. He had been sleeping so soundly that it took a few seconds for him to remember he was at *Domaine deBouillon*. He yawned and checked his watch – it was eight-thirty – then he turned to get up but a sharp pain in his wounded arm stopped him short. He waited a second for it to subside then reached for his camera beside him on the bed. It was gone. But his Blackberry never left his pocket. He moved to the tall window and used it to shoot the scene unfolding below. A dour undertaker in a faded black suit was standing beside a long black hearse. Doubtless Jules's body was in the back. Melisandre came out of the house and greeted him.

The sad little mortician bowed and kissed her hand, and she cupped his face and raised his head as she spoke to him. Linus had witnessed enough of this devotion lately to know that Melisandre was a powerful and widely respected woman. Aside from her apparent wealth, he still wasn't sure why.

The mortician bowed again then drove toward the back of the house. Melisandre went inside. Linus went to the side window to watch the hearse. It didn't stop at the garage, as he expected. Instead, it ambled onto a dirt road and went up through the vineyards, then disappeared over a nearby hill. Linus wanted to know where it went. He washed as best he could with an arm that wasn't as much weak as it was tender – especially when the stitches were stretched – then assayed his bloodied, tattered clothes.

Another car was coming up the drive. He went back to the window and saw Melisandre's friend, Veronica Franco, getting out of a chauffeured sedan. Linus started shooting pictures again as Melisandre emerged from the house and the women embraced. Veronica's long, thick hair was pulled back and knotted. Her face was pale and her eyes sunken red. Indeed, Melisandre looked no better. They talked quietly and walked, arm-in-arm, inside.

Linus rifled the closet and drawers for a complete set of clothes and got dressed. As he was taking a suit coat, he realized that it was just like the one Jules was wearing on the night they first met. Then he realized that everything he was wearing had once belonged to Jules.

He didn't like the idea of greeting the women in the dead man's clothes. But his old clothes were blood spattered and torn beyond salvage. So he finished dressing, looked again – unsuccessfully – for his missing camera, and headed downstairs.

As he approached the salon he heard muffled voices. Passing slowly, he saw Veronica sobbing as Melisandre doubtless was trying to tell her what had happened on *Montsegur*. Linus wondered which story she would tell. Technically, Jules's death was a murder-suicide – Jules had actually committed suicide *and* murder simultaneously.

But who would see it that way? A more likely story was that Jules was killed in a struggle with his captors, who were liable for murder. Either way, Linus was certain it warranted an official inquiry.

But, like at other times in this intrigue, there wasn't an "official" anywhere to be found. Melisandre and her comrades again seemed to be operating with impunity, at lease in total secrecy. He opened the front door of the *Château* and stepped out into the warm sunshine. The skies were blue and dry, the air was standing still, filled with birdsong and the sound of his own feet crunching on the gravel. He entered one of the small patio gardens that lined both sides of the house and sat on a stone bench. Within minutes, Melisandre arrived to join him.

"Is it always this quiet?" he asked.

"Everyone here is pretty much in shock," she said. Linus nodded and said,

"I saw Veronica." Melisandre seemed too downcast to comment, and the pause which followed seemed long. Finally, she said,

"I'll find you some coffee if you like."

"Thanks. And you wouldn't happen to know where to find my camera, would you?" Melisandre nodded and said,

"I would."

She walked him to a small garden off the dining room where a breakfast tray was waiting. She asked how his wounded arm felt and commented that Jules would be glad to see his things put to use – a wistful comment, but also meant to put him at ease. A housemaid brought Linus's camera.

"I'm sorry about that," Melisandre said. "I erased your video from *Montsegur*. I hope you understand."

"You had no right," Linus protested.

"True," she agreed, "only a great necessity." That much, Linus knew, was indisputable. Melisandre wanted to have the spin control – though he thought it more likely that she lifted, and not erased, his photo files. "Your hotel key was in your car. I'm having your things brought here," she added.

"Am I being kidnapped?"

"You are welcome to stay, but free to leave at any time. But I think you'll find it more interesting if you stay." Linus knew she was right. There were many things he hoped to discover before leaving *Domaine deBouillon*. "Today is very busy for me but are you available for dinner?" she asked. Linus, of course, was.

His car was available if he needed to go someplace, she said, though she recommended against driving "with that arm". And she also offered him the run of the winery and said she'd arrange a lunch in the vineyard for him. Her hostility had turned to hospitality. She finished her coffee, stood up and said, "I'll see you in the salon, at eight." Then she turned and left him to his coffee and croissants.

Chapter 15. DINNER for TWO

The clock on the mantle chimed faintly eight times as Linus entered the front salon. Right away he noticed that the donor figure painting of the naked woman –Melisandre – reclining with a book by a candle and covered only by her hair, was missing. A large mirror was hanging in its place.

He also noticed that he was surrounded by funereal bouquets. They had been arriving all afternoon – orchids and roses, exotic lilies and gladioli, a few wreaths made of dried flowers and aromatic herbs. But one black eucalyptus wreath stood out because it was so bleak and unlike all the others. And the card was different, too. *"One that lives by other's breath, dieth also by his death."* The others just had the sender's name. This one was poetic, handwritten, and signed "W.K." Linus was sure it was from Wolfgang Kohlhertz.

He heard steps in the marble hallway coming toward him so he pinched and pocketed the card. But it wasn't Melisandre who had come to collect him, as he expected. It was Veronica. Her eyes were still sunken but the redness was gone. She was dressed in half-mourning – simple black shirt and slacks – with maybe a bit of rouge on her ashen cheeks. She managed a muted smile as she greeted him with a handshake and touched the sleeve of his coat – the one he had taken from Jules's closet. Surely Veronica recognized it, though she didn't say.

"I heard you were very heroic, and badly wounded," she said, then asked if he was okay. Of course, he said he was. They went to the dining room patio where Melisandre was seated under an arbor, warmly lighted by candles on the table. A young man with strong hands and tanned forearms was clearing a dinner from the table. Linus knew it was Veronica's dinner, since it had barely been touched.

"I hope we meet again under better circumstance," Veronica said as Linus sat. She bade them "*Buona notte*," and went inside.

"She's very shaken," Linus noted.

"She made many difficult phone calls today," Melisandre noted sadly.

"Was she related to Jules?" he asked, and Melisandre said, "No, but very close."

She said that Veronica *was* a Venetian diplomat's daughter, as she had claimed. But her alias – the name of an ancient Venetian courtesan – was meant to separate her advocacy work from her family. She was, foremost, the founder of a system of "safe houses" like the one near Lindow Abbey, Melisandre said. "It's called Das Giudecca, after the Venetian island where prostitutes were given safe haven," she said, adding that, ironically, the island was now the site of a women's prison.

He confronted her with the sob story she told him about the murdered lover and the family rejection, *a la* Saint Margaret of Cortona. But Melisandre was anything but contrite. It's not her habit to mislead, she said, but it's also her privilege to protect her privacy. "I don't feel *obliged* to answer even a *single* question," she assured.

"Can't you at least tell me who you are?" he asked, figuring that, by now, Melisandre must've realized that he wasn't going to go away.

"There is really nothing remarkable," she began. She said she was the daughter of an English businessman-slash-adventurer and an American pediatrician. She was an only child, her childhood was interesting and comfortable, and she became a doctor. She was never married, and had no children.

"A pediatrician?" he asked.

"Dermatologist. Dermatological surgeon, actually. And, yes, it's more than acne ointments and rosacea cream," she explained.

She said her family traveled a lot but lived mostly in Boston. Her father, an only child, and her mother, an adoptee, were dead, as were her grandparents – which pretty much left her all alone in the world.

"My parents were killed on Interstate eight-eighty in nineteen eighty nine . . ”

"Cypress Freeway in San Francisco – Oakland, to be exact. Collapsed in the earthquake," he said. Melisandre nodded solemnly. Her telling of the story had a ring of sincerity but Linus still wondered if he was hearing another canard.

She said she no longer had a formal medical practice and was currently the director – not just spokeswoman, as she said before – of *Novangelis*, a private, gender-based philanthropic foundation. "I still make use of my medical skills, though I've developed many other skills as well," she noted.

"Some very interesting ones at that. You ride that motorcycle like a pro. And that taser gun is a nifty little toy, too," he said. Melisandre shrugged and said,

"Not all are maidens that wear fair hair."

The young guy in the apron came and gave them each a big white plate with a roasted bird in a small puddle of brown sauce. He carved off a piece – it was capon – and asked, "Did Jules always carry a gun?", then put the piece in his mouth.

Melisandre said she didn't know when he started carrying a gun, though she did know that it was never loaded. Linus shook his head with disgust.

"Don't you think you're being reckless? Empty pistols and stun guns are no match for real bullets."

"And a notebook is?" she retorted.

"I'll take a hidden, insurance copy of a notebook full of evidence over a stun gun or an empty pistol any day," he said and added, "You'd be surprised how powerful information can be."

"Maybe so. But how many women do you think have been saved from a beating – or worse – just by threatening to expose their batterer?" she asked, and Linus had to admit, probably none.

"Why does Kohlhertz think he can get paid for killing you?" he asked, bluntly referring to what was said atop *Montsegur*. Melisandre was dismissive.

"When you go up against the likes of slavers and pimps, which we often do, you're bound to make a few serious enemies," she said.

She knew she had logic on her side. But she also knew that Kohlhertz didn't mean slavers and pimps when he talked about people who'd pay to have her killed.

"Jules said he used genetic fingerprinting to authenticate ownership claims for stolen artifacts. But that's not the full extent of it, is it?" Of course, to the best of his knowledge, it was. But he hoped that the phrasing of his question might lead her to believe that he knew more.

But Melisandre seemed prepared for the question. She said that the *Novangelis* foundation was founded by a family which traced its roots back before the crusades, and is funding a study on their lineage. "Researching old burial sites, records, historical documents. That type of thing," she said, adding that they were experimenting with genetic fingerprinting to verify genealogical data. Linus began to think that his theory about the map he found in Melisandre's Berlin headquarters – that it plotted research locations – was gaining weight.

"Since this is *Domaine deBouillon*, then it's the family of Godfroi de Bouillon, I take it?" he said. Melisandre nodded but she didn't mention the fact that Godfroi was thought to be a Merovingian, and thus descended from Dagobert II, the king mentioned in the Rennes-le-Château scrolls. Linus suspected that attempting to establish the bloodline was more than just an exercise in documenting the family tree.

He asked about the eye disorder called *Aniridia*, which he discovered through documents he found at Lindow Abbey, but Melisandre said she knew nothing and suggested that it was something of specific interest to Jules.

"So what does it all mean? What is your mission?" he pressed.

"To protect and give voice to the un-entitled and the powerless," she said. It was a noble notion but actually revealed little.

"History is littered with hundreds of millions of similarly intentioned people, screaming at the top of their lungs. Look around. Can you honestly say it has made a difference?"

"Is that how you rationalize being a *paparazzo*? With cynicism?"

"The cynicism comes with experience," he said. But somehow,

Melisandre's remarks were penetrating his shell, and he had little stomach for defending his current occupation as 'celebrity photographer'. He finished the last few bites of his dinner and pushed away the plate. "Are you still as committed to your cause, after what happened to Jules?" he asked, washing down the last swallow with a gulp of wine.

"Even more so," she replied, her eyes bright and steely.

"Why did he do it? What made him jump off a cliff to save you? Why did he trade his life for yours?"

"I don't know. I wish he hadn't," she muttered, though Linus was sure that she *did* know why Jules had given his life, and just as sure that Melisandre wasn't going to reveal it. Not now. Maybe never. He'd somehow have to figure it out on his own.

"Who was the guy Jules took with him?" he asked, meaning Kohlhertz's thug.

"No other bodies were recovered," she responded.

"You mean the other body was gone," Linus stated. Melisandre didn't respond. "Someone took it?" he asked. Melisandre's expression remained taut. She looked him straight in the face and said,

"There was no other victim."

"Don't be ridicu ... "

"Jules's untimely accident is a tragic shock to us all," she stated, sticking to the scripted response. Clearly the truth had not yet come to light officially and Melisandre was gambling on him to clam up. Linus prudently played along.

"What do you know about this Kohlhertz guy?" he asked. Melisandre seemed to know little beyond what Linus knew – that his name sounded very German but his accent very American. "In fact, loosely translated, the name Kohlhertz means black-heart, which sounds very phony," she said. Of course, she also knew that he had somehow come into possession of an ancient artifact – a scroll – the importance of which was supposedly still unknown.

Linus told her that, in their Berlin tussle, he thought Jules had yanked out a sample of Kohlhertz's hair – obviously for a genetic fingerprint. He didn't tell her that he'd copied the ensuing DNA report from a file at her Berlin headquarters. Melisandre said they checked Kohlhertz's DNA against as many law enforcement databases as they could but nothing came back. Even so, there was plenty of evidence against him. So why was he still on the loose?

Melisandre said if not for the scroll, Kohlhertz would've been "long gone". Gervan knew it was important, she said, but he didn't get a chance to tell them why. So as long as Kohlhertz had it, he'd be walking around – and presumably not alone.

"Don't you have a copy?" Linus asked. He already knew Jules – and Fischer – had one.   Melisandre said she had a "copy of what Gervan was working on", though didn't know if it was the entire text. But, she said, even if they solved the script, the actual document might be needed to establish its veracity.

Yet both Linus and Melisandre agreed that Kohlhertz's deal-making attempt was confirmation that he didn't know what he had, and that he knew he'd never decipher the scroll on his own.

And they also agreed that Kohlhertz was very dangerous

The waiter returned and cleared the dishes. Melisandre dismissed him for the evening then suppressed a deep yawn. The sadness was again becoming pervasive. The *Château* was on a funereal footing. A great friend had been lost. And it was obvious that people weren't sleeping well. She sat for a moment, staring distantly at the vineyards, and Linus said,

"I think I'll turn in and read." The weary Melisandre must've welcomed that, he thought. She offered to walk him to his room.

They ascended the front staircase and Linus admired the old *Château*'s flawless condition. Polished oak details and cherry furniture with plush brocade coverings appointed every room. Melisandre said it belonged to the foundation and they were very particular about its upkeep.

When they reached his bedroom, Linus turned to say good night. "I'm sorry about Jules. I wish I'd known him better," he said. For the first time, he saw tears well in Melisandre's eyes. But she dammed them before they fell, and thanked him for the sentiment.

"There's a private service for Jules in the morning," she said, assuming he'd want to attend. She offered her hand and said, "Good night, Mister Mercator." Linus shook her hand and said,

"Good night." Melisandre then turned and entered the bedroom across the hall.

August 2nd.
Domaine deBouillon. Day 12.
Vera's Grief

Veronica followed the light of her lantern up the dirt road, away from the *Château* and into the vineyard. She turned onto a footpath and climbed a hill to a small cave near the top, where the path passed through a flower garden surrounding the cave's entrance. The opening was very small and the tall woman had to stoop to get through.

She pulled back the hood of her cloak then lifted the lid of the plain, sanded-wood coffin. As the body of her lover came into view her heart pounded harder than the hammer which would nail shut the lid. For four years she had been Jules's confidant and most ardent supporter. For four years she had looked forward to a time when life would return them to the serenity of the vineyards. Together.

And return them it did, though not as they had envisioned.

A huge tear rolled out of her eye and landed on the breast of his white linen shroud. His face was pale but the undertaker had masterfully closed a jagged gash on his left cheek. In her mind, she kissed him goodbye – as she had kissed him goodbye so many times before. And with trembling hand, she reached out and once more stroked his thick hair.

The subterranean chill suddenly made her shiver and she pulled her cloak closed. In several hours, shortly after sunrise, a small crowd of workers and friends would gather outside the cavernous sepulcher. Melisandre would reassure them that Jules did not die in vain. And each would remember him for his inspiration and valor. It reminded the woman from Venice of an old Italian adage, that the best way to gain praise was to die. In Jules's case, all the praise would be true, and fitting tribute to a true friend.

But by the time it was all being said, Veronica, the greatest friend of all, would be miles away.

The Hillside Sepulcher

Linus looked up at the denim gray, pre-dawn sky and the brightening red sunrise beginning to flare just beyond the rolling vineyard hills. Melisandre was in front of him, holding her white and gold smock above her ankles as she traversed the stony path to the top of the hill. He had awakened early this morning, his mind filled with questions and caution about Melisandre. She seemed sincere but he'd made that misjudgment before, and he didn't intend to repeat the mistake. Skepticism would be his shield.

Her claim to be a mere director of a foundation was one of the things that made him most skeptical. The depth of servitude and homage that surrounded her struck him as much more than simple worker-to-boss respect. Even the most popular boss didn't see this much fawning. No, Melisandre was more than just a good boss. She was someone – or *something* – else. Something special.

He had also witnessed *another* curious event this morning. Just after he woke up, a car pulled up and parked in front of the house, its driver waiting beside the open back door. The passenger surprised him. It was Veronica. Not coming, but leaving.

She handed the driver a small piece of luggage then got in. The driver then handed the bag back to her, closed her door, and drove her away.

"I saw Veronica leave this morning," he recalled to Melisandre as they climbed the path.

"She said her farewells privately," Melisandre replied, then added, "I imagine the thought of seeing Jules closed up forever in a cold tomb was too much." The sadness and finality of it struck Linus deeply, too.

A thin morning fog was settled in the vineyards and a pungent aroma of incense filled the air as they arrived at the hillside tomb. Two men in coarse work clothes were standing beside the large stone tablet which would be rolled into place to seal the cave. Jules's shrouded body was laid out on a bed of smooth stones just outside the opening. The scene was Biblical, and Jules' corpse eerily Christ-like.

Three dour women – two wearing aprons and probably house staff – watched from a few feet away as Linus and Melisandre arrived. But there was no one else. No grieving relatives. No sobbing children. No bishops or clergy. A knot tightened in Linus's gut as he viewed the body, wrapped in white linen and surrounded by flowers and ferns. Only the ashen blue face was visible. A smoldering brass censer was set near the feet.

The three women moved closer, folded their hands at their breasts and bowed deferentially before Melisandre. She acknowledged each of them then stood over the body with her head down and her eyes closed. Linus was heads up, examining the small gathering of men and women, all standing silently with their heads bowed. Then Melisandre spoke, her voice strong and clear.

"Oh, lift me as a wave, a leaf, a cloud. I fall upon the thorns of life. I bleed. A heavy weight of hours has chained and bowed, one too like thee: tameless, and swift, and proud."

She opened her eyes and pulled a necklace from inside her smock – a small crystal bear on a gold chain – then knelt down and draped the necklace around Jules' head. She touched his cheek with the back of her left hand while wiping a tear from her cheek with her right, then stood up and nodded at the two men. They came forward, picked up the litter and carried the body it into the tomb.

The three women gathered up the flowers and followed. A few moments later they all returned. With great effort, the men un-wedged the giant stone and it rolled into place with a deep thud. Then the others left, leaving Linus and Melisandre behind. Linus approached the tomb and touched the stone sealing the entrance, surprised by the sadness he felt for a man he barely knew.

"Blessed and sweet repose," he said.

"I think you would've been good friends," Melisandre said. They stood a silent moment, then she took his arm to walk him away.

When they got back to the house Melisandre led him into the garden where tables were set for a breakfast gathering of about twenty. She chose one and sat down, but Linus remained standing.

"Please excuse me, but I need a few minutes," he said as the house staff brought food and beverages to the tables then took their places.

"Is everything okay?" Melisandre asked. Linus nodded reassuringly and left the garden.

The Chatelaine's Boudoir

Linus hustled upstairs to his room then waited and listened to see if anyone had followed. With the entire staff at the funeral breakfast in the garden there'd never be a more perfect moment. He crossed the hall, unlocked Melisandre's door with a credit card and slipped inside and began making images with his camera. The large *boudoir* was comfortably furnished with upholstered chairs, thick carpets and a big canopied bed.

On the wall across the room, the big donor figure painting of Melisandre that he had first seen in the downstairs salon, was hanging between two sconces. Seeing it close up like this, the near-naked, candle-lit pose was even more erotic – a side of Melisandre that Linus hadn't otherwise noticed. On the one hand, it *did* seem like a *boudoir* painting. But he couldn't help but wonder if there was another reason it had been moved, if there was something about it he should realize. He made an image to study later.

He crossed to the big walk-in closet and fingered through the clothes – everything from elegant evening gowns to studded leather jumpsuits. Fashion broadband, as it were. He rummaged through some drawers and found many wigs of varied lengths and colors. The collection was beginning to look a lot less like wardrobe and a lot more like costuming. Or perhaps disguise.

He'd already seen Melisandre change from the conservative, carefully coifed, soft-featured woman he met at *Blauer Apfel* in Berlin, to the extremist, spiked peroxide blonde, leather-suited biker he confronted at the *Tour Magdala* in Rennes-le-Château.

He carefully replaced everything the way he had found it then went to the bath. Melisandre had an unusually wide array of cosmetics, especially ointments and *parfum*. But the most curious item was the case of contact lenses – no less than twenty different shades. Suddenly Linus realized why he'd noticed her eyes so much... because one minute they were radiant emerald green, and the next they were burning cobalt blue. All thanks to contact lenses.

He panned the scene with his camera then left the *boudoir* and snuck out of the house for a private phoner with Fischer.

Schwarzwald Rendezvous

Linus switched on his phone as he walked down the drive toward the gate. The voice-mail indicator was flashing. There were several missed calls – but no messages – from Fischer. There was also a voice message from Dark Star, his photo agency in New York, again begging for the Jamie Richards photos. And there was also a message from Jamie Richards, also begging for the Jamie Richards photos. He ignored them both and dialed Fischer.

"We were told at your hotel that you checked out," Fischer said, adding that he was concerned and berating him for being out of touch. Linus apologized then gave him a brief recap of the martyrdom on *Montsegur* and his stay at *Domain de Bouillon*. "There have been some serious incidents with potentially serious consequences," Fischer informed. "The sites you copied from the map, which we considered as possible places where sacred thefts have occurred... "

"But they weren't."

"Correct. At that time," Fischer explained.

"And now? Sacred thefts?"

"Something. I don't know exactly," Fischer said. "In the past two days, three places from the map have been crime scenes, the latest last night, with the murder of a woman described as a researcher, who apparently stumbled into a burglary and was killed."

"Sounds like a Kohlhertz operation," Linus noted.

"Yes, but to what end?" Fischer asked. Linus looked back at the house. Melisandre was coming out the front door and walking toward him.

"I have some ideas but someone is coming. I can't talk right now."

"There's more," Fischer said, and he told Linus to leave as soon as possible and meet him at a place called *Land Haus* in the Black Forest. Melisandre was getting closer.

"I've got to go," Linus said.

"Leave immediately. It is a long drive," Fischer exhorted, and Linus said he'd call from the road. Just as Melisandre drew within earshot, Linus ended the call and pocketed the phone.

"Everything okay?" she asked. Linus nodded. "You weren't in your room," she said. Right then, and despite Melisandre's efforts to pretend otherwise, he knew he was being watched. She took him back through the kitchen and made another pit stop in the first aid room, where she checked him for fever then changed the bandage on his arm. "Temperature normal and no sign of infection," she said as she examined the puckered skin around the sutures. She swabbed it with an anti-bacterial then waited as it dried.

"What happened to my car, by the way?" he asked as she worked.

"Going somewhere?"

"I'm afraid the rental company will want it back," he said with a smile, then added, "And I can't stay *forever*." She told him it was parked near the garage behind the house, and again that he was welcome to stay as long as he liked. As she finished with the new bandage, Linus apologized for missing breakfast and said he thought he'd hit the shower and then consider the options for a day trip.

"Whenever you feel like it, just ask one of the staff and they'll find me," she said from the bottom of the stairs as Linus went up. Melisandre then went about some business in the vineyard offices.

Linus went to his room and packed.

Fade to Gone

He found his car, keys in the ignition, right where Melisandre said he would – near the garage behind the *Château*. The domestic staff was out in full and one of them said *"bon jour"* as Linus loaded his bags into the trunk. But no one seemed interested that he was leaving – *with his luggage*. Too uninterested, in fact. It made him wonder if he was doing just as they expected – and wanted – him to do.

It was just after eight a.m. when he left *Domain de Bouillon*. He stopped in the first village he hit for a *café au lait* and a bite, checked his map, then headed northeast to *Alsace*, skirting along the jagged *Jura Mountains* on the French-Swiss border. A few hours into the trip he placed the promised call to Fischer.

"Obviously, she's working for the Merovingians," Fischer said, when he learned of Melisandre's purported genealogical study. The connections between Godfroi de Bouillon, hero of the first crusade; *Domaine deBouillon*; *Industrie Ursa*, named after the Merovingian bear symbol; and Dagobert II, the Merovingian king mentioned in the cryptic Rennes-le-Château parchments, was simply too strong to conclude otherwise. But her simple explanation that it was an "academic exercise" by the wealthy old guard of the *Novangelis* Foundation got weaker as Fischer filled in some history.

Clovis I was the most famous Merovingian, he said, the one who converted the Franks to Roman Christianity between 481 and 511. In appreciation of his services to the cross, the Catholic Church of Rome gave Clovis I the title of Holy Roman Emperor – a title he was assured he could pass down to his descendants.

But when Clovis died, his empire – and power – was divided

amongst his four sons, and the power diluted. "Thus they became known as *les rois faineant*, the enfeebled kings," Fischer said. Alas, with the subsequent murder of one of those descendants, Dagobert II, in 679, Merovingian powers fell away from the true bloodline – the descendants of Merovee and his grandson Clovis I – as it was usurped by fringe political elements and *poseurs*. "The new line of rulers eventually led to Charles Martel, the hero who turned back the moors at the battle of Poitiers in 732," Fischer said.

Though the Church had pulled its support away from the Merovingian bloodline long before – when they effectively inaugurated the Carolingian Dynasty by openly favoring Charles Martel's son, Pepin the Short, over the heirs of the Merovingian King Childeric III – the final blow came in 800 when Rome proclaimed Charles the Great, Martel's grandson – aka *Carolus Magnus*, aka *Charlemagne* – as Holy Roman Emperor, formally breaking their centuries-old promise and deposing the Merovingians once and for all. Or so they thought. And that's when the Merovingians went from being the "enfeebled kings" – *les rois faineant* – to the "lost kings" – *les rois perdus*.

Yet, despite official condemnation from the French ruling class over the centuries, the Merovingian descendants managed to remain connected. One reason for this, Fischer said, was their long history. Merovingians considered themselves descendants of Noah, of the Ark fame, and members of the exiled Benjamite tribe from the old testament. But another, perhaps darker reason for their survival existed as well.

"Strong cases have been made for a Jesus bloodline, and the Merovingians claim to be the direct descendants," Fischer said. He added that they were also known as the sorcerer-kings, evoking an aura of mysticism and clairvoyance, and were said to be capable of telepathic communication with nature and beasts. "They supposedly possessed miraculous curative powers and could heal with their touch," Fischer expounded, adding that, like Solomon, Merovingians felt that their *virtu* resided in their opulent tresses, which they were loathe to cut – labeling them the "long-haired monarchs".

Again – as it was in Melisandre's circles – hair was an important symbol.

The bee and the bear were others, and Fischer said there was also a cruciform birthmark which supposedly had been passed down through generations of Merovingians. "There's no doubt in my mind. She's working for them, probably for the *Priory of Sion*," Fischer repeated. The name – which he had forgotten about – caught Linus's attention.

"What's that, Priory of *what*?"

"Sion. It's a group from Paris," Fischer said. "They've been claiming exclusive right to the French throne for years, based on supposed secret documents which prove their Merovingian lineage. This sounds like their operation."

"Except it isn't," Linus stated. "At the induction ceremony in the woods, Melisandre made a speech and said she had received intelligence from Paris that the *Priory of Sion* has secretly named a successor. In context, Melisandre was saying that they had to redouble their efforts against this competitor. What they're competing for, I don't know."

"Hmmm. They're making conflicting claims. Obviously," Fischer responded. In any case, it all was coming together nicely except for one thing: Kohlhertz. He certainly wasn't of royal lineage, though possibly the type of person who a secret society like the *Priory of Sion* or, for that matter, *Novangelis*, might employ. And with the promise of a more detailed discussion soon and in person at *Land Haus*, Linus ended the call.

He drove over the *Rhine* near Basel and went up into the *Schwarzwald*, the Black Forest, a dense, high-altitude forest of majestic conifers in southwestern Germany. By the time he saw the sign for Tiefenhausern, the small village where *Land Haus* – the inn Fischer set for their *rendezvous* – was located, he had been traveling for twelve hours with no more than a few catnaps along the way and more than five hundred miles behind him. And the long hours of solitude afforded him the thinking time to form one more theory.

He began with the premise that Melisandre had already found a missing treasure – either from the Temple of Solomon, the Visigoths, Cathars, or Templars, since they were all potentially the same. And maybe she did so by using Kohlhertz's scroll. So now she must keep Kohlhertz from doing the same while, in the meantime, capturing the original scroll and establishing a bloodline and, thus, rightful ownership or whatever she had found. It was a nice, neat theory, but he couldn't quite swallow it all down. Something about the size and militancy of the *Novangelis* organization seemed to suggest there was still more.

The main road bypassed the center of the village and continued on through the hills. A few kilometers past the town he saw a sign for *Land Haus* and slowed down. Distant mountain vistas flashed off and on in the moonlight as gusty winds opened holes in the thick cloud cover. In a cloudburst, large gobs of rain splattered on the windshield.

He turned onto a narrow dirt road through a field. *Land Haus*, a stone country house surrounded by stone walls and fields, was nestled in a patch of trees and flowering shrubs just ahead. He parked beside the only other car in the small gravel lot. The warm light from a lamp over the wooden door cozied the place up. Through the cross-hatched windows he could see Fischer and Ute seated at a candle-lit table. He set his Blackberry to secretly capture audio of the meeting then slipped it into the breast pocket of his jacket. As he entered, a young man in an apron poked his head out from the kitchen. "*Guten Abend*," he said.

"*Guten Abend*," Linus replied and said, "I'm with them," pointing inside toward Fischer and Ute, sitting alone in the glow of the fireplace. The innkeeper understood and waved his hand to usher Linus ahead, then returned to his kitchen duties. Linus joined his compatriots at a table by the hearth.

Chapter 16. The RAID on LAND HAUS

Fischer and Ute watched as Linus struggled out of his jacket. "Just a flesh wound but healing nicely," he said. He told them about intercepting the ransom note – and Melisandre, when she came to collect it – then saving her life at *Montsegur*. Wounded in the process, Melisandre, the doctor, stitched him up. Like Linus, they were startled by the depth of Jules's devotion when he told them how he had sacrificed his life.

He said Melisandre was a gracious host, – though rather un-graciously lifted his camera out from under his sleeping nose then returned it stripped of his images. His update included the erotic donor painting – now hanging in the *boudoir* – and the wardrobe full of disguises and colored contact lenses. And he commented on how much her appearance had changed in the last two weeks alone.

He also recounted Jules's eerie, Christ-like entombment at dawn, and the depths of Vera's grief. In the end, all they could conclude was that Melisandre's behavior – the taser, the extreme outfits, and racing motorcycles around the countryside – was well outside that of a foundation director, as she had described herself. Fischer filled a goblet with *rot wine* – red wine.

"There is grander scheme in this," he said. And maybe as many as four murders in fourteen days, Linus thought – the latest a church researcher in Bayeux. Within the past two months, similar crimes were reported at LeMans and Rheims, though no murders, Fischer said. Their connection was that they were all at churches in northern France and all involved a theft of records – mostly birth and death recs, such as those being researched by the murder victim in Bayeux.

Melisandre's stated interest in genealogical study – which they all agreed was about Merovingians – and Kohlhertz's meddling in her affairs, possibly in someone else's name – painted a stark picture.

"One eccentric philanthropist is trying to prove a Merovingian bloodline and claim the throne of France, and another is trying to prevent it," Linus mused. And, he theorized, since Kohlhertz's scroll had put him into Melisandre's circle – perhaps by coincidence, perhaps because the scroll's content interested her – he was perfectly positioned to be recruited by her foes. Not the slavers and pimps she claimed were her prime opponents, but a completely different enemy.

"The *Prieure de Sion*, *Priory of Sion*," Ute said, and Fischer nodded.

"The Priory claims to have proof that Christ survived the crucifixion. They date back as far as the 11th century and for a time, until the ceremony at Gisors known as 'the cutting of the elm' in 1188, they used the Knights Templar as their military arm. Then, beginning sometime between sixteen twenty or thirty, a secret society called the *Compagnie du Saint-Sacrament*, which resembled a neo-Templar group and was founded by a French nobleman, was said to be closely associated with the Prieure de Sion.

"But in 1665 they were charged with 'un-Catholic activities' by Louis XIV and disbanded, but supposedly managed to hide their secret files somewhere in Paris. Naturally, they've never been found."

However, Fischer said, a collection called *Dossiers Secrets* of the *Prieure de Sion*, was somewhat well known though widely considered incomplete, and thus inconclusive. "A briefcase containing the complete *Dossiers Secrets* disappeared after a courier tried to deliver it to someone in East Germany but was turned away by authorities," he said, adding that the courier was found dead on the railroad tracks, apparently thrown from the Paris-Geneva express. "That was in 1967. The courier's name was Fakhar ul Islam," Fischer added. Linus then asked if they had learned any more about Gervan's scroll. Fischer read from his notes.

The alchemy part of the text, he said, was a formula for sealing something in a composition that was, essentially, a type of clear glass.

An insect became the gallant though unwilling subject of their attempt to duplicate the process, he said. "It worked poorly, though we only tried once," the professor added, leaving the question about bio samples open. Indeed, he noted that fleshy corpses have survived thousands of years frozen in glaciers, and buried skeletal remains thousands of years more. Why not something encased in glass? They wondered if anyone else had taken the scroll solution that far.

"Maybe they think some special Merovingian sample has been preserved in this way," Linus guessed.

"Why stop there, *Herr* Linus," Fischer asked. "The Merovingians claimed to be descended from Noah, and some say from Christ himself."

Fischer further explained that the text portion of the scroll bore interesting references which he didn't completely understand – yet. The *Cave of the Seven Sleepers* was mentioned, he said, recalling the parable of seven young Christians, entombed in a cave by the Roman emperor Decian in the third century. "They awoke and emerged two hundred years later during the reign of the Christian emperor Theodosius," he explained.

"Then there is a line from the Book of Proverbs," he continued, handing Linus a small, open bible. Linus read the highlighted passage:

She standeth in the top of high places,
by the way in the places of the paths.
She crieth at the gates.

Only the last sentence was in the scroll, Fischer said, though he was certain that the text was incomplete and that another portion existed. "There is a references to a stone, or tablet. I believe that the second half of the text exists as an inscription in stone. Someplace... " he said.

"Near the Cave of Seven Sleepers," Linus offered. Fischer shrugged and said,

"We will find out. It is on our ..."

But before he could finish, Linus held up his hand. Something passing outside a window across the room had caught the corner of his eye. It was a windy night. Maybe it was a tossed branch, he thought. But he thought not.

Suddenly Ute's eyes jerked to the window behind him and she gasped. Linus turned to see a pair of eyes cut out of a black mask staring in. He looked around the room – a grim, black-clad figure was filling every window frame. Linus slipped his Blackberry under his seat cushion then grabbed a handful of Fischer's notes and flipped them into the fire. The front door crashed open and, within seconds, they were surrounded by baton-wielding, black-hooded commandos. The three were easily overcome and bound to their chairs with a soft rope, like curtain cord. Then all three were photographed.

Fischer scowled as his face disappeared beneath a black sack. Ute angrily tossed her head, shouting *"Nein! Nein!."* It was the last thing Linus saw before *his* head was sacked as well. As he sat in the blindness of the hood, Linus heard the resisting innkeeper being dragged in. A table crashed, some dinnerware splattered, then the ruckus ended. The objective had been met. The victims were bound, bagged, and helpless. Hard-heeled steps clicked out of the room then returned a few moments later – though two sets of heels were clacking this time. Someone had been waiting outside for the all clear, Linus thought.

The footsteps stopped near his chair. His eyes scanned the darkness for a stress in the fabric, or a pinhole – some chance to catch a glimpse of his captors. The hood was completely opaque. But his eyes began to get a bit watery as he whiffed a faint aroma. Chamomile. Maybe a perfume or cologne, maybe the residue from a strong soap or shampoo. It was his only allergy, and the last time it struck was when he was at the *Blauer Apfel* bar. With Melisandre.

Paper rustled as the intruders photographed what notes were left on the table. Hopefully, the most important stuff was in the fire. All of it was in their heads. Linus wondered how far their captors would go to get it out. A pair of hands frisked away his wallet and keys. Doubtless they'd find his cameras and computer in the trunk, but they wouldn't find anything useful unless they got his hidden Blackberry. Which they wouldn't... as long as he could stay seated.

After a few moments of silence the clacking heels left the room – the commander had left, he thought. The trio sat still, awaiting their fate. But nothing else happened – for a full ten minutes. Linus realized that they might be alone. He jumped in his chair, moving it about six inches, then braced for a reaction. Still, nothing happened. "They're gone," he said. As quickly as the raiders had swarmed, they had vanished. "Who's near me?" he asked.

"I believe I am on your right," Fischer said.

"Don't move," Linus instructed. He pulled his tied hands over the back of the chair and stood up but slipped on a saucer and stumbled to his knees. He crawled over broken dishes until he bumped into Fischer, then fingered along Fisher's chair until he found his tied wrists. The knot was simple and Linus had it off quickly. Fischer jumped up sputtering and pulled off his hood.

"Who else have you brought with you, *Herr* Linus?" he snapped as he freed Ute but ignored Linus.

"Goddammit Ervin! Untie me!" Linus protested. Fischer rubbed Ute's wrists then turned to Linus and pulled off his hood.

"Did you draw them a map?" he groused as he plucked at the knot on Linus's wrists. Ute freed the innkeeper, who began ranting.

"What makes you so sure you and Ute didn't lead them here?" Linus retorted, rubbing his wrists, surveying the table. Oddly, everything was there – notebooks, documents, personal belongings. The innkeeper continued his diatribe as he righted tables and salvaged dinnerware. Linus retrieved his Blackberry from under his chair cushion and said,

"They photographed our notes. Did you hear?" Fischer nodded. Ute, sweat beading on her forehead, caved into a chair, righted a goblet, filled it with wine then drank it down.

"Who was it?" she said through the last swallow. The innkeeper made a last angry comment and stormed out of the room. Ute looked alarmed. "He's going to call the police," she said.

"Did you register with your real names?" Linus asked. Ute shook "no."

"I do not think we want to be here when the police arrive. We must leave immediate... " Fischer began. Linus raised a finger to shush him, found a pen and turned to a blank page in his notebook. *There may be listening devices in the room* he wrote. *Get your things and meet me outside.*

They bailed into the dark parking lot and checked their cars. Linus's trunk was ajar, bumping gently in the warm wind. His keys were still stuck in the latch but his bags had been rifled. His laptop was sitting atop his strewn clothes. The CD burner was still open. They had dumped everything off onto discs. But nothing was missing, from either car. The raiders merely wanted to acquire their information, but not deprive the owners of it. And, from the shoddy restraints, the trio figured they were supposed to free themselves quickly.

"So they can track us," Linus said, and the others agreed – though Ute seemed most affronted.

"We're not aggressive enough. We must do as they do, investigate these map locations and take anything of importance," she protested.

"By what means," Linus asked, somewhat unconvinced by the sudden boldness of the bookish curator.

"By whatever means necessary," she demanded. Linus smirked and muttered,

"Great."

"If you're not up to it..." she said, in his face.

"I've already taken my bullet. You next? Maybe you won't be so lucky."

"I am not afraid. Why do we need you at all? We already know how to make photographs!" she retorted.

"*Bitte. Bitte,*" Fischer implored. "We have enough to concern us without making enemies of each other." Fischer knew that now, more than ever, they'd need Linus's young legs – and muscle. The stakes were going up and the game was turning deadlier. Ute backed off and turned away. "Perhaps she is right," Fischer said to Linus. "If there is something of interest, perhaps we can be more offensive, but without taking drastic risks." Indeed Linus's only aversion was to recklessness, and not necessarily to risk.

"The map covers a wide area. Where would we begin?" he asked. Ute moved back into the conversation, still peeved.

"Northern France. The Merovingian seat. They want to establish a Merovingian bloodline. That's where they'll be," she asserted.

"I suggest we concentrate on the city of Stenay, in the *Ardennes*, as it is an ancient Merovingian stronghold," Fischer said.

"That's one," Linus responded.

"And the city of Tournai in Belgium, where the tomb of King Childeric was discovered," Fischer added.

"Not on the map," Linus responded. But since it was an important Merovingian location and near Stenay, Fischer thought it was worth a look.

"Much of the Merovingian culture has been moved there. Any Merovingian genealogists would have a station there," he said.

"Okay, then. That's two," Linus said. Ute spoke up.

"Two only," she said. Fischer caught her inference immediately.

"Ute, we should *each* take an assignment... " he began.

"No. I go with you," Ute said.

"But our chances are better if we each... "

"No!" she insisted. "*He* can go alone," she stated, pressing her finger onto Linus's breast. "But I stay with you." There was no use arguing. Anyway, Linus knew Ute was right – the younger woman should stay with the older man. They decided that Linus would do Tournai. Ute and Fischer, Stenay. The pressure to hurry was building.

"Use e-mail. I'll send you some images so you can be on the lookout for certain faces," Linus said, then reminded them that whoever pulled off tonight's raid had *their* pictures as well. "Change your appearance. Hair color. Beard. Clothes. Eyeglasses. It's almost certain they'll try to follow," he warned and added, "Take an indirect route. Change cars often. Lose them."

"We'll manage," Ute snarled, objecting to his lecture. She spun on her heel and headed for their car.

"What's up with *her*?" Linus asked. Fischer took Linus's hand, squeezed hard and looked deep into his face.

"Gervan was her father," he said. Linus wished he had known sooner. He looked into the Fischer's gray eyes.

"We were lucky tonight, Ervin. Be careful," he said. With an open palm, the good professor Fischer patted Linus's chest and said,

"You too, *Herr* Linus. You, too."

Chapter 17. CASING *Saint Brice*

August 3rd. Tournai, Belgium. Day 13.

"There! Shoot that!" the driver said, pointing out the windshield of the van, coffee sloshing over the brim of his cup. His partner raised his camera and got the shot – two young women entering the basement of *Saint Brice*, one of Tournai's oldest churches. One woman had a briefcase and the other was carrying a handbag.

"Look at the way she's scanning," the guy said. "And look at her hand in her bag like that. She got a gun in there," he added as his rocky-featured partner continued taping. For two days they'd been skulking around the medieval streets and ancient passageways of Tournai, impersonating phone workers in their blue jump suits and matching van. They arrived early and stayed late – always in the shadow of the ancient church. Always with a clear view of the office entrance at the rear. The women went out of view. The driver flipped open his handi – Euro name for cell phone.

"They've arrived," he said, and, "They've added security." The person on the other end responded. Give them all day, he said. Let them do their work. Then make a move after sundown. The driver grunted "Okay" and folded the phone.

"What do we do?" his partner asked. The driver said,

"We take them tonight."

The Merovingian Seat

Linus made it out of the Black Forest and through the hills south of Strasbourg without being stopped by the police, who undoubtedly would want to question him about the strange commando raid at *Land Haus*. He didn't see anyone shadowing him either, but kept his guard up just in case. He was almost two hundred miles away from the *Laud Haus* inn now, hoping that Fischer and Ute had made it just as far – far enough to be safe. They hadn't broken any laws. No international dragnet would be cast to snare them. And two hundred miles was well beyond the reach of the local constabulary. So Linus began to relax.

As he pushed through the dark countryside the forest thinned and the landscape opened up. The roads were narrow but they were empty, smooth and fairly straight. It was just after two a.m. – nineteen hours since his day began with Jules's funeral at *Domaine deBouillon*. After driving twelve hours to meet Fischer and Ute at *Land Haus*, Linus had expected a restful night. But the mugging at the hands of the masked commandos left them only one choice – to drive as fast and as far as possible, right away. Four hours and two hundred miles later, the "as far as possible" point was coming up quickly. He had to find a place to stop and sleep.

A secluded turnout and a reclining car seat was looking every bit as inviting as a suite at the Ritz. He pulled onto a dirt tractor path, left the windows open a crack and locked all the doors, but he left his keys in the ignition – in case he needed them in a hurry. Then he peeled off his jacket and rolled up his sleeve. The gunshot wound on his upper left arm looked angry and distorted from overuse, but uninfected. A few threads of catgut were twisting awkwardly out of their little puncture holes and the blood seepage painted a crusty trickle all the way down below his elbow.

He peeled off the bloody gauze then wrapped and tied a clean handkerchief around the wound. Then, with Blackberry set to wake him in four hours, he lowered the seat, lay back and fell asleep.

It was just after seven a.m. when the alarm went on. The day was bright but his car was cool in the shade of the trees. It seemed as though only an instant had passed since he closed his eyes – not much for rest, but enough to get the adrenaline flowing. He'd need it. The trip to Tournai, a small city in southwestern Belgium, would take twelve more hours. He rubbed the sleep out of his eyes, yawned, started the car and began driving.

A few miles away he found a place to wash-up and grab a quick breakfast, then he pushed northwest toward Belgium and the *Ardennes*. It was afternoon when he passed signs for Stenay – destination of Fischer and Ute. He figured they were probably there by now, checking into a hotel. But Tournai was still about three hundred miles away.

He had taken enough twists and turns to spot even the ablest tracker and was confident that he wasn't being tailed. But his car had been seen by too many people, he thought – at Rennes le Château, *Montsegur, Domaine deBouillon*, and possibly by the innkeeper at *Land Haus*. It was time for another change.

Thinking about the hundreds in drop-off fees he was racking up and the long relationship with a big credit card balance he was going to have if this story didn't pan out and pay off, Linus found an outlet of his rental agency and swapped for another BMW, this time dark blue. It was after eight o'clock and already dark when he got into Tournai.

He passed through a small industrial zone then followed the river *Shelde* through the outer city and into the medieval center of town. He checked his mirror as he rolled along the narrow, cobble-paved streets, still confident that he hadn't been followed but watching just the same.

The quaint shops and bistros on both sides were closed. Dim nightlight shone through their curtained windows. Some of the apartment windows above them were already shuttered for the night, others were showing warm light through drawn curtains. Only a few cars were moving, only a few people were on the street. As in most medium-sized European cities, activity dropped off sharply after dusk.

He pulled over to the curb near an alley and stopped the car, looked around then opened an interior light and checked his map. Most of the historical sites and monuments were clustered around the old city – the city centrum. So were the churches – at least seven of them.

He fired-up his Blackberry, made an internet connection, then found the official website for Tournai. The city had a population of under 100,000 and was noted for tapestries, textiles, machinery and motors. The old city's rich and long history made it a Mecca for tourists, historians, scholars and archaeologists, the website said. He clicked on "culture" and a new text loaded. When he got to the paragraph about churches, two stood out as Merovingian sites which might be of interest to someone doing genealogy. The first, *Saint Piat*, was built atop the vestiges of a sixth century Merovingian basilica. The other, of even more obvious interest, was *Saint Brice*.

Saint Brice was built where the tomb of the Merovingian king Childeric was discovered in 1653. The basilica digs at *Piat*'s may be the best place to study Merovingian architecture, Linus thought, but Childeric's tomb meant that *Saint Brice* would likely be surrounded by graves. And graveyards meant burial records.

He located himself with the GPS on his Blackberry and charted a course to *Saint Brice*, then pulled up a few pages about Childeric's tomb. It was found in 1653 at the edge of a cemetery near *Saint Brice*. A quantity of life-sized gold bees – like the ones on the gates at *Domaine deBouillon*, symbol of the Merovingians – were recovered from the grave. Curiously, Napoleon Bonaparte had some of Childeric's bees sewn into his coronation vestment. Linus saved the information to a file then signed off. Childeric's tomb – and whatever else he could dig up – was waiting for him across town.

Saving a Life – or Two

Linus parked his car on a narrow cobblestone street then slipped into the shadowy burial plot at the foot of *Saint Brice*, a massive brownstone church. It was after sunset and the small churchyard, nestled in the ancient village of Old Tournai, was deserted. Above him, the three dark spires spiked up into the night, flood-lighted against a black sky. He shaved close along the side wall toward a basement window then bent down for a look inside. Two women were in a small office. The window was dirty and the light was dim but it was enough for Linus to see their faces. One was slightly built and had long, straight hair. She was wearing glasses and a dark overcoat and holding a large *attaché* case as though she was ready to leave. Her face was unfamiliar.

But the *other*, with her cropped hair, yellow-trimmed beret and dark, form-fitting clothes, was a familiar type. Her back was to him but as soon as she turned Linus saw who she was – the driver of Melisandre's getaway car on the night Jules died at *Montsegur*. An big ancient-looking book or log – probably death records – was on a nearby desk.

He felt his way through the darkness and hid behind the thick shrubs ringing a small crucifixion on a marble garden pedestal, then settled down and waited with the tire-iron from his trunk cradled on his lap. After about twenty minutes, the basement office lights went out. Linus crouched tighter into his hiding spot as one of the woman – the one he recognized – climbed the steps and looked around, then beckoned the other woman forward. They walked across the churchyard, past Linus and toward the gate.

Suddenly, a blue van with its lights out sped forward and skidded to a halt just ahead of the women on the sidewalk. The doors flung open and two hefty guys in jumpsuits leapt out.

"*Vas-y! Vas-y!*" the first woman shouted as she squared herself in the path of the two men. The one carrying the *attaché* turned and ran back through the churchyard, past Linus and out the other side. Her companion stayed and fought the attackers like a ninja. Her kicks, spins and punches took them by surprise and she landed blow after blow with her fists and feet.

One of the men tried to side-track her and pursue the escaping companion but the bodyguard knocked him to the ground with a kidney kick. It was a stunning move, but it came with a price. The other guy caught her open side and landed a blow across her head with a black baton. The woman crumbled to her knees. She tried to recover but they kicked her to the ground. Linus's chest pounded. His grip on the tire iron tightened. He had imagined using it to protect *himself*, and didn't really want to use it at all. His hope that they'd leave her alone once she was down kept him frozen in place. Indeed, the kicking stopped. One guy took off through the churchyard in pursuit of the companion.

Then Linus heard the snap of an opening switchblade and saw the guy take a knee beside the semi-conscious victim. He grabbed her hair and pulled her head back to expose her neck, like he was going to cut her throat. Linus had seen enough. He charged out of hiding and slashed the heavy tire iron down on the knifeman's forearm which snapped with a loud, sickening pop. The would-be killer screamed in agony. Linus backhanded the iron across his jaw and left him in an unconscious heap in the gutter.

He kicked the knife down a storm drain then found a gun in the assailant's boot and dumped that, too. The guy was still alive but his mouth was bloody, his jaw broken, and his forearm dangling like a snapped twig. In short, no longer a threat – to *anyone*. Linus checked the woman's bloody face. She was groggy but probably okay. He dragged her off the sidewalk and into the churchyard. Then, with tire iron still in hand, he took off after the others.

He raced into the dark passageways that were the ancient city's streets. At a small square where three passages converged, he stopped and listened, struggling to quiet his own heavy breaths. An image of the other woman, slumped in a doorway with smashed glasses and a slit throat, flashed his mind and he figured it was hopeless. But then he heard a faint crash, like a case of bottles spilled on a cobblestone street. Maybe he *hadn't* lost them after all. He jogged toward the sound then stopped at the next junction. This time it was a single bottle skipping across the stones that he heard, and it was very close.

He peeked around the corner and saw women's feet sticking out of a doorway, then hurried ahead. It was her, from the church. A large, bloody lump had risen on her forehead but she was alive. Her eyes fluttered as she fought to remain conscious and struggled to get up. Her *attaché* was gone.

He checked for stab wounds and serious bleeding, found none, then laid her head gently down and ran after the mugger. He slowed at each bend in the passage until finally, around the third corner, he saw a dark figure walking briskly and carrying an *attaché*. It had to be him. Linus followed at a safe distance.

About two blocks away the guy ducked into a back alley, out of sight. Linus crept up to the entrance and craned his neck for a look around the corner. The guy was crouched behind some crates, rifling the contents of the *attaché* in the beam of a small flashlight. Linus waited until he was fully engrossed in his plunder then approached him on soft steps, tire iron poised. He was about four feet away when the guy sensed him and looked up. His astonished face twisted with fear as he realized – too late – that there was a tire iron headed for the base of his skull. One stroke and the guy was face-first on the cobblestones. Linus pulled the *attaché* case out from under him, stuffed the spilled contents in into it and hurried out of the alley.

He walked at almost a jog as he maneuvered back through the labyrinthine streets and passages. He had to get to his car without passing the church as surely the police were all over the place by now. He looked skyward with every twist and turn until he saw the tall steeples of *Saint Brice*. As he expected, faint blue police lights were flickering along the eaves. He backtracked, then cut sideways through some alleys and passages until he came out on the street where he was parked. He stayed close to the dark, stuccoed buildings as the church, then the police and crime scene, came into view. He was close enough to be seen, but not too close to sneak away – if he could get his car moving without starting it. Luckily, the road behind him was slightly sloped.

When the cops were all turned away, he got in, disabled the dome light, turned the ignition one click and shifted into neutral. Then, with one foot out the open door, a good shove got him off the curb and rolling into the street. He leaned out and steered and, as soon as he was going fast enough, shifted into reverse and popped the clutch. The engine jump-started. Linus swung backward into an intersection, shifted to forward, clicked on his headlights. And calmly drove away.

Linus raced out of Tournai, into the countryside, then checked into the first hotel he found. As he stood in the bathroom replacing the bloody handkerchief on his wounded arm with a small towel, he noticed the uncontrollable tremble of his hands. The violence invading his life was taking a toll. He had been in tight spots before and had seen what violent humans could do to each other. But beating people over the head with a tire iron was way out of his league. Tonight he had reached the other side of a bridge that, so far, he had avoided crossing. The lines separating the good guys from the bad guys were blurring. He couldn't decide who was more dangerous; Kohlhertz and his gang, or Melisandre and hers.

Or perhaps the real danger was coming from within himself. He was even questioning whether Fischer and Ute were trustworthy.

And to make matters worse, his "big story" was beginning to look like a run-of-the-mill, evil versus evil, struggle. One greedy, power-hungry faction fighting with another greedy, power-hungry faction. Another battle between degenerates, waged in obscurity and, in the end, worth only a few lines. But something kept telling him to continue his pursuit, to find the truth.

As soon as he was cleaned up he turned to the liberated *attaché* case on the bed – probably filled with a bunch of dull death records from a time long past, he thought. He sat on the bed and began sifting the contents.

The first thing he found was a small ledger bearing names with their birth and death dates. They were listed in ascending order, beginning in the fifth century and ending in the seventh. Beside each date there was another name, probably a cemetery or village, probably the location of each grave.

Only five pages out of about fifty were filled, and there were only six names on each page. Obviously, these were the culls for a larger record, maybe graves slated to be exhumed, he thought. Other than that the ledger yielded nothing concrete.

Next he pulled out a thin report folder. The first page was a cover sheet with a simple headline. The next five pages were maps with locations marked and numbered in red. Linus recognized many of them as places he saw plotted on the map in Melisandre's Berlin headquarters. Several pages with brief descriptions of each site, listed by country, followed:

LOCATIONS OF PRIMARY FOCUS

FRANCE

01. Paris – church of La Madeleine, Ile-de-la-Cité;
    several items of interest possibly present.
02. Arques – Near Rennes-le-Château – tomb similar to that
    depicted in Poussin's "Shepherds of Arcadia" painting.
03. Aix-en-Provence – Church of Saint Maximin.
04. Verdun – c1024 / church founded.
05. Bayeux – c1027 / church founded.
06. Bellevault – c1034 / church founded.
07. LeMans – c1040 / church founded.
08. Rheims – c1043 / church founded.
09. Besançon – c1049 / church founded.
10. Rennes-le-Château – c1059 / church consecrated.
11. Vezelay – Abbey Church of Ste.Marie-Madeleine: crypt
    below transept, circa 9th century.
12. Stenay – aka Satanicum – Merovingian capital, location
    of royal palace,   (Childeric tomb at St.Brice in Tournai, Belgium).

ENGLAND

13. Exeter – 10th century: Cathedral at Exeter said to   contain one item.
14. Wiggenhall – Cemetery consecrated; dwelling place of
    Hermit Joan in early 13th century.

SPAIN

15. Oviedo – 11th century catalog lists presence of one item.

ITALY

16. Venice – Church of Saint Elena: possible location of two items; Franciscan
    church also claimed as one time location of one item.

INDIA

17. Mari – small village, with nearby mountain – Pindi Point –
    on top of which is the tomb called Mai Mari da Asthan.
18. Srinagar – small village in Kashmir, location of tomb called Rozabal.

Though Linus didn't have any strong, specific reasons to doubt Melisandre's story about her genealogy project, few of the places on the list struck him as having strong Merovingian connections. He fished through the *attaché* case again, came up with a bunch of travel receipts and a few phone numbers – things he would copy and keep for later investigation – but nothing which provided any immediate answers.

He stuffed everything back into the case then opened his Blackberry and checked his e-mail. As expected, there was a message from 'Anfortas'. Fischer and Ute had made it safely to Stenay and sent the name of their hotel. There was also a video message from Jamie Richards, the actress – another plea to purchase his compromising photos. Linus watched then deleted it and checked the time. It was about eleven thirty. Fischer and Ute would be in their rooms. He switched to phone mode and dialed. Fischer, sounding fully alert and wide awake, answered on the first ring.

More Message Revealed

"Herr Linus," Fischer said without saying "hello", having recognized the number being displayed on his "handi", or cell phone. "I take it all is well?" he asked. Linus replied,

"All is reasonably well."

"And Tournai?"

"More violence."

"Hmmm."

"At *Saint Brice*. Two women, one I recognized. She was with Melisandre at *Montsegur* when Jules the priest went over the edge. Two thugs showed up and jumped them. One of the women was almost murdered."

"Almost?"

"Yes. No one was killed."

"But they saw you."

"Not the women, no. But I have a feeling the two thugs will remember me for a very long time," he said.

"I see. Kohlhertz's men?"

"I don't know. That would be my guess. But who's man is *he*?"

"Perhaps his own. Perhaps not," Fischer said. "Irregardless, he will tire of your interference, *Herr* Linus. He will want to kill you now. This I am certain."

"Ah, maybe," Linus semi-agreed, deflecting the concern. "I snatched a briefcase full of documents. I'll give you copies. So what's happening in Stenay? Any sign of Melisandre or the Veronica woman?"

"No. And yes."

"Are they there?"

"Possibly, but I haven't seen them. Ute and I visited the *Musée Archeologique* this afternoon. There was a man I had seen before, I didn't recall where. So I approached and asked. He had given a lecture some time ago and I was in attendance. He is an expert in ancient documents. And one of your countrymen.

"One year ago he was in Berlin as a visiting lecturer at the University. I reminded him of that and he was very engaging. Naturally, I asked if he was working here in Stenay and he revealed that he has been commissioned for a private project."

"Private project for whom?" Linus quizzed.

"He did not say. So I pretended I also had been approached for such work, by a woman whom I did not know, and that I could not accept the commission because of other commitments. He made a joke about being second choice, so I assumed ... "

"That the person who contracted him was a woman."

"Precisely."

"That's very good, Ervin. You are very sly," Linus said.

"Then I will be flattered, *Herr* Linus, as I am sure in your circles that is a compliment. I further suggested we meet for lunch tomorrow and asked for his hotel. He said he was a guest at a private residence nearby and said he'd contact me when he had a free moment. Naturally, I gave him an erroneous address."

"I bet he's working for Melisandre."

"We would not bet against you."

"Too bad we don't know where he's staying."

"Ahhh, but we do, actually. Ute followed him. He was taken in a car – with a female chauffeur, incidentally – to a large stone house in the Belgian forest. It is about thirty kilometers from here."

"You *are* getting good at this, Ervin."

"Aft er a time one is bound to develop instincts, *Herr* Linus. Willingly or not," he said then added. Linus's wheels were turning.

"Thirty kilometers ... about twenty miles." he said. "Is Ute still there, at the house?"

"No. I called her back."

"Why?"

"She was needed."

"You should've let her stay and watch for awhile."

"Yes. That was my intention. But something very important has arisen."

"Like... *what*?"

"I have been working on the message of Gervan's scroll. I believe I have discovered the location of the second half of the message," he said. It was major. Linus was surprised. "You recall that I said the scroll mentioned the Cave of the Seven Sleepers?

"Seven entombed Christians, released two hundred years later," Linus said.

"Essentially. And also the line from Proverbs?"

"She crieth at the gates," Linus recalled.

"I don't know why it did not occur to me sooner, how the two may be connected. There is a grotto near Ephesus, in Turkey, which is believed to be ..."

"The Cave of the Seven Sleepers," Linus interjected.

"Correct. And, as concerns, "she crieth at the gates", I have discovered – perhaps I should say I *believe* I have discovered – that the *she* in this case is the inscription containing the second half of the message... "

"Which is located someplace near the entrance, or gate, to the grotto known as the Cave of the Seven Sleepers," Linus concluded, and Fischer added,

"Near Ephesus, in Turkey. I have already dispatched Ute. She took a late flight and should arrive there by morning. If she finds something she will call then return immediately."

"That's good news," Linus said. If the lead panned out, it would also mean that his trust in Fischer and Ute wasn't misplaced.

"I must caution you not to become overly optimistic," Fischer said. "We must wait and see if Ute is successful then evaluate whatever new material we acquire."

"Of course," Linus agreed. "In the meantime I think you should stay out of sight. And keep your cell phone charged. I'm going to contact Melisandre... at least find out where she is. Probably at that house in the forest."

"I think so as well," Fischer said. "Then I will speak with you anon. *Gute Nacht, Herr* Linus," he added, and Linus replied,

"G'night Ervin. And thanks."

Re-connected

Linus toggled to the number for *Domaine deBouillon* and pressed "dial". A woman answered. "*Allo.*"

"Melisandre, *si'l vous plait.*" The brief pause that followed made him wonder if he had been recognized, as though his call was expected. Finally she replied – in English.

"Who is calling please?"

"Linus Mercator," he said, followed by another pause.

"*Madame* is not available this moment, *Monsieur* Mercator, but she did leave a message in case you would call. She has gone to Belgium and invites you to join her there if you wish," the woman said. At first Linus was surprised by the easy invitation. But on second thought, apart from the rudeness of his abrupt exit, Melisandre had no real reason to avoid him – at least none that he knew. And plenty of reason to find him – whether she knew it or not. In any case, it was what he wanted so he accepted.

The woman directed him first to Stenay, in Belgium, then on to "the lodge" in the *Ardennes* where Melisandre was staying. "When shall I tell her you will be arriving?" she asked.

"Tomorrow evening, no later than nine," Linus replied, though he knew he'd go there much sooner, watch the comings and goings, then try to catch them off balance. The woman said she would relay the message. Linus hung up and called Fischer again.

"Your hunch appears to be right," he said. "I've been invited to meet Melisandre someplace in the Belgian *Ardennes*."

"It's the house in the forest, that Ute found," Fischer conjectured, and he gave Linus the name of his hotel in Stenay.

"I'll pick you up in early afternoon and we'll go have a look," Linus said, and Fischer replied,

"Good. Sometime after lunch."

Exhaustion was bearing down hard but Linus wanted to do one more thing before sleeping – a quick internet search on the city of Ephesus, where the Cave of the Seven Sleepers was located. Where Ute had gone. He found an abstract at an online magazine site focusing on Mediterranean cities.

Eph-e-sus (ef'i-sus). - Ancient city of Greek Asia Minor in present-day western Turkey. Once a major seaport commerce center on the Aegean Sea. Its temple, dedicated to Artemis or, in Roman times, Diana, was one of the Seven Wonders of the World. Saint Paul visited the city on his missionary journeys. ALSO: depending upon the source, the place where Mary Magdalene died and was interred near a grotto known as the Cave of the Seven Sleepers.

The last sentence tingled along his neck. Ephesus, and the Cave of the Seven Sleepers, was possibly the final resting place of Mary Magdalene. It was a name that was surfacing more and more lately. Linus figured it was time to explore how the Magdalen fit into the equation.

Chapter 18. The LODGE in SATANICUM

August 4th.
The Ardennes, Belgium. Day 14.

Fischer was running for the car as soon it pulled into the hotel
parking lot. Linus had overslept – all the driving and fighting had laid
him low – and was an hour late. The old professor didn't seem to
care.

"News from Ute," he said as he climbed in and locked the doors.
Ute had reported that the Cave of the Seven Sleepers was at a ruined
temple, which was built at the grotto in the first century, and is now a
museum. "There is a weeping woman statue which was found near
the cave."

"She crieth at the gate," Linus said. It was the line from Proverbs
that was in Kohlhertz's scroll.

"When Ute first found nothing, she decided on a less elegant
approach and tipped it upside down. And there it was. A text, carved
into the bottom of the pedestal," he said, beaming. She had already
sent pictures, he said, and was on her way back with rubbings. Linus
got a large brown envelope from the back seat and handed it to
Fischer. It contained info from the recovered *attaché*.

"I picked this up last night in Tournai. Some of it overlaps their
map," he said. Fischer sifted the contents with interest as they drove
out of Stenay, through the hilly *Ardennes* and into Belgium. Stenay
was once known as *Satanicum* and was an ancient Merovingian
capital, Fischer said, adding that they were in sacred part of the
Ardennes called the *Forest of Woevres*.

The landscape became darker as the tall pine groves grew
thicker. Linus slowed, checked his directions, and said, "I think this is

it," as they passed by a driveway into the trees on their left. A large rock at its side was carved with the profile of a bear – Ursa, the Merovingian totem.

"Ute photographed that. This is where the documents expert was taken," Fischer confirmed.

"Drop me off, then hook up with Ute as soon as she gets in," Linus said as he turned into the entrance. The driveway wound for about a quarter of a mile before the gray stones of the house came into sight. It wasn't a grand *Château*, like *Domaine deBouillon*. It was more of a lodge made of field stone and rough-hewn wood, overlooking a small valley. A blue sedan with an open trunk was parked out front and a uniformed woman – the driver – was loading a suitcase as a man got into the car.

"That's him, the documents expert that Ute followed," Fischer said. "His name is Archer."

"Looks like he's going someplace."

"Not too close," Fischer warned, afraid he'd be recognized. Linus stopped well away from the sedan, opened the door and got out. Fischer slid in behind the wheel as Linus grabbed the *attaché* then leaned on Fischer's open window.

"Let's do this. Tell Ute we'll meet her in Paris, then follow that car and see where they take this Archer guy," he said as the sedan rounded the circular driveway then headed out. Fischer dipped his head as it passed.

"I'll call you later," he said, then he drove off in pursuit. With the liberated *attaché* in hand, Linus headed for the front door. A woman about fifty in a plain black skirt and white blouse answered the door. He said, "Linus Mercator to see *Madame*." She checked her watch. "I'm sorry. I'm early," he apologized. The woman smiled pleasantly.

"Well it's a sight better than sorry I'm late then, isn't it," she said, sidestepping to let him in. She was Irish, with a brogue. "If you would like to wait in here I will inform *Madame*," she said, depositing Linus into an expansive room with exposed beams, peaked ceiling, and a huge stone hearth. The wall to his left was a bank of

French doors onto a patio with a long view of green fields rolling gently away to a tree line beyond. The sky was a gray and white canopy of clouds. Nothing outside was moving, not even birds. The only sound was the ticking of an old wooden clock on the mantle. Until Melisandre entered.

"Linus. How nice of you to be so early," she remarked.

"Eager to see you," he replied. She smiled disbelievingly. Her appearance had changed again since he'd last seen her. Her hair – still short – was its original soft chestnut brown and not spiked blonde. And for the first time since they'd met she was wearing jeans. Her blouse was plain and crisply pressed, her brown boots freshly shined.

"Where did you go?" she asked. His departure from *Domaine deBouillon* was abrupt. She took his outstretched hand then leaned forward and kissed his cheek. Suddenly his allergy was activated and his eyes were itching. An image of the commando raid flashed in his head. He was catching the delicate scent of chamomile in her hair – same scent he caught while sitting at *Land Haus* with his hands tied behind him and his head in a thick black sack. At best it was a curious coincidence. At worst, damning evidence.

"I'm sorry I just disappeared like that," he apologized.

"How's the wounded arm?"

"Ah, healing nicely I think."

"Good. I was just about to go for a walk. Care to join me?" she asked which, of course, he did. Her eyes fell on the *attaché* case he had set on the floor. Clearly she knew exactly what – and whose – it was. "Perhaps you'd like to wash up first?" she asked, nodding toward the case as though it were his luggage.

"I think this belongs to you," he said as he picked it up and gave it to her. Melisandre didn't ask so Linus figured she knew where he got it. And though she must've wanted an explanation for what he was doing at *Saint Brice*, she didn't ask that, either. Linus was sure she'd get around to it eventually. Melisandre took the case, thanked him and, leaving the room, said,

"I'll just be a second to change my shoes."

Linus and Melisandre left the lodge and walked a well-worn path along the edge of the field beyond. "I was told that an unknown person intervened heroically in Tournai. Saved one life, possibly two," Melisandre said as they walked.

"Heroic probably isn't the right word," he replied. "The two women are okay?"

"They're fine."

"What about the two creeps?"

"One was taken into custody at the church. The other hasn't been found."

"Who were they?" he asked.

"Unfortunately *Herr* Kohlhertz still thinks we have something he wants," she said, implying they were working for Kohlhertz.

"And you're certain you don't? Have something?" Melisandre shook her head. "The scroll Gervan was working on?" Linus questioned further.

"Kohlhertz has it. I have a copy," she said.

"Sure. But do you know what the scroll means?"

"No. But I may have some new information very soon."

"Like ... ?" Melisandre smiled. She had said enough and wasn't offering details just yet. Of course, she was unaware that Linus knew she had engaged another expert as Gervan's replacement. "If it turns out to be important I'll tell you right away," she said, though Linus doubted that she'd be so forthcoming.

"So, is Kohlhertz under arrest yet?" he asked.

"No. But he's on the run," she replied, and Linus didn't bother to register his astonishment that the cops still weren't involved.

They walked for about a quarter mile, up along a ridge which overlooked the thick, green-black forest. The trail leveled off near a big elm in a small clearing. Melisandre stopped and sat on a rock beside the tree. Linus stood beside her, overlooking the view. "Fairly impressive... as forests go," Melisandre said, and Linus agreed. "This was once a very sacred place for Merovingians. In fact," she said as she stood up and rounded the big elm's trunk, "take a look." She pointed out what was left of an old carving. "Kind of hard to see now, but it was a bear."

"Ursa, the Merovingian symbol," Linus said.

"Dagobert the second, who may have been the last of the great Merovingians, lived in a palace near here with his Visigoth bride, Giselle de Razes. His kingdom covered most of what is now France, Germany and Belgium." Linus knew about Dagobert via Fischer's tutorial on the Merovingian dynasty and the mention of Dagobert in the mysterious parchments from Rennes-le-Château. And he remembered that Dagobert had been assassinated – while sleeping under a tree.

"On December twenty-third in 679, Dagobert, on a hunting trip, lay down under a tree for a midday nap and was pierced through the eye by a servant with a lance," she said. Linus looked at the large elm under which they were seated.

"This is Dagobert's tree," he said. Melisandre half nodded, half shrugged. Though it seemed more likely that it was a *descendant* of the original elm, the prospect was nonetheless haunting. "So what's your connection to all of this? Are the people behind your foundation trying to re-claim the throne of France?" Linus asked.

"I suppose you could say they were. But mostly they are just trying to re-establish their family tree, bring in the extended branches, to make sure the history isn't lost. Settle estates. Things like that. It's more a matter of pride and practicality than of power."

"I still don't see how a woman from way back in Boston gets mixed-up with neo-Merovingians."

"Well, as I say, it's only a very small part of what I do," she reiterated. She said that the *Novangelis* Foundation's interest in charitable work is much more intense than their interest in genealogy. But since Kohlhertz blundered into their lives, the bloodline search has taken on "much undeserved grandeur." Linus was – as ever – the skeptic.

When they got back to the house a small fire was burning in the hearth. Melisandre tossed her coat on a couch then stood drying her damp feet by the flames. Linus took off his jacket and joined her. "Thank you for returning the attaché case," she said as she rubbed the dampness out of her hands.

"Don't be *too* grateful. I went through everything that was in it," he confessed. Melisandre was unfazed.

"To find out who owned it, of course," she said slyly. "So how did you know to bring it here?"

"I recognized one of your *Novangelis* group. Your 'New Angels', as it were. One of the woman at *Saint Brice* last night was also the driver of your car at *Montsegur*."

"How did you happen to be in Tournai in the first place?"

"I want to do a story about the Rennes-le-Château mystery, so I came to learn about the Merovingian connection. Showing up at just the right time, that was luck," he stated, then asked, "And you think those guys were working for Kohlhertz? Is Kohlhertz working for someone else?"

"Who?"

"The *Priory of Sion*," Linus blurted. Melisandre looked troubled – for some reason – but not surprised. She didn't deny knowing about the secret society.

"I suppose it's possible, but judging from what I've heard of them I doubt they'd get involved with someone as ham-fisted as Kohlhertz," she said. Linus, unconvinced, and knowing that *most* goons-for-hire were ham-fisted brutes, thought, 'why not?'. Then Melisandre asked for – and got – a full accounting of what happened last night at *Saint Brice* – complete with graphic, bone-crunching, arm-dangling details of that split second when a mugging almost turned into a murder. Luckily this one didn't make that transition. Linus wasn't shaken to the core, so to speak, but Melisandre could see in his eyes that his mind would play those disturbing images many times in many nightmares. A few silent moments passed then Linus stood up.

"I should go now. Can someone call a cab for me?"

"It's getting late," she said, though it was only about six o'clock. "You can stay here tonight if you like. I'm not your enemy, Linus," she assured. The offer wasn't a total surprise. He smiled. "The information I'm expecting about the scroll should come within a day or so. It may be something of value for your story," she added.

Linus was beginning to wonder if he was being considered as a replacement for Jules. He figured he had nothing to gain by leaving, possibly much to gain by staying. So, once again, he accepted.

"I'm sincerely sorry for what you had to do in Tournai but I can't deny that I'm glad you did it. You've helped me twice, and very profoundly each time. I won't forget," Melisandre assured. About this much, at least, Linus knew Melisandre was sincere.

She said she'd tell Ailene – the Irish woman – to make up the guest quarters, then Melisandre left the room. Linus stood up and started looking over some of the titles on one of the large bookcases flanking the stone fireplace. Some of them were in French, others German. Most were in English. All were by, or about, women: The Good Earth, by Pearl Buck; Ma Vie, Edith Piaf's autobiography; Emily Dickinson; Charlotte, Emily and Anne Bronte; Germaine Greer.

Religion was well represented, too, in books about the likes of Margaret of Cortona – of course; Mary, mother of Jesus; the Magdalen; Phoebe and Junia; Paula and Marcella. And Melusine, the niece of Godfroi de Bouillon. And there were many other books by and about women from all walks of life. Melisandre returned and said, "Ailene is just having some sheets put on the bed. I'll show you up," and Linus dutifully followed.

"Ever read anything by or about men?" he asked. Melisandre smiled.

"Sure. George Sand," she said, referring to the pen name of Amandine Aurore Lucie Dupin, Baroness Dudevant, the French writer whose novels, plays, and essays focused on freedom and independence.

For women.

"Orly," Fischer said. "They went to Orly airport in Paris then he boarded a plane to Turkey," he added. He was talking about Melisandre's hired documents expert that Fischer had followed that afternoon. Linus was on the balcony of his upstairs room, overlooking the grass fields behind the lodge, his phone to his ear.

"They're catching up," he stated. "What's up with Ute?"

"Ute will be back tomorrow morning at seven o'clock." The thought of Melisandre's guy arriving in Turkey then Ute departing on the same plane was oddly amusing.

"We need to hurry, *Herr* Fischer," he said. He then recounted his visit to Dagobert's tree that afternoon and said Melisandre told him that the lodge was located approximately where Dagobert and Giselle had their palace.

"She appears more forthcoming with her Merovingian connections," Fischer observed. Linus agreed but added that maybe the Merovingian bloodline wasn't her central concern after all, and not as important to her as they thought.

"Stay there. Get a hotel in Paris and we'll meet Ute there tomorrow morning," Linus instructed. Paris was a four hour drive from the lodge so he'd have to get an early start.

"How will you get there?"

"I'll see if I can borrow a car. If not, I'll get someplace where I can rent one," he answered, though from the looks of the big garage-cum-chauffeur's quarters near the house he was confident there would be an extra vehicle around. He came in off the balcony just as Ailene, the house manager with the brogue, was delivering a tray of sandwiches. She asked if there was anything else – there wasn't – so she said good night and left.

He lay on the bed and toggled through his messages. There was another video from the actress, Jamie Richards. She was very beautiful, and very well spoken though she sounded a bit nervous. "Mister Mercator. You know who I am, and what I want. But you may not know all of my motives. The photos you took of me at Klaus's studio in Berlin may damage my box office power and have a negative impact on my earnings. Frankly, I don't expect much sympathy on that count. But money isn't my only concern. You see, all of my life I've dreamed of doing something important to help other people, mostly children, perhaps as part of a charitable foundation, perhaps even starting one of my own. Your photos could cause me to lose that dream.

"But I don't expect you to work for free and I'm still willing to make up for your losses if you don't release those pictures. It's not a bribe. Just a fair deal. Please don't take away my dream over something as insignificant as this. My posing really is separate from who and what I am. Please consider as much when making your choice."

The recording ended with her leaving a number and an address. Linus's finger hovered over the 'delete' key but, for some reason, he saved the message instead. Then he had a hot shower and ate a few of the small sandwiches on the tray. He wanted to be in Paris at about ten the next morning, which meant leaving the lodge before six. He made a few more notes then set the alarm on his Blackberry for 5:30 next morning.

August 5th. Day 15.
Skipping Breakfast

Linus awoke well before sunrise and even before the alarm. A thin layer of fog blanketed the rolling hills beyond his balcony, waiting for the warmth of daybreak to cook it off. Linus planned to disappear with it. He dressed quietly then left a note on the bed. He was restless, it said, and had decided to get an early start on his sightseeing tour. "I'll be back in evening," he wrote, then he headed for the large, barn-like garage with chauffeur's quarters on the second floor.

The office door wasn't locked. He slipped in and took one of the sets of keys that were hanging in a cabinet and tried them until he found the match – a new Daimler coupe. He pushed the switch to open the garage door – which must've woken at least the chauffeur upstairs – then hopped in the coupe and headed for the gate. As he raced away over the empty morning roads he wondered if they'd try to follow – as they would had he announced his departure time in advance. His meeting with Fischer and Ute, in a hotel on *Place du Tertre*, in *Montmartre*, Paris, was four hours away. He pressed harder on the accelerator. The car had plenty of power and got him away from the lodge quickly. He was sure he'd be long gone before anyone had a chance to give chase.

Chapter 19. In the SHADOW of SACRÉ COÉUR

It was a mild, sunny morning when Linus reached Paris. He parked on the shady *Rue Marcadet*, at the foot of *Montmartre*, and began climbing the long, concrete staircases up towards the basilica of *Sacré Coéur*. It was just after ten thirty when he reached the top and crossed through the small square known as *Place du Tertre*. The painters, portraitists and street performers were just setting up their easels, cases and canvasses. And the tourists were beginning to trickle into the square.

Linus hurried through the square to the highest side of *Montmartre*, went left along a narrow street and sighted a sign on a tiny, townhouse-style building saying '*Hôtel du Tertre*'. That was where he'd find Ute and Fischer. They were in room 13. He hurried upstairs to the modest suite with a panoramic view of Paris. Ute was sitting at a table near a window, poring over photographs and notes. She looked up and Linus said "hello."

"Guten Morgen," she replied. Fischer ushered Linus to the table.

"There are many important questions to discover," he said, picking through his notes about the inscription that Ute had retrieved from the Cave of the Seven Sleepers in Ephesus, Turkey. Fischer said he found what appeared to be a reference to "a sample", and he believed it to be a blood sample, preserved using the glass-encasement method described in the alchemy part of the scroll. "Though I am not sure who the sample donor is, exactly," he said. Linus noticed that Ute was pursing her lips.

"But you have a theory," he pressed. Fischer exhaled and sat at the table.

"It is not based on what we have found in the texts. It is based on something *you* gave me, *Herr* Linus," he said. Ute pushed around some papers until she found the list Linus had liberated from the Tournai *attaché*.

"An interesting pattern has finally emerged," she said, sharing the document across the table. She ran her finger down the numbered items and counted. "*Eins*. Paris. Church of la Madeleine on *Ile-de-la-Cité*, said to have a piece of Mary Magdalene's forehead, if you can imagine, which was supposedly touched by Christ after he rose from the dead and met Mary and the other woman in the garden."

"*Noli me tangere ...* do not touch me," Linus said. Christ had said it to the women. Ute nodded, then went on.

"*Zwei*. Arques. It is a village near Rennes-le-Château, where there is a tomb once considered a possible location of the Christ cadaver." Linus had already heard this from Jules. It was the tomb on the grassy knoll where he and Jules hid out after their farm house encounter with Kohlhertz. Ute continued with her list.

"*Drei*. Aix-en-Provence, also in southern France. In twelve-seventy-nine, some monks claimed that the body of Mary Magdalene was found in a crypt at the church of *Saint Maximin*," she said. Then she ran her finger down the list, from number four through ten. "Verdun, Bayeux, Bellevault, LeMans, Rheims, Besançon and Rennes-le-Château. All have churches founded under the patronage of Mary Magdalene.

"And here, *elf*," she continued, pointing at number eleven – Vezelay. "The Abbey church of *Sainte Marie-Madeleine* gained immense wealth during medieval times by possessing several Magdalene bones, which were kept in a crypt below the transept of the building."

"Vezelay is a most interesting Magdalene center," Fischer interjected. "Pilgrims *flocked* there with offerings in her honor. The Abbot levied taxes and fees on foreigners and rented booths to merchants and vendors on Magdalene feast days."

"Nice racket," Linus remarked.

"Very profitable," Fischer observed, adding that Vezelay was of particular interest to female penitents, who would post lists of their sins on the altar and gain immediate absolution. "Repentant prisoners did likewise with their chains and iron collars. So many, in fact, that they were forged into fences and railings for the church!"

Ute then slid her finger down the page, past number 12 – Stenay, the Merovingian capital – to number 13, and said,

"*Dreizehn*. Exeter, in England, a tenth century king named Athelstan puts a finger of Mary Magdalene in the cathedral there," she said. She skipped number 14, the cemetery of Mary Magdalene in Wiggenhall, England, and went to number 15.

"*Fünfzehn*. Oviedo, northern Spain, location of some of Mary Magdalene's hair ... "

"Same hair she used to wash Christ's feet, no doubt," Linus mocked. Ute nodded. Fischer was amused.

"Sixteen," Ute continued, unconsciously switching to English. "In Venice, a nobleman named Arnold von Harff, who died in 1505, said he saw a large bone from the breast of Mary Magdalene at the church of *Saint Elena*.

"Also in Venice, a finger of Mary Magdalene is believed placed under an altar at a church honoring *Saint Maria Maddelena Penitente*.

"And yet *again* in Venice, a phial containing a mixture of Mary Magdalene's spikenard ointment and some of the blood of Jesus was said to be held by a Franciscan church there, at least until the eighteenth century," she said. The amount they'd discovered was very impressive.

"All this since yesterday afternoon?" Linus asked.

"Sometimes that which is hardest to see is that which is right before your eyes," Fischer said with the faintest smirk. Ute tugged at Linus's sleeve, her finger still on the list, and said,

"Seventeen. Mari, small village in India." She moved her finger across Fischer's notes as she read. "Atop a nearby mountain called *Pindi Point* there is a tomb called *Mai Mari da Asthan*, which means *final resting place of Mary*."

"We're not sure if it refers to Mary Magdalene or to the virgin Mary," Fischer said. "One account claims that local Muslims call it the grave of Issa's mother. In Islam, Christ is considered to be a prophet. The Koran says that he did not die on a cross but lived to travel through India and the east, with his mother. And he is commonly called Issa." Ute cleared her throat and resumed.

"Eighteen. Srinagar, a small village in Kashmir," she said, pointing to the last entry on the list. "There is a tomb called *Rauza Bal*, which means *tomb of a prophet*. An inscription at the entrance says it is the tomb of Yuz Asaf, which means leader of the healed. Yuz Asaf is the name that Moslems called Jesus during his supposed travels in Persia." she said. She straightened out and pushed back from the table. Fischer chewed on his briar pipe.

"Do you see a pattern, *Herr* Linus?" he asked, unaware that Linus had already recognized the Magdalene's rising importance.

"Their primary interest is Mary Magdalene, particularly Magdalene relics. And not Merovingians," Linus said, and he reminded them that the Cave of the Seven Sleepers has been cited as a possible Magdalene burial place, as well. Fischer shifted his pipe to the other side of his mouth.

"By some accountings, there are enough body parts out there said to belong to the Magdalene to assemble five complete corpses!" he chuckled. He further noted that hundreds – maybe *thousands* – of organizations around the world were dedicated to Mary Magdalene. "Most are charitable, but some are political, too," he said, and Ute mentioned the Catholic woman's group in Germany called *Gruppe Marie von Magdala*, dedicated to equal religious rights, including ordination, for women – which sounded very Cathar-like.

"I wonder how many of them come under the umbrella of Melisandre's *Novangelis* group," Linus said. It seemed like a natural core for assembling an army in the battle for woman's rights.

"But do not discount the Merovingian connection," Fischer said. "They like to think of themselves as the descendants of Jesus. And who do you think is most often mentioned as the mother of Jesus' children?" he asked. Linus smiled and said,

"Mary Magdalene, of course. And since the body of Christ is vanished, but there *are* alleged parts of Mary Magdalene scattered all over Europe, Magdalene relics are the logical place to start a genetic catalog," Linus surmised.

"Or so it would seem," Fischer agreed. Ute, however, was more skeptical.

"But how could they possibly connect anything using genetics?" she said. "The samples are very old, the gene pool many generations diluted." Linus offered the first opinion.

"I see two important things they could possibly learn," he said. "They could genetically fingerprint all the Magdalen relics they can find, then group the similar ones together. I suppose that would give them at least some idea of which ones might be authentic.

"Then, if they were able to find any Merovingian relics which were genetically matched with their Magdalene relics, they'd have a connection, and one that would lend credibility to their claim," he proposed. Ute was still skeptical.

"But the Merovingians are so scattered, and their throne so heavy with imposters," she said. "The odds of finding a match must be astronomical. And the odds of bringing a genetic fingerprint forward to a match in the present are even worse! They'd have to test everyone on the planet," she objected. But Fischer, more intrigued, was willing to suspend his disbelief.

"This is all true, Ute. But perhaps they could accomplish *some* goals, depending upon how many people could be convinced of the veracity of the claim and the test results," he said. "If they have indeed discovered some proof, some documentation, of the Christ-Magdalene liaison, then these things together with the genetics would be *very* convincing."

"What could be proof?" Linus queried.

"Certificate of marriage," Fischer said. "They were common at the time. And then there is the claim that the Rennes-le-Château parchments contained incontrovertible proof that Christ didn't die on the cross, that he married and gave rise to a bloodline which exists to this day," he noted, opening a wide door to the possibility that Melisandre and her cohorts had come into possession of the missing parchments – and their secrets. Linus found it all too fantastic.

"So Jesus somehow wriggles his way out of a tight spot with the Romans, marries Mary Magdalene, spawns a passel of kids, and they all ride off into the happily-ever-after, like Ozzie and Harriet," he said. Ute and Fischer were puzzled.

"Ozzie *und* ... .?" Ute questioned, shaking her head.

"American television family," Linus mumbled. They still didn't see the humor. He didn't bother to explain. "Imagine what it would mean if someone could reasonably prove lineage from Christ?" he mused.

"The second coming," Fischer said solemnly.

"And it is a *woman*. God forbid!" Ute said sarcastically.

"All the patriarchal churches would be reeling. The whole idea of Biblical inerrancy would be smashed to bits. A lot of Christians wouldn't like that, but I bet a lot would," Linus observed. But Fischer saw a darker side to it all.

"The changes it could engender would eclipse any other event in religious history, possibly in all of human history," he said, eyebrows arched. "Worse yet," he added, "think of someone like Kohlhertz in control of that proof. The sale price would be staggering!"

"So would the potential for extortion," Linus noted. They all knew the theory that Saunière, abbot at Rennes-le-Château, a poor parish priest suddenly living like a king, used his discovery to blackmail the Church of Rome.

"So maybe Jules the priest *was* undercover for the Vatican, to put them on the inside track in case something was discovered. Certainly they'd be interested in any proof of a Christ bloodline, *especially* if it could be brought forward to the present," Linus said.

"To suppress it?" Ute wondered.

"At least to control it. There'd be some serious concerns to be thought through before something like that could be made public – if it ever could at all," Fischer said, and he suggested that perhaps Melisandre was working for the Vatican as well. But Linus thought she was too independent..

"Not for the Vatican directly, I don't think. She said she met Jules through Gervan, who was working on something for them both, and Jules offered to share his resources in exchange for hers. I believe that."

"You believe too much from this woman," Fischer objected, jabbing his pipe stem into Linus's chest. Ute gently pushed Fischer's pipe away and said,

"I believe *Herr* Mercator has understood your point, Ervin." Her intervention on his behalf surprised Linus. This quiet, deliberate woman was appearing more belligerent toward him every time he saw her – until now. He took a deep breath, massaged his eyes with his fingertips, and said,

"Let's get back to basics. So the scroll says there is a preserved sample, perhaps of blood. Whose, we don't know. But do we, or will we, know where it is?"

"With more study, I believe so," Fischer said. "The scroll contains a line which refers to the holder of a special *gnosis*, or wisdom, as also being the holder of the well, or receptacle," he reported. Linus had an epiphany. His throat tightened. Fischer's words – "*... the holder of this gnosis is the holder of the well*," echoed in his mind. He had all he could do to hide his alarm. The revelation hadn't spread to the others. Linus's heart pounded. He didn't want to tell them what he was thinking – yet. He didn't want them to know. He swallowed hard and retained his composure.

"Patience and study will pay off, then. As long as we can stay ahead of the competitors," he said. Fischer nodded but seemed a bit wary. Perhaps Linus hadn't hidden his surprise so well after all..

"And we know they've got a man in Turkey now, following in Ute's footsteps, no doubt," Fischer said. Ute told them that she tried to cover her tracks and asked the curator to keep her work confidential, but there was no guarantee that whoever came looking wouldn't find something on their own.

"Did Gervan travel to Ephesus?" Linus wondered. Ute shook a solemn "no". "Then what was *his* big discovery? Melisandre said he left a message about an important discovery just before he disappeared. He wanted her to come to the shop right away."

"I would not be surprised if he located an ancient reference to the inscription Ute found on the base of the statue," Fischer speculated. "Gervan was a paleographical genius and knew *dozens* of lost languages," he assured.

"He must've discovered the location of the scroll's second half. Yes, that must've been it," Linus agreed. "He wouldn't have been so excited just discovering that the second half of the message was at the Cave of the Seven Sleepers. I say Gervan figured out the whole riddle but didn't get a chance to tell anyone." Linus noticed that Ute seemed far away in her thoughts. He had all but forgotten that Gervan was her father. He reached to her hand, beside him on the table, and touched it lightly. "You've done so much, and so well. Thank you," he said. Ute smirked and withdrew her hands to her lap.

"Your interests are in writing a big story to make you wealthy and popular, *Herr* Mercator. With this, I do not wish to help you," she said. "My interest is in learning what my father found and why he died for it. And in seeing his killers punished. If our actions serve our mutual purposes, so be it," she concluded, then she stood up and left the room. Linus was both puzzled and perturbed.

"I could understand her hating me if we spent some time together. But in just the few hours...?"

"I don't think it is hate you are seeing," Fischer said.

"It sure ain't love," Linus quipped. Fischer smiled broadly.

"Perhaps not," he said, "though I've seen many a happy union begin just this way," he chuckled. "I think she is reassuring herself that she is doing this for her own reasons, not for yours."

"Fine. Writing is what I do," Linus mumbled. "Who says you can't write a book *and* serve justice?" he groused.

"No one, *Herr* Linus," Fischer assured, then added, "Just be sure that you *do* serve both masters and Ute will turn around. Are you returning to the *Ardennes* today?"

"Ya. Melisandre said she was waiting for some potentially exciting news about the scroll and would share it with me. I'm sure she's referring to whatever that American expert she hired is going after in Turkey. I can't wait to see what she tells me."

"A big lie, I should expect."

"You're probably right, Ervin, but it won't hurt to play along for now. And you? Can you stay here in Paris for a few days?"

"I can."

"Good. And Ute?"

"Back to Berlin. She has been neglecting her work at the museum. I told her to go back and I will let her know as soon as I find something."

"Okay," Linus said as he checked his watch. It was almost noon. "What say you, me and Ute have some lunch and try to glue ourselves back together as a team."

"Splendid," Fischer said as he stood up. Again, he laid an avuncular hand on Linus's shoulder. "Despite your hard-shelled cynicism, my American friend, I suspect that your motives are not *completely* mercenary," he said, grinning at his deliberately left-handed compliment.

"Thanks a million," Linus muttered and Fischer said,

"*Mein* pleasure."

Seek and Ye Shall Find

Melisandre was reading in a comfortable chair when she heard approaching steps. A light rap on the door followed. Ailene entered, carrying a cell phone. "Mister Archer," she said. It was the paleographer – ancient documents expert – calling from Turkey. Melisandre took the phone and Ailene left the room.

"Yes?" Melisandre said . "Why won't he cooperate? ... I see ... Are you sure you've looked everywhere? ... But you are still confident that there is something there? ... More time won't help you find it on your own? ... I understand. Alright, then. We'll be on the first flight in the morning ... Right. From Paris. Orly. Good. See you then," she finished. And she ended the connection.

The Wrong Way From Stenay

The *Forest of Woevres* was black and empty when Linus

returned that night from Paris. It wasn't late – just after nine o'clock – yet the lodge seemed deserted. Aside from the house manager Ailene, a chauffeur, a maid and Melisandre, Linus hadn't seen another soul. Four people seemed far too few for such a big lodge, he thought. It gave him the uneasy feeling that there were others, out of sight but nearby, ready to be called. Ailene was waiting for him when he got to the door.

"Good evening, sir," she said with a pleasant curtsy.

"Hi. Where is everyone?" he replied.

"'Tis very quiet. Lovely," she said. Linus nodded. "There's a supper in the oven should you be wanting one, mister Mercator"

"That would be grand," he said, and followed her to the kitchen. Using a towel for a mitt, Ailene took a *cassoulet* out of the oven and put it on the chop-block table set for two. Linus pulled up a stool and helped himself as she poured him a glass of red wine. "Aren't you joining me?" he asked as he dug into the delicious meal. Ailene shook 'no' then pressed the intercom button and said, "*Monsieur* has arrived." A few minutes later, Melisandre came into the kitchen.

"Hello there," she said. "You've been gone a long time. Did you find *so* many interesting sights?"

"I ended up going to Paris."

"Have you been before?"

"Yes. Often," he said. He didn't want to chit-chat. He wanted her to tell him about her "potentially important news" regarding the scroll. Ailene put a wine glass in front of Melisandre and she shared Linus's *cassoulet*.

"I had some interesting news today," she said as she poured some wine. "An expert in my employ says that the scroll message is actually in two parts."

"Really," Linus said, feigning surprise – though probably not too well. But at least he knew that *she* was telling the truth.

"The text of the first segment speaks of another message, and some sort of secret wisdom or knowledge," she explained. Again, information which he already knew to be true. Fischer had said the scroll refers to "the holder of a special gnosis, or wisdom, as also being the holder of the well, or receptacle". So far – so good, he thought. Melisandre was still being truthful. But then the other shoe was dropped.

"Any idea where the second half is located?" Linus asked. Without hesitation, Melisandre said,

"Jerusalem." Linus struggled to pretend he believed her.

"I'm going there tomorrow to purchase it from an antiquarian who has no idea what it is, exactly. He thinks I am a private collector," she said. Linus nodded approvingly as the possibilities raced into his head. He wondered if she was being misled by her expert. Or maybe her expert was simply mistaken. Or maybe there *was* something in Jerusalem, like a copy, which he and his colleagues had missed.

Yet he couldn't help think that the most likely case was that Melisandre was simply lying again. "You'll want to come with me? To Jerusalem?"

"Sure. If you don't mind," he said, sipping wine. They ate and chatted for about an hour. He asked her about the 'MD' tattoo he'd seen on Kohlhertz's wrist during the fight in Berlin and she said she had recently heard a rumor about some sort of secret, pagan society called the *Massa Damnata* – Masses of the Damned – which referred to the human cesspool from which they recruited their members. Aside from that, she knew nothing – though they agreed that Kohlhertz would fit the *Massa Damnata* profile.

Finally they separated and went to bed. Linus wasn't sleepy so he opened his Blackberry and gave himself a tutorial on religious relics. The body parts of prominent religious figures were at the apex of their potency during the middle ages, he found. When Saint Thomas Aquinas died, his monks decapitated then boiled his corpse to preserve it.

The power of such relics extended far beyond spirituality. To own, for example, a finger of Saint James or the head of Saint John, was *priceless*. Great wealth accrued to the abbeys with such possessions. Pilgrims would travel great distances to receive indulgences through items of such *puissance* – indulgences for which they would pay dearly. With the right amount of payola, it seemed, no sin was too heinous to be absolved.

Passion pageants, saints' days festivals, curative fairs – all centered around relics – brought large profits to their sponsors. The abbeys even rented space to vendors to ply their trades and sell souvenirs – like a modern day visit from the Pope. Sometimes a town's very existence depended upon something as simple as a clot of saintly hair.

Unfortunately, such good business led to corruption. *Sacré Furtá* – Sacred Thefts – were common. Monks from poorer abbeys would conduct nighttime raids and steal relics from other abbeys. Then they would cite some obscure scripture or event in history to claim rightful ownership. Or, worse yet, they would rationalize their misdeeds by claiming that 'God would have prevented it were it not meant to be' – a lot like the Islamist rational for blowing up busses and babies, Linus thought.

In any case, most relics were counterfeit, since those which were genuine were scattered and lost like many other treasures from this age. Fischer's comments from their *Montmartre* meeting were echoing in Linus's head: 'By some accountings there are enough body parts said to belong to the Magdalene to assemble five complete corpses!' he had said. Apparently the small matter of whose hunk of cadaver they were really worshipping was of little consequence to the truly devout. He switched phone modes then composed an e-mail to Fischer:

TO: Anfortas
FM: LP-Merc
SUBJECT: Travel plans
Her expert says the other half of the scroll is in *Jerusalem*. Supposedly taking a two o'clock flight to Israel tomorrow from Orly. Find the departure gate and look for me at the nearest security checkpoint leading into the gate area. When I see you, follow me.

Fischer, who must've been working online, replied immediately.

TO: LP-Merc
FM: Anfortas
SUBJECT: Travel plans

I'll be there by noon.

August 6th.
Orly Airport, outside Paris. Day 16.
Ditched

Fischer was standing inconspicuously off to the side, near the security check-in for gates 20-35. He made eye contact with Linus and nodded. But just as Linus was about to excuse himself to the men's room, Melisandre suddenly stopped.

"Would you mind waiting here for just a minute?" she said, glancing toward the signs for the lavatories. Linus figured it was a lucky stroke – Melisandre was getting herself out of the way. She disappeared through the throng toward the lav. Fischer approached and handed Linus a book.

"You'll find this interesting," he said. It was titled *Mary Magdalen in Myth and Metaphor*, written by Susan Haskins. Linus slipped it into his carry-on.

"Either she's getting me out of town for some reason, or giving me the slip," Linus said.

"Maybe both," Fischer suggested.

"Yeah. But if I get on that plane, keep an eye on the lodge."

"Anything else?" Fischer asked. Linus shrugged and said,

"You?" Fischer shook 'no'. "Then you better get out of sight before she comes back," Linus said. Fischer blended into the crowd but watched from afar. Linus was looking down the concourse for Melisandre when someone tapped his shoulder from behind and said,

"*Monsieur.*" A trio of *gendarmes* in blue uniforms, the word *"securite"* embroidered on their shoulder patches, was in a semi-circle behind him. The leader said something in French.

"*Excuse moi. Je ne parle pas Français,*" Linus replied. His

French was decent, actually, but pretending it wasn't was sometimes useful.

"May I see your passport?" the *gendarme* asked. Linus reached into the inside pocket of his jacket and handed it over. "Where are you traveling today, *monsieur*?" the *gendarme* asked as he leafed through the blue US passport.

"Israel," Linus replied, realizing that the other two *gendarmes* had circled around beside and behind him. "Something wrong?" he asked.

"May I look in your bag," the lead *gendarme* asked. Linus handed that over as well, still watching for Melisandre. The *gendarme* dug through the bag. Fischer was still hanging in the background, scrutinizing the unfolding scene. "Is this your property?" the *gendarme* asked, holding a gold medallion hanging on a gold chain. It was a bee medallion, the Merovingian bee. Linus shrugged and shook 'no', trying to look surprised. But he knew what was going on and wasn't surprised at all. He had been set him up as though he'd stolen the pendant – probably when the chauffeur put his bag in the trunk that morning as they left the lodge.

"That came out of my bag?" he asked.

"*Oui, monsieur.* Will you come with me, please," the *gendarme* said.

"But my flight ... " Linus protested.

"You may continue your journey shortly," the *gendarme* said as his partners closed in. Linus had little choice and was led away from the gate area. In the corner of his eye, he noticed Melisandre watching from afar. Making no attempt to intervene. He pretended not to see her. As he passed Fischer, Linus motioned toward Melisandre with his eyes. Fischer looked and saw her, then nodded – he would watch her and see where she went.

The *gendarmes* locked Linus into a small, fluorescent-filled office where he sat alone for the next six hours, thumbing the same dog-eared copy of *Paris Match*, before he finally heard keys in the lock. A *gendarme* entered, carrying his travel bag. He placed it on the table and stepped aside as an official in a plain suit came in behind him. The suit sat opposite him, put Linus's passport on the table and slid it across.

"This morning, just before you were detained," he began, slowly reaching into his jacket pocket and pulling out the medallion, "we received a phone message that this valuable item was stolen from a private residence in the *Ardennes*. We were given your name and description, *monsieur*, and told you would be attempting to board a flight for Israel. So we acted on the information we had. However, when we reported the item recovered, and you detained, we were told there was some confusion about whether the item was actually stolen, and that attempts to reach the owner were underway. Naturally, we had no choice but to hold you until the matter could be resolved."

"Has the matter been resolved then?" Linus asked. The police official nodded, his face a regretful frown.

"Just this moment we confirmed that this item was meant as a gift to you. A surprise gift, *monsieur*," he said. Linus shifted in his seat.

"Well, I *am* surprised," he said with a grin as he hung the chain around his neck and dropped the gold bee into his shirt.

"With our apologies, you are free to go," the official said. Linus shook his hand to show there were no hard feelings, gathered his belongings and left. He was surprised to see Fischer in the waiting area outside the security office.

"It became obvious what was happening, *Herr* Linus. The Melisandre woman met a friend, the woman you photographed outside the *Château* at *Domaine deBouillon* ... "

"Veronica?"

"Yes. They boarded a plane for Turkey."

"So much for Israel," Linus huffed. A smile broke over his face. "She ditched me *again*," he said, shaking his head. Fischer didn't see the humor in it. But Fischer wasn't aware of how badly Melisandre had just played her hand. Linus began walking through the terminal toward the exit.

"You are going after them?" Fischer asked.

"No," Linus said as he picked up his pace. "In fact, she'll be chasing *me* very soon. All the way to the States," he said cryptically.

"You're returning to America?" Fischer asked. Linus nodded. Then Fischer made what should've been a startling announcement. "I believe I know where this blood, or relic, or genetic sample is hidden," he declared. But Linus was unfazed, as though he hadn't even heard. The wise old man quickly concluded what that meant. "You have realized this too, eh *Herr* Linus?" he asked. Linus stopped walking. Smiling with great satisfaction he nodded slowly. Indeed he had more than a strong hunch about where the coveted relic was hidden. He started walking fast again. Fischer hustled to keep up. "Do you have it? The sample?" he asked. Linus shook "no" – which was only half true.

"But I will. Very soon," he said confidently. They arrived at the exits and paused. The evening was dusky beyond the glass doors. Fischer was staring at Linus, squinting his eyes, sizing him up.

"You are a crafty one, *Herr* Linus," he said. "But I warn you, be sure that you are as clever as you think. And choose your actions carefully. You are dealing with the potential for unspeakable power. Do not underestimate the will of your opponents."

"Don't worry, *Herr* Professor. Kohlhertz *and* Melisandre will get what they deserve, and very soon," Linus assured. "And you can tell that to Ute as well," he added. And Fischer said,

"Good luck, Linus." Linus took his hand.

"Take Ute and go someplace. Underground. Couple of weeks, that's all. I'll tell you when it's safe. Watch your e-mail. When I'm finished, we'll have a big celebration dinner in Berlin," he said. The old professor was still skeptical. Linus was making this sound all too easy, he thought. But he'd said all that before. So he held his tongue, released Linus's handshake, and headed home.

Linus went back into the terminal to lay a trap and set a juicy bait.

Chapter 20. The BAIT

Linus struggled against a tide of baggage-laden air travelers as he made his way back toward the gates, formulating his plan as he went. He had to accomplish several things and contacting Kohlhertz was at the top of the list. He would lure Kohlhertz with something a guy like Kohlhertz would find irresistibly appealing – an act of betrayal. Posing as one of Melisandre's followers, Linus would offer the translation of the scroll message – *and* the location of its treasure – for a hefty price.

And he needed to play it so Melisandre would intercept the transaction. Then she'd be caught in his web as well.

He stopped in a news shop and assembled his props – a magazine with an internet service promo, a souvenir package of note cards, and a fifty-franc calling card for the phone – then headed down the concourse to a large, crowded food court filled with people passing their layover time with light snacks or coffee. He was glad it was crowded – good cover for his next step, he thought.

He looked around and found his pigeon – a middle-aged guy in a gray suit near the middle of the eating area. A garment bag and Burberry trench coat were slung over the empty chair beside him. He was reading a newspaper, and Linus couldn't see his face until he reached for a bite of his cake and a sip of his coffee. This would be the guy, he thought. He was so absorbed in his newspaper that he'd never suspect a thing. All he needed now was for the guy to get a bill.

He set up his phone for taking pictures then waited for twenty minutes until, finally, good things began to happen. The waiter came to the table and spoke. The guy looked over his newspaper and shook "no". The waiter departed, but returned a few minutes later and left the check. The man looked at it. This was the moment – cash or credit? The guy reached for his wallet then slipped out a gold *VISA* card. The waiter went away then returned shortly with the receipt, got a signature, and left the customer his card and a copy of the receipt on the table. The guy went back to his newspaper. Linus made his move.

He sidled through the scattered tables and chairs and, as he squeezed past, he bumped the table hard and the credit card fell on the floor. Apologizing profusely, he bent down, snapped a picture of the card – both sides – returned it to its understanding owner then hastened down the concourse and blended quickly with the surging crowds. He ducked into a cluster of public telephone cubicles, plugged his laptop into the data/fax jack and opened a trial internet account with the promo from the magazine. When the instructions asked for credit card info, Linus punched in the digits, expiration date, and name from the card he had just shot. Within seconds the connection was complete and the screen was flashing a cheery "Welcome"

He chose *"Iscariot"* for his screen name, as in *Judas Iscariot* – it seemed like an appropriate choice for someone perpetrating a betrayal. In a few moments, it was accepted. The electronic *"Iscariot"* had been born. Linus then chose "Blueapples" for his password, which was also accepted, and his faux account was active. But it would be closed long before the trial period ended, and using calling cards and public phones for his connection meant that no credit card charges would accrue. The guy who had unwittingly donated his name and card number would probably never even know. And nothing would be traceable back to Linus. He signed off then took one of the note cards he'd bought and wrote his cryptic message: *"He who lives by other's breath ... __?__ "*

It was half of the poetic line from the card on the black Eucalyptus wreath which was sent to Jules's funeral from "W.K." Of course, if those initials didn't stand for Wolfgang Kohlhertz, Linus knew his plan was dead. But if they did – which was likely – then he was in business. He wrote the name and address of the internet account sign-on page then continued with his instructions.

I have what you want. Verify your identity by completing above
phrase. Instructions:
1. Sign-on as screen name: ISCARIOT - the password is Blueapples.
2. Compose a mail message addressed to ISCARIOT.
3. Select SEND LATER then sign-off without sending the message.
4. Sign-on the same way at noon each day thereafter for subsequent
instructions. Find them by selecting MAILBOX option, then EDIT
MAIL WAITING TO BE SENT option. Your further instructions will
be written as un-sent letters addressed to WK.

It was a simple read-and-delete set-up. Instead of communicating via e-mail, they would share an account and message back and forth via e-mails that would never be sent – no copy would exist on any server, and no routing information could ever be retrieved. The messages would be deleted.

He then wrote the exact same message on another card and took two envelopes from the package and enclosed both notes. He figured he had two good chances of hooking up with Kohlhertz. On one envelope he wrote, *W.KOHLHERTZ / URGENT*. This was the one he'd leave at the farmhouse – Kohlhertz's lair – where he and Jules had their fight.

Then he dug out the florist card from the Eucalyptus wreath and, on the other envelope, wrote: *W.KOHLHERTZ / URGENT and IN CARE OF* – followed by the florist's name and address. This one he'd deliver to the florist shop in Blanchefort, a village near *Domaine deBouillon* where Kohlhertz bought the wreath. He was certain Melisandre would intercept it through her local connections – especially since fresh flowers seemed to follow her everywhere and the florist would no doubt be in her circle. He also knew that Melisandre probably couldn't complete the phrase and, even if she could, she wouldn't run the risk of blowing a possible subsequent security question or code word, because a blown cover would cook the deal. And she couldn't let that happen. So she'd let Kohlhertz reply, follow him through the instructions, then intercept the deal before it was closed.

Next he opened his rolodex file and dialed the number of an old Pentagon contact, Admiral J. George Lahr. "I need you to check on something for me," he said after they exchanged greetings. Though Lahr probably would've helped him anyway, he was more than willing when he heard what Linus wanted.

Finally, there was one more call to make – to the owner of a small shop called *Clay and Kiln* in his hometown of Newburyport, Massachusetts, who was his friend and neighbor. "I'll e-mail the images. Just copy them as best you can," he told her, adding that he'd need the job completed within one week, and after apologizing for waking her at two in the morning.

He shut down his phone then leaned back with his hands atop his head, double-checking his details. The plan was in motion. Tomorrow he'd deliver the notes. The dirty deal would be underway. There was nothing left to do for now except purchase a plane ticket. But not to the States, as he had told Fischer. To Toulouse, in the south of France, and just a short drive from the farmhouse and florist where he'd deliver the notes.

Then he'd lose himself in the countryside for a few days. Take the long, scenic route back to Berlin. Read the book Fischer gave him.

And wait.

August 11th.
Berlin, Germany. Day 21.
The Wait

Linus gazed out of the window of his Berlin hotel, watching two young guys in the shade of a big tree lean in and out of the open hood of a run-down, flat-tired, mustard yellow Trabant. It was merely a place to park his eyes. His mind wasn't on car repairs. It was on *charades*. Five days ago, when he laid the bait to lure Kohlhertz and Melisandre, he was certain they wouldn't be able to resist. Now, five days later, he wasn't so sure.

He wondered if he had missed something, or if there was something he should've done differently. When he dropped one of the two notes at the farmhouse near Rennes-le-Château – where he had his encounter with Jules, the priest-*cum*-burglar – the farmhouse was empty. But not deserted. Fresh motorcycle tracks in the dirt and dishes on the kitchen sink told him that the note he was slipping under the door would find its way to Kohlhertz.

Likewise, he was certain that the second note – dropped at the florist shop where Kohlhertz ordered the wreath he sent to Jules's funeral – would find its way first to Melisandre, then on to Kohlhertz as well. So, he wondered, where were they? What was taking so long for a response?

He thought it ironic that both Melisandre *and* Kohlhertz had written him off as a meddler and a pest. Linus was sure he was ice cold, un-followed, un-accounted for. But that was about to change dramatically. Everyone was about to discover that *he* was actually the key to the entire caper. The thought brought him a wry smile

The *Mary Magdalene...* book he got from Fischer was lying on the bed, a ragged page marker hanging out of it. He was only a third of the way through and already it was a real eye-opener, connecting many things he'd seen over the past few months with many things he was discovering about the historical Mary Magdalene.

His first revelation was that Mary Magdalene was never a prostitute, let alone a reformed prostitute. In fact, the epithets *"penitent Mary"* and *"great sinner"* had been removed from the official Catholic breviary – church rule book – way back in 1978. He wondered why such an important restoration of such an important woman had seemed to pass largely unnoticed. Bad public relations? Church politics? Male chauvinism? Probably all of the above. In any case, the new image of the Magdalene he was forming was a far cry from the one he had held since childhood, the one most Catholics – indeed most Christians – probably hold to this day.

Mary was a wealthy, influential woman whose parents, Cyrus and Eucharia, were said to be descended from a line of kings. She was beautiful and fashionable, intelligent and outspoken – qualities which doubtless led to her being unfairly labeled as a whore.

She was also an activist, prominent among a handful of equally influential women who supported Christ's ministry with their money, and who opened their homes for meetings and services. Lazarus's wife was one, and she was probably friendly with the wife of a high dignitary in King Herod's court as well.

Several of the gospels place the Magdalene at the resurrection. Indeed, several say that it was Mary Magdalene who first encountered the risen Christ, who told her to carry word of the resurrection to the Apostles, earning her the appellation *"Apostola Apostolorum"* – Apostle to the Apostles.

She was also present at the crucifixion when Joseph of Arimethea supposedly caught some of Christ's blood in a cup – a possibility which raised the hairs on Linus's neck in light of the scroll message touting the existence of some type of "sample."

He discovered that one can't discuss Mary Magdalen without also touching on the debate over whether Christ was married – as the Magdalene was so often mentioned as his wife and mother of his children. On the one side, there was the belief that Christ was celibate – a view held mostly by those who believe in Biblical inerrancy. The other side, however, claimed it was highly unusual and unlikely that a young man of the time would be unmarried, especially one who had received rabbinical training, as Jesus had. Marriage was all but mandatory for rabbis in the first century.

Mary was also heavily featured in the so-called *Gnostic Gospels* – such as the *Pistis Sophia*, the *Gospel of Mary*, *Codex Brucianus*, the Nag Hammadi scrolls, and others – where her prominence in the establishment of Christianity was highlighted – which apparently had the church patriarchy quaking in their sandals. So the *Gnostic Gospels* were conveniently declared heretical and not included in the *New Testament*. That was in the fourth century, and it effectively condemned Mary to sixteen centuries of bad press. Like Eve, on whom the downfall of paradise was blamed, the Magdalene was labeled a sinner and a whore, saved only by the divine intervention of Jesus. It was a bad rap but one that stuck.

Linus was also amazed by the depth of Christianity's determination to exclude or, at least, limit the official participation of women. He recalled the history of the Cathars, who were originally Catholic but whose rejection of material wealth, and whose liberal beliefs in openness and gender equality, flew in the face of the church fathers and ultimately led to their massacre at *Montsegur* – a full 800 years after the Magdalene and the *Gnostic Gospels* were trounced! An amazing shelf life for *any* prejudice, he thought.

Yet the determination of those opposed to that prejudice seemed just as immense, if not as dramatic. To this day, thousands of Christians – like the German women's *Gruppe von Maria Magdala* – were promoting their own beliefs that Christ didn't exclude women from his ministry, that indeed he meant for them to have an important role. Equal in every way to that of men. Christ chose Mary to carry word of the resurrection, they say – which proves that Christ meant for women to be ordained. And now, he thought, with the Catholic church on the ropes from their immense sexual abuse scandal, perhaps their time had indeed arrived for Christian women to emerge.

He began to speculate on the Magdalene's potential importance to women's rights in religion – especially those oppressed by their religions – and to women's rights in general. Melisandre said that her *Novangelis* group was a charitable organization. But her preoccupation with all things Magdalene – particularly her intense interest in Magdalene relics – left Linus wondering how much of her work was charitable and how much was political. Was the real purpose of her work to help women in crisis, or was it to claim greater power for women in all corners of society, particularly in Christianity?

Either way, Mary Magdalene seemed like a prime role model.

And now, with much more of the historical record coming to light and much more equality being won for women in many sectors of society, the stage was set for the Magdalene's *true* comeback. The possibilities were staggering for someone who could reasonably prove a genetic link to Mary Magdalene. How many established, male-dominated churches would be turned upside-down? How many elections could be swayed. How many women – world-wide – could be propelled into positions of power? How many of the world's downtrodden, lost souls could be retrieved, inspired, and perhaps directed to... whatever purpose?

And, as during the crusades, when the Magdalene was elevated to cult status and vast armies marched in her service, how many armies could be raised and led to do any bidding on the same blind faith?

The potential for great humanitarianism was eclipsed only by the potential for even greater malevolence. And anyone with a vested interest in that Christ-Magdalene bloodline proof – whether it was Kohlhertz, Melisandre or anyone else – would let nothing stand in their way to obtain it.

He thought about Melisandre's friend, Veronica Franco; beautiful, intelligent, fashionable, wealthy, influential in politics – she seemed a perfect parallel of the Magdalene. Was Veronica the 'New Magdalene'? The 'New Angel'? Was Melisandre her campaign manager? Whatever the answer, at least Linus knew his overall hunch was right – this was a *big* story. The story of a lifetime. But it all hinged upon a positive response from Kohlhertz. And so far, Kohlhertz wasn't responding.

Linus had been back in Berlin for a day and a half now, avoiding contact with *everyone* – including Fischer and Ute – and avoiding places where he might be recognized. It was part of his effort to heed Fischer's warning about the danger of underestimating his opponents. Now, more than ever, even the slightest error in judgment could be costly.

He finished the last swallow of a coffee and put the cup on the breakfast tray. It was just after 10 in the morning and time to check his phantom e-mail account again – as he'd been doing forty or fifty times every day. At first, the absence of a response wasn't surprising. Now it was maddening.

He powered up his laptop and signed onto the Iscariot account to check for outgoing mail. His heart pounded in his throat as the window popped open and a listing appeared. At last, there was a message addressed to Iscariot. The initials "W.K." were in the subject line. Kohlhertz had taken the bait. Linus opened the message: *"He who lives by other's breath ... dieth also by his death."* The completed phrase was there. As instructed, Kohlhertz would be signing on again at noon to receive further instructions. Linus copied the message and sent it to his regular e-mail account, then began typing a response:

TO: W.K.
FM: Iscariot
SUBJECT: Instructions
An escrow amount of one hundred-fifty thousand $ US must be deposited into a numbered account on the Caribbean island of Nevis within two days, the number to be forwarded via this method in a message to *Iscariot*. Upon confirmation of said account, the translation of the entire scroll message shall be revealed, also via this method. Following said translation, you will be given instructions on when and where to pick up the object described in the scroll message. At that time, and in my presence, the money will be transferred out of that account and into another to which only I have access. Once this transaction is completed, the object in question will become your sole property. To accept this proposition, compose a message to *Iscariot* with the word AGREED in the subject line, and leave it in the MAIL WAITING TO BE SENT file as per the established method.

He clicked on SEND LATER, placing the message in the MAIL WAITING TO BE SENT file, and signed off. Kohlhertz would have it by noon – assuming that he was following instructions. He shut down his computer and lay back on the bed, hoping that 150,000 dollars was large enough to convince Kohlhertz that something important was in the offing, but small enough for him to raise quickly. It was a lot of money for a common thief – but not for one directed by an unseen hand. Like the hand of the *Prieure de Sion – Priory of Sion* – which was perhaps Kohlhertz's sponsor.

And, as thieves go, Linus knew that Kohlhertz was far from common. He figured Kohlhertz would accept the proposal, and would do so no later than early that afternoon. And the next step would be to make a date for the swap.

The hours crept by and Linus's phony internet account had become the proverbial watched pot. He checked every half hour for some indication that Kohlhertz had received the second message and the instructions. After nine hours of waiting he pried himself away for dinner – a much needed diversion. But nothing could divert him for long. It was ten that night when he got back into his room. He emptied his pockets and decided to check once more before falling asleep.

As he waited to make the connection with his laptop he anticipated failure and charted a contingency plan – start hanging out at all the old haunts, like the *Blauer Apfel*, Gervan's shop, Melisandre's Berlin headquarters, Humboldt University. Perhaps even make a return visit to Lindow Abbey and the woman's refuge called *Das Giudecca* next door. It sounded risky. He hoped it wouldn't be necessary.

He yawned and repeated the sign-on routine one last time for the day. Screen name: *Iscariot*. Password: *Blueapples*. The connection went through. The icons lit up. Linus pointed his way to the outgoing mail area. And there it was – the message to *Iscariot* with the word "agreed" on the subject line. Kohlhertz had replied. And there was more. The phrase "coded escrow" followed the word "agreed." What Linus first thought was a slow, uncertain response was actually a solid commitment.

He clicked the message open and found the name of a bank on the Caribbean island of Nevis, followed by a number identifying an escrow account of $150,000 – a bold initiative which said that Kohlhertz – or *someone* – knew the value and importance of the promised information. Linus saved three copies of the then composed a return message:

TO: W.K.
FM: Iscariot
SUBJECT: Translations
The scroll in your possession is only one half of a two part message. Your half contains an alchemist's formula for preservation of non-specific samples, presumably biological. Your half also makes cryptic references to a sample of some sort, which has been preserved using the above mentioned alchemy method. In the opinion of experts in such matters, the sample to which the scroll alludes is probably a blood sample, likely from the Magdalene, possibly also a sample of the blood of Jesus. Your half of the scroll says that the location of said sample/s can be found in the text of the second half of the scroll message, which is an inscription located in Ephesus, Turkey, near a grotto called the Cave of the Seven Sleepers. This inscription has been located and deciphered. I have recovered and have in my possession the sample/s in question. You have twenty four hours to decide. Should you not respond within that time, this proposition will be offered elsewhere.

He clicked SEND LATER and the message was stored in the MAIL WAITING TO BE SENT file where Kohlhertz would find it the next time he signed on. The original instructions were for him to sign on each day at noon, though Linus suspected Kohlhertz was too impatient and was checking for new instructions at least every hour. In any case, the bait was taken and the hook firmly set. Linus was sure that Kohlhertz would go all the way to the end of the deal, and all he had to do now was stay out of sight and wait. And just as he expected, a reply was waiting when Linus signed onto the *Iscariot* account at eight the next morning. Kohlhertz was ready to do business in person.

He signed off then checked his regular e-mail account. He had five messages from Dark Star, his New York agency, all marked URGENT, and all looking for the Jamie Richards photos.

And there were a couple more heartfelt pleas from Jamie Richards herself. Linus ignored them and went straight to the message from his Pentagon pal, Admiral Lahr. The results of the check Linus asked him to perform were positive. Linus had suspected as much since the day he scuffled with Kohlhertz near *Blauer Apfel*, when he noticed the MD tattoo and the other blotched-out tat on Kohlhertz's wrist.

He booked himself on the ten o'clock flight from Berlin-Tegel to Frankfurt am Main, then home to Boston. Then he sent a message to the Admiral that he was arriving in Boston on August 12th – followed by the flight number. He requested a squad of Military Police to meet him on the granite pier in Newburyport at five p.m. on August 16th. The Portsmouth Naval base was only thirty minutes from Newburyport. The Shore Patrol would come from there.

Next he called the *Clay and Kiln* pottery shop near Plum Island and left a voice-mail: it was imperative that the work he ordered be finished no later than noon on August 14th, when he would pick it up.

Lastly he composed and sent the next message to Kohlhertz. He instructed him to be on the Lufthansa flight out of Frankfurt am Main, which would arrive in Boston on August 16th at seven p.m. He told him he was being monitored, to take this flight only, to come alone, and that the time and place for the meeting would be in a new e-mail message shortly after the flight arrived. That gave Linus four days to get home and get ready. He showered, packed, then headed for Tegel Airport and the beginning of his flight home to the States. The trap was loaded and waiting.

Linus was ready to deal.

Chapter 21. The DEAL

Friday, August 16th.
Plum Island, Massachusetts. 10:00 pm. Day 26.

Linus stared through the darkness at the glass doors lining the beach-side of his house, pondering the ultimate object of desire – Power. In this case, the power to raise legions to crush any enemy, to alter world political processes, to change the course of history.

The power to grant life, or cause death.

And right now, that immense power was sitting in a shoe box at his feet.

His pulse throbbed as a sudden gust sprayed sand against the glass doors and the small house groaned. He tightened his grip on the pistol in his lap. Never had he felt a more palpable threat... not when he was reporting on the mob, or the IRA. Not from the street gangs, or the bikers. He had chanced upon a struggle being secretly prosecuted across the ages. It involved great blasphemies and spectacular treasures still unaccounted for after centuries of searching. It centered on ageless, unsolved mysteries, bizarre rituals and dark secrets supposedly kept by furtive societies.

It was an intrigue harkening back to an age when deceased saints were routinely dismembered, and their parts given to churches throughout the realm, an age which spawned a new type of crime, the '*Sacré Furtá*', or 'Sacred Thefts'. And now, a thousand years later, human relics were again gaining potency in a new age, the age of technology, and promising to spawn another, more deadly, age of *Sacré Furtá*. An age that, as Linus saw it, had already begun.

The wind gusted again and a white chop moiled the Atlantic. He held his breath and listened for anything more than the usual aural wallpaper surrounding his beachfront cottage – like the creaking deck. Someone was lurking outside his door. He was expecting two people tonight. The man he knew as Wolfgang Kohlhertz was the invited guest. The woman he knew as Melisandre was the crasher.

Melisandre would do anything to keep his deal with Kohlhertz from closing – he just hoped she wouldn't do anything *too* drastic, like shoot him. He wiped his clammy forehead and lifted the pistol. There was another footstep on the deck. Then another... walking toward the door. This was it. The steps paused. The door began to open. A tall, square mass filled the frame. It was Kohlhertz, right on schedule. He was holding a gun, surveying the room. Linus, invisible in his shadowy corner, moved onto the edge of the chair and planted his feet.

"Right on time," he said out of the darkness. Kohlhertz startled and crouched.

"Who's there?" he demanded. Linus reached up and snapped on a lamp, revealing Kohlhertz's square, grainy face. It smiled wickedly. "I *knew* it was you," he said with great satisfaction. "I figured you had more sense than these other dip-shits."

Linus wasn't flattered.

"My fee," he said, pointing to his computer on the desk, poised for some long distance electronic banking. Kohlhertz stepped forward and released the agreed sum from the escrow account, then stepped back. Linus used a wireless mouse to click the money into his own account. The verification was instant. Kohlhertz nodded at the shoebox at Linus's feet. "That it?" he asked. Linus shoved the box across the floor. Kohlhertz opened it and examined the contents.

"Look familiar?" Linus asked.

"I should've known this was important," he said, shaking his head as he carefully examined the clay jar that had contained the scroll that Gervan had been studying for him. "Right in front of me all the time. It's gotta be worth millions. So why sell it to me? And so cheap?"

"Because I think it'll turn out to be worthless."

"Worthless?" Kohlhertz said, smiling. Linus smiled back.

"Maybe it'll even get you killed. Maybe even tonight," he chuckled. Kohlhertz wasn't amused.

"I'll take my chances," he said, "You knew what it was all along. Why did you wait to make a deal?"

"I *didn't* know what it was," Linus said. Kohlhertz put the box on the desk.

"I knew that old bastard Gervan couldn't be trust...," he began but stopped short. Utter surprise filled his face. He moved a step forward and a voice said,

"Hands." Someone had gotten the drop on him from behind.

It was Melisandre, right on cue.

The Spoiler

"Hands!" Melisandre commanded again, and both men raised their empty palms. Kohlhertz moved back into the room, the points of a fifty thousand volt taser shoved into his back. Melisandre, in a tight black jumpsuit and veil, stepped out from behind him.

"You double-crossing son of a bitch!" Kohlhertz sneered at Linus.

"Me?" Linus chortled. "You're the idiot who led her here," he declared from his chair.

"Move away from the desk," Melisandre ordered, and Kohlhertz complied.

"Don't plan on keeping the money!" he warned Linus.

"Money, Linus? That's what this is all about?" Melisandre scorned.

"You think you make me feel guilty, Melisandre? You, who ditched me, lied to me, and spied on me?"

"So you're getting your revenge by selling out to a murderer?"

"You have your agenda, Melisandre. I have mine," Linus retorted. Melisandre made a move toward the box on the desk. Linus jumped to his feet, brandished his pistol and shouted, "*Leave it!*" Kohlhertz was surprised. Melisandre, too. She backed off, aiming the taser back and forth between the two men.

"You're out-gunned, Melisandre. Drop the taser."

"Don't do this Linus. The consequences are..."

"I understand the consequences *completely*. All hundred and fifty thousand of them," he assured. "*Drop the taser,*" he shouted.

"You won't shoot... " she began. Linus pulled the trigger. A bullet ripped past her and splintered the door jamb. Her face filled with angst and dripped with sweat. "Don't *do* this, Linus. I'll double the money," she said.

"Deal's a deal," Kohlhertz admonished.

"*Shut up!*" Linus commanded. He fired again, this time right at her feet. Melisandre jumped back. "Put the taser on the desk or I'll shoot your hand off!" he said. Melisandre tossed the stun gun. Kohlhertz lurched forward and grabbed the box off the desk. Then he pulled his pistol and raised it to strike her. Linus stepped up and jammed the muzzle of his gun under Kohlhertz's jaw and said,

"Don't." Wisely, Kohlhertz didn't. Linus took away Kohlhertz's gun and backed off. He retrieved the taser and tossed it across the room.

"Who the fuck's side you on here, anyway?" Kohlhertz whined.

"My side," Linus replied.

"At least give me my gun," Kohlhertz said. Linus straight-armed his pistol to inches from the bridge of Kohlhertz's nose. Kohlhertz raised his palms and said,

"Never mind. I'll go, I'm going." So Linus backed off again. And Kohlhertz didn't hesitate. He tucked the box into his jacket and bolted out of the house. Linus kept him covered all the way, out the door and across the sundeck. But when he was close enough to her, Melisandre made her move. She dove for his gun. Linus seized her wrist but she fought like a tigress, clamping onto his shooting hand, holding the gun aimed at the ceiling.

"Whoa! *Wait!*" he implored. But Melisandre wasn't backing off. He yanked his gun hand out of her grasp. She punched at his face and head. He didn't want to get pummeled but he didn't want to hit back, either. Strategic retreat was his only hope – until he tripped and tumbled backwards into the room. "*It's a fake! I gave him a fake!*" he said in a subdued voice. His words began to get through and Melisandre's attack subsided – though by now he was flat on his back with her elbow crunching his larynx. "It's a set up," he choked. She let up the pressure. "Take my gun. Here. But let me up. It's important!" he said.

Melisandre took the gun and covered him. Linus sat up. "Quick. The phone in the top drawer. Give it to me," he said, rubbing his throat. Melisandre hesitated. "*Give it to me, dammit!*" he insisted. She kept him covered but handed over the phone. It was direct connect. Linus pressed the button. "Dune grass," he said – a pre-arranged password.

"Go ahead."

"Subject is fleeing, presumably by land."

"We're moving on him now. The armed forces of the United States thank you sir." Linus set the phone aside and relaxed – still under Melisandre's gun. Both were drawing heavy breaths but she was looking very confused. Linus pulled himself across the floor and leaned against the sofa.

"You can lose the hardware," he said. She looked at the gun, then at Linus, then lowered the gun – but didn't let it go. Linus was checking his lip for blood from her punches. "You *are* crazy... trying to fistfight a guy with a gun," he said. Melisandre's patience was thinning. She raised the gun again.

"Quickly. What just happened here?" she insisted.

"I just sent Kohlhertz to prison, probably for life," he said. "I found out who he is. When we mixed it up that day in Berlin I noticed a tattoo on his arm which had been inked over. It looked military, like a shield," he explained. "So I sent his genetic fingerprint to a friend at the Pentagon. All soldiers are genetically fingerprinted, for identification.

"His name is Mason Crill, Corporal Mason Crill. He was listed as missing in action during Iraqi Freedom. Now that he's alive again, the Army wants to have a long talk with him," he explained. He pulled himself up onto the couch. "I'm thinking this Corporal Crill discovers an ancient hiding place in the desert, steals the scroll and whatever else is there, and skips. Then he runs to Germany, where he was based before the war, and opens shop as Wolfgang Kohlhertz. Pretty basic, really."

"So you gave him a fake?" Melisandre asked. Linus nodded.

"I had the real one all along. But I didn't know what it was, and it didn't occur to me until after you ditched me at Orly. It took awhile, but I figured out the Mary Magdalene connection from the places on your map. So many were associated with Magdalene relics. It was the only explanation. You've been recovering samples and cataloging them genetically. That way, you can arrive at a reasonable probability of which ones came from the same corpse which, presumably, could then be presented as likely to be authentic," he said, adding, "How'm I doin' so far?" Melisandre didn't respond. "Then my colleagues... "

"That would be *Herr* Fischer, and Gervan's daughter Ute," Melisandre said, showing she'd done her intel homework.

"... Fischer and Ute. Yes. They deciphered enough of the scroll to get us to Ephesus and the Cave of the Seven Sleepers, where Ute discovered the second half of the message. It was the line that said *"the holder of this gnosis is also the holder of the well"* that tipped me off. Not at first, but the more I remembered old Gervan's bruised face that day in his shop, the more I realized that Gervan had figured it out, too. The *jar* – not the text – was the key. And he was determined to keep it out of Kohlhertz's hands so he pawned it off on me."

"Gervan called me that day, just before Kohlhertz got him," Melisandre said. Linus nodded.

"I'm sure he was going to give it to you. But when things got shaky he ended up giving it to me instead. But what you don't know is that he also wrote down the name of the *Blauer Apfel* cafe and slipped it in with the packaging. His way of leading me back to you, I suppose. You see, it was July 22nd. He knew you'd be at the restaurant," he said.

"Then you obviously know why," she said. "And you also know what the scroll revealed." Linus nodded solemnly and said,

"I do. It's a sample of some sort, possibly Mary Magdalene's blood. Possibly Christ's, too."

"If that sample yields a genetic fingerprint which can be matched to the Magdalene relics we've collected... " she began.

"It will make a very persuasive case," he finished, and added, "But I kept asking myself, to what end? The only logical answer was a bloodline. I figured you had to be trying to establish a bloodline."

"I told you about the Merovingian genealogical research ... " she began.

"Oh, I suppose you *are* interested to see if the two bloodlines cross, since the Merovingians claimed to be descendants of Christ, and Mary Magdalene is most often mentioned as Jesus' wife and mother of his kids. But the Merovingians weren't the main focus. The main focus all along was the Magdalene. You and your friends are seeking to establish her bloodline all the way to the present, with or without the potential of Jesus Christ as her consort. It's the only logical conclusion," he said. Melisandre still wasn't reacting but Linus knew he had her – almost.

"But something still nagged at me," he continued. "Even if you possessed something which could arguably be a genetic fingerprint of Mary Magdalene, how would you find a match among today's population? You couldn't start doing random genetic tests on the entire population. So where would you check? There aren't many genetic databases around. Most people aren't fingerprinted genetically. It just isn't a routine part of life, at least not yet. So even if you did a cross-check with all known genetic databases, the odds against finding a match in such a small sample are astronomical," he said. Then he looked into her eyes, her bright blue eyes, eyes which he'd seen variously as blue, green, and azure, and he asked, "Am I making sense so far?"

"It's an intriguing theory," she conceded.

"So I wondered ... what could possibly narrow down the potential matches. And the answer was right before my eyes – or, should I say, *your* eyes," he said.

"The more rare the Magdalene fingerprint, the fewer potential matches. In other words, if you had discovered that the Magdalene fingerprint had some sort of rare genetic condition, you'd have a narrowed population of possibilities, a population of people with the same condition, people for whom there may already be an organized medical database," he said. "And if it was an *observable* genetic condition, like a physical defect, the group could be narrowed even further," he added.

"Very imaginative, Linus," she said.

"You know, that may be the first compliment you've ever paid me," he quipped.

"Maybe the first you've earned," she replied. Linus shrugged. He left the couch and walked toward where she was half-sitting on the edge of the desk. She tensed up as he approached. Linus paused. "Reee-lax, Melisandre," he said impatiently.

"I'm just not sure what you're up to," she replied. "Where is the original container?"

"It's safe," he assured as he toggled into his laptop note files and found the entry he wanted. He read it aloud: "Aniridia. A congenital abnormality, Aniridia is a semi dominant disorder caused by a mutation of the PAX-six gene, in which development of the iris, lens, cornea and retina can be disturbed. It is a disorder of variable expressivity characterized by iris hypoplasia." He looked into Melisandre's eyes again. "In other words, misshaped irises.

"All those internet documents from Johns Hopkins and the *Human Genome Project* I saw at Lindow abbey," he said, still searching in her eyes. "Jules was into this before you, tracking stolen artifacts and relics. And he was using genetic fingerprinting to catalog relics, weed out the counterfeits. It's my guess he discovered that the ones he considered to be authentic Magdalene relics also had the mutation for aniridia. That's when he realized it might be possible to establish a bloodline, at least make a reasonable claim to one. So he started searching," Linus said. He began pacing in a small circle.

"It must've been a huge task," he mused. "He'd have to contact all those afflicted people and convince them to be fingerprinted genetically, though many of them probably already were," he said. He stopped pacing. "I wonder what he used as a cover story... medical research?"

"He was a priest. People were willing to believe him," she said.

"*People* believed him," Linus repeated, then added, "*you*, for example. I knew you were important, and everything you told me about the charities and the *Novangelis* Foundation was plausible. But when all this stuff about Magdalene relics and bloodlines came up, my first thought was that Veronica was the candidate. She seemed regal, was wealthy and fashionable... influential... all qualities reflecting the historical Mary Magdalene. Everything I knew about Veronica, added to what I learned about the Magdalene, made me believe that she would be the one.

"But the more I learned the more it all fell into place, beginning all the way back to July 22nd, the night we met. That party at *Blauer Apfel* was in *your* honor. It was the feast day of the Magdalene," he said. "Yet you walked me right into the middle of it. Pretty sure I wouldn't make that connection, weren't you," he stated.

"Very few people would," she said.

"I suppose. In any case, you were right. It was all right there and I didn't see a thing," he said. "That parade of admirers – the flowers, leather shoes and gloves, perfumes, wine... and all those gold colored scarves," Again he referred to his notes and read aloud. "Mary Magdalene ... guardian of gardeners. Patron of ointment mixers, scent makers and apothecaries. Protectoress of glove makers, coiffeurs, seamstresses, shoemakers, whittawers and wool weavers. Patron of drapers at Bologna, of the water sellers at Chartres, of wine producers near Bolzano," he listed then, from memory, he summarized, "As well as patron saint of prisoners, reformed prostitutes, distressed and exploited women in particular, and penitent sinners in general. Her liturgical colors are white and gold, like the robes you use in your ceremonies and all those gold scarves your followers wear. Mary Magdalene. *Beata Peccatrix* – the Blessed Sinner.

"The fealty and dedication you inspired. The militant obedience, too, especially from other women. And that long hair you had when I met you... right out of the Golden Legend, where Mary Magdalene rejects all worldly possessions, including clothes, and spends the rest of her life an anchorite, covered only by her flowing, golden hair. That was the source of symbolism at the ceremony by the lake, the two naked women who had purged their minds and bodies of worldly distractions," he said. Melisandre was standing up straight, listening and watching. "The way their fitness was showcased tells me they were going into the commando unit, and not the choir," he quipped, then continued.

"But even the donor portrait I saw in your *boudoir* at *Domaine deBouillon* should've been a tip off. I knew it was your likeness, but I didn't know about the reclining pose, the sheer gown. The long, flowing hair, all part of the erotic Magdalene persona that was popular in the middle ages. And the lighted candle and open book... classic symbols of the *Contemplative One*, another Magdalen persona." He stepped closer and looked into her eyes. "What color are they today?" he asked. "I finally figured out that the colored contact lenses were for disguise. Only I didn't know what they were covering," he said. They were staring at each other, their faces only a few feet apart. "It's you, isn't it," he said. Melisandre didn't respond. "*You* are the one, the match. The New Angel. *You* are the new Magdalene," he stated quietly.

They were eye to eye and close. She stared at him a moment longer then gently moved him back, lowered her head, removed the contact lens on her left eye and looked up again. Her left iris was beautiful, bright blue – but misshapen. Aniridia. Linus leaned in for a closer look. Her iris was shaped like an apple. A blue apple! "Blue apples at dawn," he muttered, quoting the translation of the Rennes-le-Château parchments.

"You have been very clever, Linus Pauling Mercator," she said.

"For a celebrity bloodsucker. Isn't that what you called me?"

"I may have said some things ... "

"No," he corrected. "You *did* say some things." Melisandre stepped away from him. Linus sat on the couch.

"How could I have trusted you?" she asked.

"You had no reason not to," he replied. "And I saved your life. Doesn't that mean anything?"

"I knew I'd hear that, only I thought it would've been sooner," she mumbled, then added, "Was it my life you were saving, or your precious story?"

"You can't fairly suggest that I saved you just to get a story," he said as he put his foot up on the coffee table.

"All right, that's unfair. But just because someone is ethical enough to stop a murder doesn't mean they'll have the same ethics when it comes to the most intimate secrets of others, does it?"

"No, I guess it doesn't," he conceded. "But it might be an indication of character. You had me pegged as an idiot from the start and you have tried to ditch me ever since."

"This character of which you speak... the same character of the man who broke into my office... ?"

"You didn't know about that when you made your conclusions!"

"... and the man who told me he wouldn't interfere at *Montsegur*?" This time she had him.

"Lucky I did," he muttered, though he knew it was cheap.

"Sure. But you also got shot. That's what I wanted to avoid."

"How could you possibly think I wouldn't be at least *curious* about you after the party that night at *Blauer Apfel*. I'd have to be a nit wit," he said, then added, "And by the way, who *are* you, exactly?" Melisandre hesitated for a moment but then recited her dossier – most of which she said came from a diary dating back to World War Two and the Nazi occupation of France. And though it was all very plausible, Linus was compelled to remind her of the Saint Margaret of Cortona canard that she'd foisted on him a few weeks back.

But this time her assurances seemed more truthful, mostly because she now had little reason to deceive him. "I'm truly impressed that you figured out as much as you did on your own," she admitted.

"Thanks... I guess. Mostly a matter of being tenacious," he said.

"You are wrong about one thing, though. I never took you for an idiot, Linus. I liked you when we met and I never thought of you as anything less than a very awake person," she said. Linus had been expecting this ingratiating posture but made no attempt to stop her. He wanted the full treatment. "That cynical exterior of yours is very transparent. Once an idealist, always an idealist."

"Idealism is a luxury I can ill afford," he said.

"Ill afford not to have," she countered. Her persistent optimism just wasn't popular with him right now. This episode wasn't over, not by a long shot. The stern look on his face must've said so. Melisandre dropped the pretense. There was still one very important matter to be resolved. "You gave Kohlhertz, or whatever his name is, a fake?" she asked. Linus nodded. "Do you know who has the original?" Linus nodded again. "Would you be willing to carry a message to them for me? Perhaps an offer to purchase it?" Linus rubbed his chin.

"Just say, for example, that it *does* have a Magdalene, or a Jesus blood sample, like the scroll said. Then what? You make the scroll public and announce your lineage?"

"At some point, maybe."

"And what if it is a close match to your genetic fingerprint. Do you claim you're a descendent of Mary Magdalene? Mary Magdalene and *Christ*? Then what? Run for office? President maybe?"

"I wouldn't expect the world to immediately fall at the feet of someone making those claims," she assured.

"Oh, I'm not so sure," Linus cautioned. "History is filled with demagogues who have risen on much lesser claims."

"True. But there may be others making similar claims.

"The *Priory of Sion*," Linus said.

"I believe they'll go public with something soon," she said.

"Sure, but they don't have the genetic proof... or do they?" Melisandre shook 'no'. "So? What? Empress? The first female Pope? President?" he quizzed.

"I think something like this transcends politics."

"Religion *never* transcends politics. Never has, probably never will. The separation of church and state is a fine sentiment but it's an illusion," he proclaimed, proving that – on some level, at least – his cynicism was alive and well.

"But this has as much to do with women's rights as it does with religion," she said. "The women of the world have yet to have their day. Have you ever wondered, Linus, even briefly, what it would be like living in a female dominated civilization?"

"Of course. I've already felt as though I was, at times," he said with a grin. "Punished and subjugated for being a man."

"I bet," she said dubiously. "But it's possible that before women can contribute equally they may have to contribute disproportionately. Men have been dominant up to now. The gender pendulum may have to swing all the way to the other side before it can effectively come to rest in the middle."

"Maybe," he said. "But it won't be an easy trip. Every revolution's road to liberation passes through the fields of treachery and vengeance. Why should the gender revolution be any different?"

"I have no vengeance in my heart, nor charges of betrayal on my sheet. I have not been so repressed," she said. "We're not talking about armed revolution. This is a revolution of the spirit. An awakening. An enlightenment. The female of the species is an untapped resource which needs to be understood, then committed to the benefit of all. Do you think it's right that women in some countries aren't even allowed to show their face in public, let alone think for themselves, or vote, or own property?"

"Not at all," he said.

"Do you know that groups like the Taliban have had women stoned to death merely for *disobeying* their husband or father? Buried up to their necks in dirt then bashed with rocks? Not stones, but large, heavy rocks?"

"I don't doubt the validity of your cause. I just wonder about your methods. Remember your history – if just the mere suggestion of service to Mary Magdalene can send thousands of crusaders to their deaths in a holy war, what could the actual incarnation of her do? What *will* you do, Melisandre. And how will you do it?"

"I don't know, Linus. Ask me something I *can* answer. Ask me if the people who mutilate, or beat, or stone women to death should be stopped. Yes. Immediately."

"By any means necessary?"

"Drastic measures may be the only way. My first concern is rescuing their victims before they become casualties. Eliminating the threat will take time."

"You would seek to bring down male-dominated societies?" he posed.

"I would seek to bring down any *corrupt* society," she answered. "And if my ability to do that is a consequence of this discovery, I can only promise that I'll advance judiciously and not plunge recklessly." She had gradually moved closer to him as she spoke, using her presence to emphasize her points. "Do you believe me, Linus?" she asked. He did but he couldn't possibly answer "yes" without surrendering some of his initiative.

So he did the next best thing. He sighed, moved Melisandre gently aside then pushed up the carpet and opened a trap door leading to the crawl space under the house. A rush of cool air filled the room as he lowered himself into the opening and retrieved a box that was wrapped in a trash-bag, shook off the excess sand, then set it right at Melisandre's feet. She didn't speak or move, even though he was sure she knew what it was. He dusted off, climbed out, put the box on the desk, and said,

"It's fragile." Melisandre peeled the plastic bags, sliced the packing tape with a letter opener and lifted out the contents – a red clay jar, the one that Gervan sold to Linus, the one which once held Kohlhertz's scroll. Her eyes widened at the sight of the glassy red orbs around its circumference. "The stuff of dreams," Linus said with muted mockery. She gently slid it back, closed the box and said,

"Maybe. The testing will tell."

"Can you get it to someplace safe tonight?" he asked. Melisandre nodded.

"You haven't said what you wanted for this," she said.

"Reward?" he asked as though he hadn't thought of it.

"Call it whatever you like," she said.

"Skip it," he said. "Just promise that, no matter where this leads,

I get the exclusive story, and as it's happening. Starting now," he stated, meaning she'd have to see a lot more of him. Melisandre naturally agreed. They shook hands. "Do you need me to drive you someplace?" he asked. She shook "no", cell phone in hand.

"I'm ready," she said to whoever was listening on the other end. Linus wasn't surprised. He knew she was never alone. A few moments later, headlights cut across the windows as a car pulled up outside. Melisandre cradled the box. "Thank you for this," she said. Linus humbly averted his eyes as she added, "You won't regret it."

"I'm counting on that, Melisandre," he said. From the look on her face he knew that her thoughts were already elsewhere. Her mission with the jar was far from over. Then, without saying 'goodbye' or 'see you later', she was gone. Linus knew that her gratitude was – this time – sincere. Unfortunately, he also knew that her gratitude would be replaced with the vilest contempt. And perhaps all too soon.

He watched from the deck as Melisandre got in a car and was driven away. He then went back inside, locked the door behind him, and started to unwind. He stood in the middle of the room and surveyed images of his salad day glories, hanging all around him on the walls – him on exotic assignments, glad-handing renowned Statesmen, receiving prestigious awards. It was a long way – and twenty years – from there to here, he thought.

He wanted to finish his last detail but didn't want to be in the middle of it and have someone barge in. So he sat. And chilled. And thought about Melisandre's latest life story. She said her mother was adopted and she never found her natural parents though she did learn that her mom was born in Paris in 1938, then adopted by an American woman near the beginning of World War Two. The woman was only fifty-one when she and her husband – Melisandre's father – were killed in the San Francisco earthquake of 1989. Exactly six years later, on the anniversary of their death, a package arrived in Melisandre's mail. It contained two old snapshots.

One was a man, woman, and a baby, in *Montmartre*, with *Sacré Coéur* in the background. 'Paris, 1939', was written on the back, she said. The other was a photograph of the same man, bare-chested, holding the same baby in the light of a nursery window. Little crystal bears bobbed from the window shade and there was a distinct cruciform mark on the man's arm. The bears were Ursa, the Merovingian bear, and the birthmark was a fabled Merovingian marker as well, she said. Of course, the baby had one too.

There were also several crude gold bees in the package – one of which, she had pointed out, was hanging on a gold chain around Linus's neck.

Then there was a small leather diary, she said, with a letter slipped inside the back cover – an affidavit from a woman swearing that she was nanny to the pictured baby in 1941, and that the diary was hers. It also swore her to secrecy on "matters described therein".

Melisandre never found out who the nanny was, and never heard from her again, she said. But the baby to whom the woman was nanny was her mother – making the man and woman in the photos her grandparents. Her look turned pensive when she spoke of the "great weight of sadness" she found in the diary, as though the writer knew the story was destined to end sadly as soon as she put pen to page one.

The first entry was *Paris, May 14th, 1940*. Her mother, Melisandre de Razes, was a year and a half old. The Nazis were only a month away from taking the city so her grandmother took her baby and escaped to the Languedoc, in what was to be unoccupied southern France.

But her grandfather, a prominent engineer, was caught up in a Gestapo round-up of scientists before he could follow. Mother and baby made it safely to *Domaine deBouillon*, a family property. But within months, the Nazis showed up to dig at *Montsegur* and at the Knights Templar preceptory on nearby *Mount Bezu*. They also had digs in and around Rennes-le-Château and Blanchefort, she said.

Knowing that the Nazis were no strangers to her history – the de Razes and de Bouillon names – and that it was only a matter of time before they came looking for her at the estate, her grandmother decided it was too risky to stay. She managed to get papers declaring her baby a war orphan, then smuggled her to Lisbon, Portugal, from where the baby was sent into the care of strangers – apparently a German officer who had succumbed to her wiles as part of her deception was killed for the cause. The nanny, and her pledge of secrecy about the baby's true identity, went with the baby as the adoption agent. Then, with little more than a hope that they'd be reunited someday or, if not, that the bloodline would be preserved, the mother ran away to join the resistance and rescue her husband. Which she succeeded in doing.

But her heroic grandmother was shot and killed a year later during a sabotage mission, she said. Her grandfather – widowed, his only child's whereabouts unknown – survived the war but died soon after it ended. The nanny's letter said it was from a broken heart.

Linus stood up and moved to a large bookcase. High on the top shelf there was an arrangement of dried flowers and beach grass in a foil-wrapped vase. He took it down, dumped it out, then peeled back the foil to reveal a glassy, red orb – like on the vessel that once held the vaunted Kohlhertz/Gervan scroll. He buffed the orb's polished surface with his thumb.

Was it really Magdalen blood?

Or maybe the blood of Jesus?

Was he holding the Biblical cup of red porphyry, in which Joseph of Arimethea caught some of dying Jesus' blood?

Was *this* the Holy Grail?

He wondered how long it would take Melisandre to realize that she, too, had a fake... probably weeks, certainly not before tomorrow. And by tomorrow the *real* jar would be locked in a safe deposit box.

He wrapped it in paper, plastic and duct tape, then opened the trap door and buried it in the soft sand of the crawl space. Then he dusted the sand from his pants, washed up, and went to his computer.

First, he cancelled the phony *Iscariot* account. Then he composed an e-mail on his own legitimate account.

TO: Anfortas
FROM: L-P Merc
SUBJECT: Herr Linus

Hello Fischer. The object in question is in good hands. Please tell Ute that Kohlhertz, real name Crill, is a deserter and a murderer, is in the custody of the US military, and will answer for his crimes, including the death of her father.

Thank you for your help. Find a good restaurant – but not *Blauer Apfel*, please! Back in Berlin soon.

LPM.

He clicked SEND then closed the laptop's lid. Then he took a camera flashcard labeled "Jamie Richards" and a bubble-pack envelope bearing her address from his desk drawer. He set them aside and scratched a note:

This is the whole show. No one has seen them. No copies exist. And now they're yours, compliments of –

L.P.Mercator.

"Probably worth millions," he groused as he folded the flashcard into the note and sealed it in the envelope – knowing full well that Dark Star, his agency, would surely dump him over this.

But there were more pressing matters, like his growling stomach, reminding him of his missed dinner. He'd mail the letter then have some late supper in downtown Newburyport, he thought. Maybe hear a live band at a bar. It was *Friday*, after all, and one of the last of the summer at that. Surely there'd be *something* fun happening ... someplace.

So Linus grabbed his jacket and went to find it.

www.ingramcontent.com/pod-product-compliance
Lightning Source LLC
Chambersburg PA
CBHW020618260626
47157CB00003B/1062